Expired Cache

LAST CHANCE COUNTY BOOK THREE

Lisa Phillips

Publisher Lisa Phillips
Cover design Ryan Schwarz
Edited by www.jenwieber.com

One

"Eleanor!"

Everything in her screamed, *ambush,* a half second before she was engulfed in French perfume and cashmere.

Ellie gave the woman a squeeze. "Ruby."

"It's so good to see you again, hon." The older woman's skin shimmered like glitter. She did her makeup like a pro, and her white hair had been trimmed to a pixie cut. Ruby had been working the same style since she'd taught Ellie's fourth grade Sunday school class. Ellie had to admit, it really did work.

"You, too."

"Smile a bit," Ruby said, "and I might actually believe it."

"I never could pull one over on you."

"Can't kid a kidder."

Someone at the far end of the coffee shop called out, "Sugar free vanilla soy latte with whip."

"Ooh, that's me!" Ruby retrieved her paper cup from the end of the counter.

Ellie glanced from the elderly woman's red skinny jeans and white sweater, to her own flats and skirt with her most comfortable jacket. When Ruby came back over, Ellie pushed her glasses up her nose.

"What brought you back to town this time?"

Ellie said, "Meeting with the lawyer. We're going over grandad's will."

Her last trip to Last Chance had been for the funeral. She hadn't even stayed overnight. This time she'd be here for a long weekend, enough to help her younger sister go through their grandfather's things.

"And your mama? Is she still..."

Ellie didn't want to get into that. "She wasn't able to get the time off work."

"I see."

Yes, Ruby probably did. Ellie tried to smile. She moved back to the map on the wall she'd been looking at before the ambush hug.

"The Founders' Map."

Ellie glanced over, her frown enough of a question.

"That's the first map of Last Chance. From the year the town started." Ruby pointed to the copyright in the corner. July 4th, 1975.

"It's fascinating."

Ruby nodded. "Long before I came to town, but I read all about it in a series the newspaper put out a few years ago." She pointed to the foothills. "This whole section of the mountains was deemed safe, and that's where all the hiking paths are now. The area above that is out of bounds. According to the signage posted."

Ellie frowned at her.

"A couple of friends and I hiked up there." She leaned close like she was telling a secret. "We didn't see anything dangerous. It was fine."

"Oh." She wasn't sure what to say.

Ellie's gaze strayed to the bookshelf below the framed picture. A dozen or so books, all used, by the look of them, had slid sideways. In the middle was a thick tome about the Civil War. *When Freemen Shall Stand* had been a runaway bestseller, written by Professor Eleanor Ridgeman. Unless, of course, the reader was one of the hordes of people who'd hated it. Despite sales, people seemed to be pretty much in two camps—they'd either loved it or decried it as an emotionless regurgitation of facts.

Ellie winced at the sight of it. She hadn't written a single thing since.

The same barista called out, "Extra shot, extra-dry, dairy-free cappuccino."

"That's me." Ellie stepped away from her old Sunday school teacher. "It was nice to see you again, Ruby."

By the time Ellie approached the door with her paper cup, the older woman had joined a friend at a table off to the side. She lifted her cup with a parting smile and stepped outside onto busy Main Street. *Everything's fine. Deep breaths.*

She took a sip of coffee. *Ouch.* Too hot.

"Your hot tea is gonna be hot, smarty pants." Her sister strode onto the sidewalk, a thermos she'd brought from home in one hand. Jess, four years younger than Ellie, was dressed in what she referred to as her "church clothes" whatever that meant. She also had her hair in a ponytail.

Ellie shot her a smile like everything was fine and sidestepped a young woman with a stroller. She glanced over her shoulder at the cars and people passing on the opposite sidewalk.

Going into the coffee shop for a drink was supposed to have settled her.

Why did she still feel like she was being watched?

"You okay, El?"

"Sure." She smiled at her sister. "Let's get to our appointment."

They headed down the sidewalk to the office of Holmford and Watts, her grandfather's lawyer. Where the will would be read. Once she got through the rest of this legal stuff, she wouldn't have to come to Last Chance again.

Her sister was Officer Jessica Ridgeman, formerly with the NYPD. Currently an officer with the Last Chance police department. As though moving to a small town and taking a job with a tiny department eight months ago could ever compare to the career of a cop in New York. But their grandfather, the previous police chief, had been terminal.

Jess was the one who had sat beside his bed those last few months to ensure he had family around him. It had just made the most sense, considering Jess lived here. Ellie lived on the East Coast.

Now their Grandfather was gone and buried. Ellie was back here long enough to get the paperwork done, help her sister pack the house and deal with the old man's things, and then she'd be off on sabbatical.

Write another book, Eleanor. She winced, picturing her boss's face right in hers. Close enough she could feel his breath. *You need to pull your weight, and we need a bestseller for this department.*

Jess glanced at the screen of her phone, then slid it into her back pocket. "As soon as we're done with Mr. Holmford, I have to get to work. We have a new case and things are starting to get interesting."

Even having grown up with a police chief for a grandfather, Ellie still didn't know what that meant.

Jess spoke again. "How are things going at the university?"

"Things are fine," Ellie said. "Why wouldn't they be?"

"If you'd actually breathe, I might believe you mean that." Jess glanced over again, assessing her.

Ellie hadn't liked that "cop" stare when their grandfather did it. She didn't like it now from her little sister.

"You get that I'm trained to interrogate people, right?"

"Criminals. Not your own sister. And we all have the right to remain silent." Ellie sighed. "Let's just get to the lawyer's office and get this done."

There had been zero choice in coming back this time, just like there hadn't been for the funeral. She couldn't have left her sister to do all this alone. Being back in the old house with her sister felt good, but the memories in and through the rest of town put her on edge. That was the only reason she felt under a microscope.

Ellie was a history professor. She didn't know how that science stuff worked, but probably whatever scientists watched that closely—that *intimately*—knew they were being studied.

"You think there's anything in the will? Besides the house, at least."

"What about his cabin, or the car?" Ellie took another sip. Hot liquid encountered the burned taste buds on her tongue and she winced.

Across the street, a man parked in his car watched them pass. *It's nothing, just ignore it.* Would she always be suspicious of every man who glanced her way? No. That was no way to live her life. She might have avoided Last Chance for years, but innocent people should never be a source of fear for her. That wouldn't be fair to someone just trying to live their life.

Ellie had been targeted specifically by one person—and his friends. But that had been years ago. And it was done now.

If she was inclined to thank God for anything, she would start with the news report she'd read a few weeks ago. The one that gave her peace. Some, at least. There was no reason for her fear now.

"Who knows what all there is?" Jess shrugged one shoulder. "But the chief wasn't exactly hiding anything. You know he never could keep a surprise."

Ellie chuckled. "That is true." The old man had ruined more than one surprise party.

Their grandfather.

The police chief.

Jess had connected with him as a cop and had called him "chief" even in middle school. Ellie had existed at odds with the old man. Her grandfather hadn't understood her.

He'd tried to help her when she needed it. But at the time, Ellie couldn't accept it. Not from him or anyone. She knew he'd felt rejected by that. Life had never given them the opportunity to fix that. They'd exchanged emails for years. Catching up on each other's news. But they'd never really made amends or worked to deepen their relationship. With Ellie's book becoming so successful, and then her busy teaching schedule, there just hadn't been time.

Ellie felt the burn in her eyes and glanced up at the sky so her lenses would transition to sunglasses and her sister wouldn't see the sheen of tears. Not that Ellie would cry. She never did. Crying didn't fix anything, and she wasn't one to wallow.

"Thanks for coming."

"I know." Ellie smiled at her sister. "You said that already."

Jess shook her head. "What with you being busy and all, I was kind of surprised you came at all, to be honest."

Ellie didn't take offense. She and her sister told the truth to each other, even when it might hurt. It was called honesty and it was key in healthy relationships.

She said, "I'm glad I came, too." Not exactly what her sister had said, but she understood the sentiment. "The will is supposed to be read to both of us."

Soon as it was done, she would get back to the East Coast and begin figuring out which New Hampshire rental house she was going to live in while she was on sabbatical. Ellie only had six months to research and then write a book about the Vietnam war.

It had better be juicy, Ridgeman.

Her department chair wasn't going to let her ride much longer, writing papers while refusing to "come into the new millennium" as though there was a void in social media that should be filled by academia. As if they should steep that low. It was tantamount to selling themselves in the name of entertainment.

Still, Ellie had to give him what he wanted or she had to get out. And there was no way she'd let him push her aside. She'd worked hard. For years. Now she was going to make him see how much of a mistake it would be to force her out.

Ellie pushed all that aside for later and took a closer study of her sister's face. She seemed over tired. Because of the big new case or their grandfather's death, or both? Jess had adored their grandfather, which was probably why she'd become a cop. Of course she would deeply grieve the loss of her mentor and the only stable male figure in her life.

Ellie hadn't needed him in the same way, but she was still grieving.

Ellie said, "I'm sorry you lost him."

"You lost him too."

"You know what I mean."

Jess shook her head again. She seemed to do that a lot.

"It's hard to suddenly have your mentor gone, a man you looked up to personally and professionally."

"It wasn't sudden, El. He fought a long battle. No one thought he'd last that long. The kind of cancer he had is supposed to take a person quickly. Viciously." Jess paused. "I actually thought he was waiting for you to come and say goodbye."

"You know that was impossible for me, in the middle of the semester." She touched her sister's shoulder. "He had you. But that also means you feel the loss more. It's okay to be upset."

Jess said, "I might be comforted, if I thought this conversation was more than an intellectual thought exercise, professor."

"I'm not a psychologist."

"No, you're not. Just smarter than everyone in the room at any given moment."

"We're outside." They were walking along the street in the center of town in broad daylight. Why was Jess comparing the two of them right now? Was Jess more distraught over their grandfather's death than she'd thought, and trying to deflect?

Her sister shook her head. "Never mind." Her attention snagged on something across the street, and Ellie saw Jess's head turn sharply. Did she see it too? Did Jess feel what she did, that there were eyes on them?

Ellie spun to see what her sister was looking at. She heard Jess mutter, "Dean" as though the name was a curse word.

"Who is that?"

Ellie didn't recognize a guy with that name from high school. He was about their age, and he was huge. His face…she'd have remembered someone with those features. Dark hair. A strong jaw. The kind of guy who knew exactly the effect he had on women.

She saw men like him on campus every day, striding past huddles of tittering college girls like they thought they were walking through busy city streets. Heroes off to war.

"Dean Cartwright."

"As in…"

Jess nodded. "He's Ted's disapproving older brother."

Ellie glanced over.

"Yes, we figured out we have that in common." Jess grinned and nudged Ellie's shoulder away. "But trust me, he's way worse. Dean was a Navy SEAL, so of course he has that hero complex all guys like that have. The 'hop to it' and 'yes sir' stuff, with the hospital corners when you make your bed. Every day. Without fail. Ted's a computer genius."

Ellie nodded as though that topic jump made any sense whatsoever. Her sister's last email had been all about the police department's super cute—apparently—tech specialist. Given the handsome level of his brother, she didn't doubt he was good looking.

"Dean just can't stand to see Ted doing anything he doesn't approve of."

"Sounds like grandpa." Ellie grinned, trying to lighten the mood.

Jess laughed. "Back in your 'wild' days, getting picked up at the golf course at two in the morning, drunk as a skunk, in junior year."

Ellie groaned. "Oh, I remember that. Officer Frampton didn't let me live that down. He made me do the perp walk and everything."

Jess was still laughing. "Classic…until you got all weird senior year. Then you never did anything."

All the humor she felt dissipated in one fell swoop.

"Shoot. Sorry, I shouldn't have mentioned it." Jess sighed. "I know something happened. Grandpa never told me what, but you changed. That was obvious."

Ellie figured that, given her sister's experience as a police officer, she might've worked out what occurred that Friday night at the home game victory party. She might have been younger, but Jess had never been dumb.

Ellie stepped off the curb onto the crosswalk.

"El, watch—"

Car tires screeched. Ellie gasped, then turned to see a champagne-colored car barreling toward her. She jumped back. Landed on her behind on the street. Her hip glanced off the curb, and her palms slid across the asphalt.

She cried out.

Her purse dropped, and the contents dumped everywhere. The car's engine revved, and they sped up and down the street while Ellie fought to catch her breath and figure out what had just happened.

"This is Officer Ridgeman. There's been a hit and run."

She twisted to her sister, blinking. Pain rippled through her side, and she cried out. When she touched her hip, it was with bloody hands. She winced, a breath escaping between her pursed lips.

"Careful." A figure entered her peripheral.

Ellie sucked in a breath and twisted, instinct causing her to jerk back from the dark figure.

"Easy." Dean Cartwright reached for her. "Let's take a look at your hands. I'm sure it's not too bad."

Beyond him, Jess frowned down at the former Navy SEAL. Ellie felt his warm hands under hers, cradling them. She yanked her hands from his and shifted back. "I'm fine."

"Ma'am—"

"I don't need any help."

He towered over her. Big shoulders. A disapproving stare, as though she needed more of that in her life.

Ellie looked at her sister, who took three steps to her and held out a hand. This was going to hurt. She grabbed Jess's wrist anyway and let her sibling pull her to her feet while Dean Cartwright straightened to his full height. Good grief, he really was huge.

And still frowning.

Ellie lifted her chin. *Ouch.* "We're good. But thanks anyway."

Two

Dean looked down into her brown eyes and everything just…stopped. Then he remembered the roar of the car engine. Jessica's cry. The car hadn't even attempted to slow down.

The injured woman was scared. Probably woozy as well, from the shock of almost being flattened in a hit and run. He glanced at Jessica and saw the resemblance in their features.

His brother Ted, who worked with Officer Ridgeman at the police department, had told him that Jessica's older sister was coming into town again, this time to hear the reading of the will. She'd flown in one day for the funeral and not even stayed overnight.

He'd seen her from across the field during the service but hadn't stayed long enough to pay his respects. Now he kind of wished he had.

"Eleanor, right?"

"Ellie." She held a hand out to shake. It was tentative. Then she realized why he wasn't going to shake her hand.

"Dean Cartwright." He swung his backpack off his shoulder and slid a water bottle from the side pocket. He twisted off the cap. "Hold out both hands."

She held them to the side, and he emptied the water onto her palms.

"Rub a little, if you can. Get the dirt off." While she did that, he pulled out two gauze pads and ripped open the packets—she could use them to dry her hands off—and then grabbed a tiny packet of Neosporin.

Officer Jessica Ridgeman, the younger sister, stuck her hand on her hip. Dean was almost positive his brother was in love with her, given how he talked about her. Truth was, they knew practically nothing about her. Or the sister. Dean had wanted to run background checks, but his brother's reaction meant he'd tabled that discussion.

For now.

Dean caught her gaze. "Hand?" He tore open the cream packet and held out his hand so she could place hers in it.

She just frowned.

"I'm certified as an EMT if that's what you're worried about."

"I'm not." She took half a step back. "I'm fine, though. I don't need help."

Yeah, she'd said that. Dean wasn't used to treating patients who couldn't admit when something hurt. Though he dealt with his fair share of alpha personalities, so it really shouldn't surprise him to come across someone inflated with sheer stubbornness. Normally he didn't find it quite so attractive.

Usually those he treated knew they needed help. In their own ways, they'd allow him to do what he could to help them.

Her dark hair had been pulled back into a bun with a silver pen stuck in it. Now loose strands floated around her face. Her glasses were askew, in a way that made him want to reach over and right them for her. Attraction stirred. The librarian thing. He blew out a breath. It had always been a weakness for him, but that didn't mean he had to listen to it.

He wasn't in the place in his life where he was ready to look for a relationship.

At least, not yet.

Dean tossed the Neosporin packet to Jessica. "Make sure she puts this on her cuts."

"Aye aye, captain."

"I might've been Navy, but I was never an officer. Thanks for the vote of confidence, though."

Jessica's eyes flashed. "It was unintended."

Ellie glanced between them. She could see he wasn't going to pretend there was any love lost between Officer Ridgeman and himself. Truth was, no one would be good enough for his brother.

Dean's watch alarm beeped. He canceled the tone and pulled his backpack on. "I have an appointment." He glanced between them but asked Ellie, "If you're good?"

He almost wanted to tack on the question of whether he could call her later and make sure. Ellie nodded, the hint of a smile on her face. "I'm good. Thanks." Like she knew exactly how she'd affected him.

Great.

"Dean!"

He twisted around. The door to the coffee shop was open, and Doctor Gilane waved a hand. Dean's appointment.

He held up one finger, and the doctor nodded.

A police car pulled over at the curb and the uniformed officer climbed out. Sergeant Basuto. He waited for the guy to make it all the way over and they shook, then Dean left them to it. As a rule, he didn't get involved in police matters. Jessica had this covered. He didn't need to get in the middle of this when he had a meeting with the doctor to get to.

One last glance back let him know Ellie had forgotten all about him. She was smiling at the sergeant in a way she hadn't looked at him.

Dean tried not to let that sting. Especially considering the fact he'd never been needy before. Why start now, with a dark haired, tiny nosed intellectual who checked every box he had?

No way was it a thing when no other relationship he'd had in his life turned out the way it had promised to be in the beginning. He was done being ditched, broken up with, tossed aside and otherwise moved on from. Dean was making his life what he wanted it to be.

He was about to start a new venture, one that would begin with securing backing from the doctor on his new project. He had plenty to do. And that didn't include wondering why a driver had tried to run Ellie down.

It wasn't an accident. It had been a deliberate attempt to hurt her.

But he wasn't a cop and Ellie Ridgeman didn't have any connection to him.

"Latte?"

Dean said, "Cappuccino."

A few minutes later, they sat at a small round table and Doctor Martin Gilane pulled Dean's portfolio from his briefcase. He set it on the table between them but didn't open it. The doctor's white hair was perfectly styled. His face was tanned like his arms and hands. A man who did good work but also regularly treated himself to exotic vacations with this wife, who was twenty years younger and closer to Dean's age than his own.

Dean had lived in this town long enough to know that Doctor Gilane knew his father. Knew some of his history.

The doctor tapped a manicured nail on the portfolio. "This is good stuff."

Dean hadn't been expecting that. He also wasn't sure what it meant. He lowered his paper cup, waiting for the inevitable "but."

"A treatment center for those suffering PTSD." Gilane tipped his head to the side. "When you came to me to sign off on your therapy hours, I can't say I thought this was where it was going. You've more than exceeded my expectations with everything you've done. You're an asset to the medical community in Last Chance, Dean."

He'd been hearing that from the doctor for a while now. The same as with all those other times, he just couldn't let the words settle in. Not in a way that it satisfied what was inside him. Dean only used the words to fuel him on.

He'd survived his childhood with his sanity intact. That had been a feat in itself. Then, Dean had gone into the Navy. He'd done one of the toughest jobs in the world.

Had he come out of that with a sense of satisfaction? Not the way most would think.

Will satisfaction come with this new venture?

God hadn't answered his question yet.

"This isn't going to be a medical facility. It'll be a voluntary residency, and a place people can attend group meetings or get one-on-one treatment that's highly specialized. I want to take on a certain client group."

People who had been where he'd been, and needed help the way he had. Dean was determined to give back. To be the man he knew he could be. Someone people wanted in their lives. Sure, he had friends. But there was so much he was missing.

Love. A family.

"The case studies are fascinating. I had no idea you've been doing all this since I helped you get licensed."

His stomach clenched. He felt like he was trying to pass an interview for the career he'd always dreamed of. "Having your support will go a long way to legitimizing a treatment center."

"You know, I'd love to put in some hours alongside you."

"You would?" The doctor had helped Dean get all his licenses and certifications, he'd been invaluable signing off on Dean's work so far.

"The chance to be on the cutting edge of PTSD therapy? Fascinating." The doctor took a sip of his coffee. "You know, I have a friend at the Pentagon. I'm going to make a call. He might be interested in taking a look, maybe secure some backing to get you referrals. Cases they'd like you to take on."

"You think so?" When the doctor nodded, Dean continued, "It's been nearly four years since I left the Navy. A lot of my contacts there have dried up." So far, he'd treated a few friends and a couple of locals who'd sought him out.

"Even with those roommates of yours, word hasn't gotten out?"

Dean said, "They all work private security now. There are occasional government contracts, but those aren't the norm."

His roommates were currently halfway across the world, working a job. Only one was home with Dean and Ted. Dividing the chores between the three of them until the rest of the boys got back was going to earn them at least a month of freedom. The house was fifteen thousand square feet. It took forever to clean all that, even with Ted's squadron of seriously modified robot vacuums.

"I'll bend some ears. See what I can come up with."

"But you think it'll work."

The doctor nodded. "More than think. This is a great idea, Dean. Something noble the town should be able to get behind."

"Thank you." That was high praise. The kind that made him want to sit taller in a way that usually didn't happen outside the military.

"You really think you can take it on, on top of your…work?"

Dean said, "Being the town's informal EMT is something I don't think I'll ever stop doing." Even if the constant phone calls sometimes drove him crazy. "Though, I've thought about shifting it to more of a concierge thing."

"You'll charge people?"

"Of course not." He shook his head. "I prefer the muffin baskets anyway."

Gilane looked at him like he'd grown another head beside the one he already had.

Dean said, "I'll figure it out. If folks know I'm working on something that can help those who need it, they might chip in and take some of the strain. Or, they'll have a mind to what I'm doing and call less for incidental injuries."

"Or you could take on a partner. Get help with the EMT duties."

"I always figured that would come from the actual EMTs." Dean shot the doctor a wry smile.

"They give you grief?" Gilane frowned. "I can speak to them if you'd like."

Dean shook his head. "It's fine."

But the doctor didn't let it go. "Anything you need, Dean. You let me know." He nodded. "No matter what it is, I'm here to support you."

"Thank you." What else would he say? He'd expected to have to fight for what he wanted in order to convince the doctor this was the right thing. "I just need a location and the resources to pull it off."

It wasn't like Dean had the money for something like this lying around. He was comfortable, and he had good savings, but wiping out his resources and living at the edge wasn't wise. What he needed were financial donors. Charity events. Annual fundraisers. People in town pulling together.

"I've had some thoughts about that, as well." The doctor pulled a business card from his shirt pocket. "This is the paralegal at Holmford and Watts. She's done fundraising for the local schools and for the hospital. I think she'd be a great resource. And that's only if she doesn't jump in with both feet to help you."

Dean took the card. "Thank you."

"I already sent her an email, so she knows you'll be headed her way."

"I actually have an appointment to see Holmford in an hour. I'll talk to her while I'm there."

"You're seeing the lawyer?"

"He didn't say why he needed to talk to me." Dean blew out a breath and leaned back in his chair. "I feel like I'm totally out of my depth, but I want to do this so I figure that's a good thing."

It was important. He could help people, long term. Make a difference in their lives past just putting a bandage on their injuries and telling them to see their doctor.

He *should* feel like he was taking on too much responsibility to start up a therapy center. That would help him move cautiously and consider the weight of what he was doing.

"Well, then." The doctor stood. "I won't keep you if you're headed to another appointment."

He still had half an hour, but Dean was pretty shocked and needed some time to just think. He shook the doctor's hand and just sat back to absorb it all. He was really going to do this.

"Anything you need, Dean." The doctor said, "You let me know."

Dean blinked, then watched him walk out. Full support with no convincing wasn't exactly what he'd imagined this meeting would be. Now that it was done, and so easily, he didn't know what to do with himself.

Anything you need.

Because the doctor believed in him? Dean had grown up with a father who said what he thought would get you to do what he wanted you to do. That level of manipulation made him sick now. He couldn't stand it. Dean wanted to believe the doctor was just supportive. That he believed a therapy center was a worthy cause. But something just didn't sit right.

After all, nothing in life was free.

Three

"One of you needs to say something."

Ellie waved off the lawyer's words. She got up and paced away from the chair, away from the lawyer and her sister. The will.

She stared at the walls, where rows of books had been arranged on shelves that stretched from floor to ceiling. No dust collected in front of them, so she knew his cleaner regularly attended to that. Ellie had the janitor who took care of her office at the university remove the books from the shelves once a month and wipe down all sides, then each book individually. No sense in allowing them to collect dust.

She inhaled the smell of leather-bound first editions and turned back. They both stared at her. Ellie took another deep breath. Absorbed the sight of dark wood furniture not too dissimilar from her office.

She curled her toes in her shoes, then stretched them out. A meditative action she often used to center herself back in the here and now.

No one saw it, which meant she was the only one who ever knew she needed that small action to get her emotions in check. All those feelings she saw trail down Jess's face, twin tracks of tears.

She strode back to her sister and crouched. "Are you okay?"

Jess sniffed. She nodded.

Ellie looked at the lawyer, Peter Holmford. "Can we just break it down, piece by piece?" He'd read the will in one long speech. Rattling it off like it was a grocery list she'd had to process on the fly. That was never good. She needed methodical. Thoughtful.

"Of course." The lawyer was an older man. Nice suit, but small town nice and not big city nice. It wasn't specially tailored. Just well made, and likely more expensive than what he could find on the rack at a big department store.

He shifted through his papers again and settled tiny reading glasses back on his nose.

Ellie straightened. She slid her glasses up her nose, wincing when her palm smarted on her cheek. Her hip—probably with a giant, purple bruise by now—also didn't feel too good.

It had taken an extra half hour to explain to the sergeant what had happened at the scene of the accident. Basuto had been a cop her grandfather respected, so she'd stayed when he'd insisted it was necessary and answered all his questions.

While Jess stood there, frowning. Her focus on the street. Cars driving by. When Ellie had asked her what she was thinking, Jess only shook her head. They were late for their appointment with the lawyer.

The word 'appointment' only reminded her of Dean Cartwright. Certified handsome hero, annoyingly overprotective older brother to the guy Jess seriously crushed on.

"The house and everything in it has been left to Jessica."

Ellie would be thinking about Dean again in a minute, given what the lawyer had gone over already, so she didn't need to worry about him right now.

Her sister twisted in the chair, those tears still coming. Ellie handed her two tissues from the box on the desk as Jess said, "I'm sorry. Ellie…"

"For what?"

"We should be splitting the house."

"It's where you live." Ellie shook her head. "There's no sense to sell it, and I don't live here all the time like you do. It's good that he gave you the house."

Her sister frowned.

"It's fine." Would she believe her?

Jess's gaze turned assessing. Still, she knew Ellie wasn't the kind of person who manipulated or lied. Not when it was important.

He said, "Your grandfather's investment account will be distributed to Selena Ridgeman in monthly installments." He frowned down at the words.

Jess shot her a look he didn't see.

Ellie nodded. *Mom.*

Mr. Holmford looked up from his paper. "If you'd like to contest any of this, that is, of course, your prerogative."

Ellie said, "Nothing so far. But that doesn't mean we won't be following that course of action. Please continue."

Jess brushed at her face, and Ellie caught a flash of a smile there. Whatever that was about.

He said, "The cabin—"

"Was left to Dean Cartwright." Disdain dripped from her sister's words as she repeated what he'd said the first time he went over the will. That definitely needed to be explained.

"I'm sorry if that is how it came across." Holmford said, "Technically that's not entirely accurate." He looked down. "The *land* surrounding your grandfather's hunting cabin has been gifted to Dean Cartwright."

Jess shot her a look.

Ellie had nothing to say about it. She didn't understand it and therefore was unable to reach a conclusion. All they had now was their grandfather's wishes. That lacked an explanation of why on earth he'd have given family property to someone who wasn't family.

Which only birthed a whole lot of what amounted to conspiracy theories. But that was ridiculous. Her grandfather and Dean weren't even related.

Maybe connected in some way—more than the visceral attraction she'd felt when he was standing right in front of her. Trying to be all heroic by treating her wounds. Like she couldn't wash her own hands. They were red now and stung. But that didn't mean she required a hero.

Ellie had been taking care of herself for years now. She wasn't suddenly helpless because a car had nearly hit her, and she'd been forced to dive out of the way.

"The cabin itself is what Eleanor has been bequeathed."

Ellie said, "I've never even seen it. I don't know anything about it, other than he'd said it was 'rustic.'" She shrugged. "We never had any interest in hunting, and I got the feeling he wanted some 'girl-free' time anyway."

Jess grinned. "He said he wouldn't carry anything that wasn't his, so I didn't go. Then mom moved us to New York because Ellie was going to college."

Ellie had often wondered if her sister begrudged that, but she hadn't jumped at the chance to move back. Jess hadn't given up her life and returned to Last Chance until their grandfather got sick enough he'd required bed rest—the point at which he'd been unable to deny any longer what was proving to be inevitable. His days were coming to an end.

She shook her head. "It makes no sense that he gave me the cabin."

Why would she want that and not the land around it? Instead, her grandfather had given her his man cave while Dean Cartwright, of all people, got the valuable part—the twelve acres around it.

"Along with a cryptic message," Jess said. "Could you read that again, please?"

Holmford nodded. "To my granddaughter I bequeath my secrets, my honor, and the trust necessary to finally wield the truth. Once and for all, what was buried will be unearthed and the story will be told. This, I leave in your hands, Eleanor, believing that you will do the right thing for all parties concerned."

"So basically he left you nothing."

Ellie knew what her sister was feeling, but she didn't agree.

"Seriously El, the house is yours too. We can share it." Jess shook her head. "This is unbelievable. I get the house, and you get his man cave. It's probably falling down, in disrepair and full of hunting junk. And the land around it belongs to Dean, of all people. This is nuts. He probably won't even let you access the property."

Ellie turned to the shelves of books and focused on one red spine among the many volumes. She took a long inhale and blew the breath out slowly.

Would Dean deny her access to the cabin? She wasn't so sure and would have to check the county assessor's records to see precisely what he'd been given.

As for what Ellie had been given, it was a chance to solve a mystery she hadn't even known existed. She could get to know her grandfather more. *My secrets. My honor. My trust.* He believed that she would do the right thing. He believed in *her*. Ellie smiled to herself. Doing that brought up thoughts of her grandfather, threatening to swirl her emotions into a tornado that only left destruction in its wake.

She pushed the feelings down and turned to her sister. "It's not nothing." Trust was *never* nothing. A sentiment she and her grandfather had shared, as hard as that had been.

Her sister made a pfft sound.

"Keep a guest room ready in the house. That's enough." She didn't need money from any of this, and she'd long thought that was the last thing to think about when someone you loved had just died. But it was how things worked, so she let it go.

"And mom gets all his money?"

Ellie glanced at the lawyer, then back at her sister. She shook her head, a small movement that Jess understood.

She responded with a tiny nod of her own.

They would talk about this later.

"I should prepare for my next meeting, given that this one got a late start. I'm afraid I'll have to wrap it up now." The lawyer stood. "Please don't hesitate to contact my secretary if you wish to talk further—about any part of what was covered here."

"Thank you." Ellie gathered her purse and held the door for her sister. They shook the lawyer's hand and offered the standard pleasantries.

As they headed down the hall, Jess looked at her watch. "I should get to work. I'm late already."

"Sorry."

The hallway opened up into the reception area. A tall desk, behind which sat a young woman looking up at the man across the counter with a rapt expression. Beside him, another older woman threw her head back and laughed. The man smiled wide at them both.

"You're not the one who delayed things." Jess's tone darkened.

Ellie saw who Jess was looking at. *I think I know who the next appointment is with.* Dean's smile fell as he saw them there.

Jess strode to the door and pushed it open. "Let's go, Ellie. There's no reason to stick around here."

He had tried to help. Why would Jess blame him for her being late to work?

Dean opened his mouth, like he wanted to say something, and then frowned as she passed by him and headed out into the sunshine.

Jess stuck her hands in her pockets. "Come on. I'll walk you to your car. You can drop me off at the police station."

Ellie walked to where they'd parked.

"I don't know why you aren't mad."

"Why would I be? Grandpa gave me the gift he thought I'd like."

Jess glanced over. "And?"

Ellie shrugged. That should be obvious. "I like it." A mystery to solve. The *secret will be unearthed.* She had to wonder what that was. Even just the wonder of it and the unanswered questions were a gift.

Now there was no denying her grandfather had understood her. Maybe he'd even known she wouldn't know how to handle her feelings of loss, so he'd given her a mystery to solve.

That alone warmed her in this season of loss. Being adrift from work, her normal universe. Rotating around familiar places, moving through those where pain flashed. Memory and trauma. All of it was intertwined—good and bad. As soon as she could be gone from here, she would feel a whole lot better.

They glanced at each other over the hood of the car. Ellie said, "What is it?"

Jess looked aside. "I don't think that car coming at you was an accident." Before Ellie could say more, she added, "At least, it's possible it might've been on purpose."

"You're right."

Relief washed over Jess's face.

"It is possible."

"No, no. I'm not talking about logic." All the relief Jess had felt at being understood was gone now. "This is serious."

"If it is, time will tell. Until then I don't plan to get emotional or make snap decisions because I'm reacting based on a freak out."

"No, I suppose you don't. Though," Jess said, "I'd pay money at this point to see you freak out."

"Not enough. After all, you only own a house. I'd never do it for so little."

Jess laughed. Good. If she was laughing, then it meant she wasn't completely worried. Just a little. And that helped Ellie feel better.

There was no way someone was trying to hurt her.

That was crazy.

Four

Dean pushed open the doors to the gym and strode inside. At least now he knew what the fresh wave of ire from Jess was about.

The receptionist frowned down at his jeans. A guy whose name he couldn't remember, who seemed to wear a muscle shirt every day of his life. Today's was pink.

"I'm looking for Stuart."

The receptionist twisted around too fast. Dean couldn't read the name tag that hung from a pin on his shirt. He moved to the computer and tapped a few keys. "Stu never checked in. Doesn't mean he's not here, though." When he turned back, Dean got a look.

"Thanks, Mark." Dean nodded. Plenty of times he'd forgotten to swipe in.

He did it now, though. Used his key card and pushed through the turnstile into the main area of the gym. For what had started as a low budget, hole in the wall place to come and spar, it had been hauled into the new century with machines and TVs. They even had a studio on one side, and keypad lockers in the locker room.

He scanned the treadmills and the free weight stations in front of the mirror. Stuart wasn't…nope. Not here.

Dean's friend might not be here, but Eleanor was. He strode to the treadmill she walked on. Admittedly, slowly. But he could see stiffness in the way she moved, even with the low speed. He walked the row in front, so he wouldn't scare her by coming up behind her.

Seriously. The woman had almost been hit by a car. She could've died today, and she was exercising?

He tried to help people, but some of them just didn't want to admit they needed assistance. Clearly Ellie Ridgeman was one of those. Too stubborn to acknowledge she could use his help when she'd been clearly in pain.

"Did you ice your hip first?" He shot her a look, trying to tamp down his annoyance.

She started. "Dean." Then pulled one of her earbuds out. "What did you say?" She fumbled the buttons on the display panel and stepped onto the sides of the treadmill.

"You couldn't even hear me? Do you know that's not safe?"

Anyone could walk up behind her and do whatever they wanted, and she'd never even know. Dean shook his head. This was a small town, but a city girl like this—dressed like a librarian, at least when she wasn't in the gym—should know how to keep herself safe.

He didn't look down at her leggings and fitted activewear shirt. They actually looked like something he'd seen Jess wear, and he wondered if she'd borrowed the outfit from her sister. He was too busy being irritated at Ellie's disregard for her own safety to contemplate how amazing she looked in that outfit.

Dean repeated, "Did you ice your hip before you came here?"

"Oh." She frowned. "Yes, I did put a bag of ice on it." The treadmill put her high enough she could look down at him. "But it still hurt, so I figured moving it would help me sleep."

She did seem tired. And she'd had an emotional day listening to her grandfather's will being read.

Dean needed to back off.

"Good." He nodded, then turned away. Stuart was the one he was here to see. Not a woman who proved seriously distracting to his focus.

Sure, he was attracted to her. She also seemed to have the innate ability to completely irritate him at a moment's notice. Not unusual, when someone didn't want him to help them. But this was different.

He wanted... Dean didn't even know. Probably he wanted her to fall in his arms, desperate for him to make her feel better.

She didn't need his hero complex working overtime. Besides, he was here to find Stuart.

"That's it?" She met him at the end of the row of treadmills, one hand on her hip. The one she hadn't landed on. "You're not going to say anything else?"

"What's to say?" Truth be told, he was still trying to figure out why on earth her grandfather had chosen to give him land up in the mountains that surrounded the town. Talking about it would only mean he'd say or do things that he hadn't thought through, yet, and that always led to hurt feelings.

Not that she was the same as every other woman he'd ever met, but he'd yet to find one that was different—who didn't get hurt by thoughtless words.

Besides, he didn't need to lay his stuff on her right now. She was carrying plenty given the day she'd had. Nearly getting seriously hurt, possibly even killed. The resurgence of all the grief she was probably feeling.

Dean felt his features soften. "I'm sorry you lost your grandfather."

"Thank you." Her voice was gentle.

It made him want to shift closer, offer some kind of bumbling attempt at comfort she probably also didn't need. So Dean shifted away slightly and tried to dial down the Navy SEAL presence he had.

She leaned against the side of the treadmill. "How well did you know him?"

Now there was a question. He didn't want to brush off a relationship, but what had there been between them? "We knew each other. When he started to get really sick, before Jessica moved home, he would invite me over. I'd sit with him on the back porch, and we talked a lot. About our lives, and the things we'd experienced."

"Really?"

He nodded. "Did you know he was a frogman?"

"One of the first Navy SEALs?"

Dean ignored the way her eyebrows pointed toward each other, above her glasses. "Your grandfather was a Navy SEAL, like me. During Vietnam he was part of a squad of Navy guys who were some of the first SEALs."

"Wow." The wonder on her face was beautiful. As though she found simple stories of great things completely fascinating.

Dean nodded. "He was a pretty impressive guy, even though he didn't always agree with me on that. Still, I got him to tell me stories, and we swapped some experiences."

He smiled, remembering the old man's insistence that he was "just a regular guy." As though the things either of them had seen could be considered normal stuff. The wars they had fought were very different. There was hardly a comparison between mid-twentieth century and the twenty-first century, in terms of combat.

"Then Jess came home?"

Dean said, "He'd gotten bad enough Conroy talked to him. Jessica came home, and he was moved to the police station. He didn't need me as much. Though, I still checked in."

But Ellie hadn't come. Not until the funeral, so far as he knew.

"He never mentioned you," she said. "And yet, he gave me a cabin and you the land around it."

He'd rather have pointed out that he'd been here and she hadn't, even though Ellie was the one who was related to the old man. Only, how would that help? He'd mentioned her a couple of times, pointed her out in pictures, but hadn't said much about her or her mother. Or Jessica, until she came home and Dean saw her for himself.

Something about the three women, or Chief Ridgeman himself, meant he'd kept family business to himself. That was his choice. Some people told everyone they knew about the loved ones in their lives. Others, like Dean, did not. After all, no one in town knew about his father. Did they?

"Jessica probably hates me even more now."

Not that he cared, of course. Officer Ridgeman was young, and she could have whatever opinion of him she wanted. What did that have to do with him?

At least, that's what he would have tried to tell himself before.

Before Ellie.

Now he had more of a connection to Jessica. Not just through his besotted brother, but also through her sister. A woman he could honestly say he genuinely liked—and who he wanted to like him.

"She doesn't hate you. She's always had strong opinions, especially when she thinks wrong is being done."

"What wrong am I doing, exactly? She's neglected to explain that to me but seems to have decided that however I'm helping Ted manage his life—and all the things he deals with that she has no idea about—is apparently the wrong approach. The reality is, she has no idea."

Her lips pressed into a thin line. At least he hadn't made her cry.

"Sorry." Dean didn't want to talk about Jess. "I'm glad he gave you the cabin." Was she glad? He didn't know. What he did know was there was no way he wanted any of her grandfather's belongings. He could hardly believe the old man had given him the land, except that Dean had told him about his dream.

"He knew I wanted to start a therapy center. Maybe your grandfather figured if he gave me that land, I'd be able to finally move forward with it."

He didn't even know what to do with that, or how to feel about being given a gift that huge. The acreage was worth a lot of money.

Maybe Jessica just wanted it all to stay in the family.

"If your sister did hate me, I'm not sure I'd blame her." Dean had to admit that, at least. Maybe Jessica was planning on contesting the will.

Would he even fight it, especially since he hadn't been expecting this and wasn't sure if he even wanted it?

Yes, it was the answer to a need he'd had. A place to start his therapy center. But considering he'd never even walked the property, Dean didn't even know if it was a good place to build a facility.

Not to mention where on earth he'd get the money for that, outside the doctor and his friends

Or had Ellie's grandfather planned on him selling the land, using the money to start his venture elsewhere? He didn't even know. Surely the chief would have put that in the wording of the will. He meant for Dean to keep the land.

For whatever reason had been in the old man's mind at the time.

Ellie was about to say something when a door slammed open across the gym. A slender woman wearing a neon yellow tank top and tiny shorts bounced in. Dean focused on her face while she crossed the floor. She was frantic. "There's a guy outside, and he's waving around a *gun.*"

Several men crowded around her.

Dean left them to it and moved to the hall where she'd emerged. The EXIT door at the end had a keycard swipe entrance. He hit the bar and pushed outside, but never heard it click behind him. Before he could glance back, Dean spotted Stuart over by the trees.

"Dude! Stuart, what's going on?"

Stuart swung a handgun in an arc, pointed up high. He had to have squeezed the trigger because a shot went off.

Dean ducked. He heard a squeal behind him and turned to see Ellie crouched by the door. If anyone came out, she was going to get shoved over onto her face.

"That was loud." She shook her head, more surprised than scared. "I forgot it was that loud."

"Go back inside." He turned to see Stuart scan the rear parking lot, his eyes glassy and unfocused.

Stuart's skills were deadly enough that he wouldn't miss if he wasn't planning on it. If Dean was going to get him to stand down, it was going to take everything he'd learned about post-traumatic stress disorder. Stuart's case was intense, and they'd only barely begun to work together to manage it.

He glanced back at Ellie. "You need to get out of here."

Five

He turned away from her. Ellie's legs didn't want to move. She pushed off the wall and tried to stand, head low so she could hopefully avoid being shot long enough to call Jess. Well, the police at least. But her sister was on duty at the moment, so it might well be Officer Ridgeman who responded.

Ellie looked around for her phone. She'd dropped it, pretty sure it skidded across…

There.

"Stuart, it's Dean." He was at least four car lengths away and taking command of the situation, but not without a thread of urgency in his voice.

He was still a hundred percent Mr. Hero. All, "I got this." Didn't need the little woman hanging around and getting hurt when he could take care of it himself.

She crept to her phone which was under a car. Teeth gritted, she leaned her good hip on the ground and reached for it.

"How's it going?" He asked the question as though he and Stuart were both out for an evening stroll and had just happened to run into each other. Not what it actually was—eleven at night in a dimly lit parking lot with his friend waving a gun around.

Fear ran through her. She wasn't going to ignore it. Doing so would mean that she missed any warning signals her instincts wanted to throw her.

"Good." Stuart's voice was breathy. "I'm good."

"Yeah?"

"Yeah, man. I'm good."

She wasn't sure she believed it. Ellie leaned around the back bumper and looked at them. Dean's stance was all caution, but he still appeared relaxed. His friend was constantly moving. Hand shaking, sweating as he ran his other hand through his hair. Feet moving.

She'd taken a body language class to help her understand nonverbal communication. It had been incredibly informative, but she was having trouble remembering now what all the stances and facial expressions meant.

Stuart looked around. "They're coming. We need to get out of here and hide."

"Good idea." Dean reached out an arm like he was going to lead the way. "Let's—"

Stuart lifted the gun and pointed it at Dean.

Ellie sucked in a breath. Would he shoot?

"You're one of them, aren't you?"

"No." Dean's simple answer. "I'm on your side."

"I can't know that. They've messed with my head."

"I know that." Dean gave him a nod like the other man didn't have the power to take his life with the slightest twitch of his finger. "You can trust me, Stu. I promise you, I'm telling you the truth. I would never betray you."

"Someone else's here. They're poised to attack."

Ellie realized then that she might need to stand up, make her presence known so Stuart would figure out she wasn't a threat. Problem was, it wasn't even remotely what she wanted to do. Would she actually stand up and face his friend? Certainly not. There was no way she'd pop up and be seen, let alone get within arm's reach of him. In the line of fire. She had to be honest with herself. The only reason she wanted to do it in the first place was to prove to Dean Cartwright that she might be helpful. Useful.

But that meant going over there *and* getting involved. Neither of which she wanted to do. Nor did she think Dean would be exactly impressed by her.

Too bad.

Dean wanted her to leave? Not before she called 911 and—*wait a second.* An idea occurred to her. A way he might be able to get this guy to stand down.

"No one else's here," Dean said. "I promise it's just you and me. But it's time to go, okay? My car is out front, and we can go get coffee. Maybe a piece of pie. Just chat about stuff."

All while the gun was pointed at his chest.

"No. You're one of them." Stuart ran a hand over his chest, like rubbing a painful spot. More vigorous than she'd have thought would feel good. His eyes were glassy, too. As though his grip on reality was tenuous.

And growing more so with every minute.

Ellie's hands trembled. She nearly dropped the phone while navigating to an app the students in her Intro to American History class told her she just *had* to have. She'd only used it once, since. But the app had a text box where she only needed to type in a few sentences. She did that now, then selected the voice she wanted to dictate her message. As soon as she gave it the green light, the app would read her message aloud.

Usually it sounded kind of robotic, but this time she used one she hadn't tried before. Nineties War Movie Drill Sergeant.

A few seconds later, with the volume turned to the max, Ellie held the phone so the speaker was pointed in the direction of the two men.

At the very least, it might give Dean a decent distraction to get that gun away from his friend.

At most, it could serve to get Stuart to stand down and realize that Dean wasn't the threat here. His memories—his trauma—and the fact they still held sway over him could wind up seriously hurting somebody. If not kill them.

"Jeopardy, this is Foxtrot." The voice thundered words she'd heard before but wouldn't know the first thing about saying them correctly. Hopefully it would work so she wouldn't have to resort to praying to a God she wasn't exactly on good terms with. She'd have to apologize and ask for forgiveness first for ignoring Him for so long in favor of intellectual pursuits.

The phone speaker buzzed. "We're taking heavy fire. We have multiple casualties and are pinned down. Repeat. We are taking heavy fire. Does anyone copy? We need—" The voice cut off, the interruption perfectly timed. Two shots followed, not so authentic. They sounded like a poor attempt at beatboxing.

Ellie winced.

The final words came after. "We need help!"

Dean turned back to his friend. His hands moved so fast she couldn't see what he did before he had the gun. A move he'd been trained to do so thoroughly he barely had to think about how to do it.

Ellie's body sagged against the side of the car, and she nearly wobbled, landing flat on her bottom from where she was crouching. Not good. She didn't want to get Jess's clothes torn up and dirty from rolling around in a gravel parking lot.

Twice in one day, at the scene where police were called. Was that what this would come to?

Dean said, "Let's go, Stuart."

His friend's shoulders slumped. He didn't have the gun, but that didn't make him appear any less deadly. Not the kind of man Ellie would want to meet alone on a night like this. Too many shadows reminded her of yet another night.

That memory from long ago was little more than a blur, sensations. Smells. Pain.

She shook off the memories she carried around. Like that would make them go away. Instead, she focused on what was around her. The feel of the car against her shoulder. Cool air, tickling her skin. The way she could shift her toes in her socks to center herself.

All just tactics to be present in the here and now.

She braced against the car and stood.

Dean's friend had turned away. He looked at the gun in his hands for a second, then shoved it in the back of his waistband. Dean looked up, his attention to her like a shock to her system.

She stepped back, colliding with the car, their gazes still locked. No, there might not be enough room in this spot, that was fair, but this wasn't exactly about not having enough space. And she knew it. Maybe she would never know exactly what it was about Dean that kept her fumbling, but she was going to find out.

He's stolen part of our inheritance, El.

As though this man was some kind of usurper, instead of a man who'd been a friend to her grandfather at a time when he'd had no family around him. Just Jess, on the NYPD, and Ellie busy with university life. Teaching. Studying.

Dean's brows shifted together. He mouthed, "You okay?"

Ellie didn't want to get into something that wasn't top priority right now, not when he should be taking care of his friend. Stuart was clearly in greater need than she was.

She turned away so he could get back to what he needed to do. After opening the driver's door of her own car, she spotted him pulling out onto the road. Stuart sat beside him.

Exhaustion weighed down on her, so by the time she got back to the house and crawled into the bed they'd made her in the guest room, Ellie fell into a fitful sleep. She dreamed of a car, speeding toward her. Dean sat in the driver's seat, waving a gun around. Which made no sense.

She tossed and turned until she woke to the garage door rolling up. Jess was home.

Ellie couldn't sleep anymore, not without adrenaline-laced dreams, so she took a hot shower. By the time she was out, her sister had cooked breakfast and the coffee pot was both full and steaming.

She poured herself a cup and sipped from it. "Bless you."

Jess laughed. "What's on your plan for today?"

"I've decided to go a whole day without thinking about Dean Cartwright." When she turned and saw her sister's face, Ellie said, "What?"

"Nothing." Yeah, right. "You just…I knew it. That's all. Yesterday, I could tell you thought he was attractive or something. You were mooning over him."

"This isn't not thinking about him. Addendum. No talking about him either."

"Fine." Jess shook her head and turned back to the toaster. "Those Cartwright boys."

Ellie figured she was thinking about Ted, as she'd likely be angry or at least irritated if that was the case. Rather than if she was thinking about Dean. Maybe Jess had pushed everything from yesterday aside already while she had worked a long shift. Maybe she'd forgiven Dean.

"Are you going to eat and then go to bed?"

"Nah." Jess handed her a plate. "I'm too wired to sleep."

"I think getting wired helped suck up the last of my energy, so I *did* sleep." Even though it hadn't been particularly restful. "Bad shift?"

Jess scrunched up her nose. "It's been like this the last month or so. There's a local guy we're trying to get a bead on, but he's been one step ahead of us since we first learned his name."

Their grandfather had gone through weeks like that when a particularly tough case took his attention. Trying to help a victim in need. Catch a vicious killer targeting innocent residents. Of course, he'd never told his granddaughters, or their mother, about specific details. Just that it was a time when work took his attention.

She'd seen enough crime dramas on TV to imagine. And read enough history books to know all the awful things humans did to other humans because some people just seemed delighted by creating new ways to terrify others.

"Feel like hiking with me?"

Jess said, "Grandpa's cabin."

Ellie didn't bother asking how she'd guessed. "Once we're there, I can look around while you take a nap. If you want."

Bonus, hopefully Dean was busy with his gun-wielding friend and wouldn't know they'd gone tromping through his land. Or maybe he was asleep. Probably resting like a happy baby, sound asleep in his bed…wherever. She didn't need to think more about that, or she'd find herself imagining him wearing very manly teddy pajamas.

"Okay, deal." Jess grabbed something from the top of the refrigerator and slid it on her belt. A gun, in its black holster. "I'm in."

Ellie shivered. Why was she seeing guns everywhere she went right now? It was enough to make her want to freak out.

Or think she was in some sort of danger.

Six

"Tell me what you can smell." Dean lifted one foot and set it on the opposite knee, then leaned forward to stretch the stiff muscle.

Stuart sat in front of him. They were both on second-hand office chairs facing each other. His friend had a blindfold across his eyes. They'd both drawn a line at securing him to the chair, but had considered it given the rough night he'd had last night.

Sweat rolled down Stuart's forehead.

"Take a deep, long breath in. Hold it." Dean paused a second. "Sigh it out. Tell me what you smell."

"Sweat. Gunpowder and beer."

"What can you hear?"

"Two men arguing."

Dean frowned, knowing Stuart couldn't see his expression. This image of his was new. Could it have been from last night?

"They grabbed me. I tried to fight back, but they cut my Achilles tendon."

That was from his last mission, the one where Stuart had been caught by the men he was attempting to infiltrate. He'd been betrayed by someone in the CIA. As an officer for the agency, Stuart had expected to be backed up by the people he worked for. Instead, he'd been cut loose and left to die.

Stuart had managed to get to a phone, long enough to call one of their team members who was also an old friend. Dean had accompanied them to retrieve Stuart from that war-torn country and get him back to the US in one piece. They'd managed, but only barely.

Now Stuart was determined to figure out why he'd been burned by the CIA. What he'd done, or hadn't, that meant they'd cut him loose. Stuart reasoned that it was something he knew, but didn't realize he did. So he wasn't able to tell them what it was Dean was supposed to help him dig it out of his subconscious. After that, he'd be in better standing with the agency.

But if Stuart's post-traumatic stress had been detonated last night by something he'd seen in town and not his past experiences out of country, then Dean had more than one problem to contend with.

"Go back to the two men arguing. Were they inside, or outside?"

"I can see the stars. One of them shoved the other, and he fell into his bike. It tipped over and scraped on the ground. That made the fight worse."

"Can you hear what they're saying?"

Some context might help, but it could have just been a fight about a spilled drink. Or a woman. Stuart had been walking last night, which he often did to clear his head. Though normally, he tended to steer clear of people. If he'd passed by the biker bar across town, he might be recalling a fight he'd merely overheard. Dean could use the tip line and hand the information over. Could be helpful to the police in one of their cases, or maybe it meant nothing at all.

The cops in town were all solid. He trusted each one, and they called often when they needed help. There was a crew of four EMTs in town and one ambulance. On occasion they were all busy, and if that was the case, Dean was called. After a while, people started calling him first, especially if they didn't want to occupy the EMTs time, didn't want it to be official, or maybe, if they didn't want to leave a paper trail.

Stuart's biceps flexed. He shifted his legs and turned his head side to side. Erratic, nervous movements that often preceded the moment he began spiraling into a state where he was harder to reach. Unable to respond.

"Listen to the sound of my voice." This was where the blindfold sometimes worked against them, and he'd occasionally had to ask Stuart to remove it. To center himself back in the present. "You're in the town of Last Chance, and you're with me. You are safe."

Stuart sucked in a full breath and sighed it out. Without being asked. He was learning how to manage the panic in its early stages. "One of them said he wanted out. That's when he got shoved. The other man…"

Dean gave it a few seconds. Then he said, "What did he say?"

"He kicked the man in the stomach, three times."

Dean's abdomen clenched in sympathy. It always did.

"He said no one quits west and lives to tell about it."

Probably a gang, or a place they lived together. Their motorcycle club, maybe. Dean wondered if it was worth having Stuart take the brain power and energy to describe both men when this could very well be nothing. Stuart was already agitated. It could make it worse by hindering his recovery.

"That's good."

Stuart pushed out another breath.

"Where did you go next?" As he asked the question, Dean's phone buzzed in his pocket. He ignored the call for right now. If it was an emergency, then the person would likely immediately call again.

"I followed them. The big man dragged his friend behind the bar. His boots made grooves in the gravel."

"Did you intervene?"

Stuart flinched in the chair. As though he was bound, which he wasn't at the moment. The former CIA agent had been tied to a wooden chair when they found him, though. The blood… Dean pushed aside those thoughts or he'd be heading to his place of panic.

"I waited at the corner, pressed against the siding. I got a splinter in my arm."

Dean couldn't see one in his arm right now, as he wore a long-sleeved running shirt.

"The big man kept kicking him. He was going to beat him to death."

"Stuart." Dean wasn't sure what to say. He knew Stuart had seen a man killed that way during his captivity. He could be reliving that. Blurring past and present so that he wasn't able to remember accurately.

"There was so much blood." His whole body shuddered, but he held back the whimper. Dean saw his throat bob as he swallowed it down. "Lights flashing. It was so hot, and he was crying. I couldn't get to him."

Useless platitudes wouldn't help, regardless of how badly he wanted to tell Stuart that he'd done what he could, or that he was safe now. Dean knew what it felt like to know you could have—or should have—done more. That inaction or a deficit of your skill had cost someone their life.

"Keep breathing."

Stuart gasped. "I had my gun out." He shook his head. "I didn't even know I had it, and then I was pointing it at him. I stood over him."

Dean stilled.

"I pulled the trigger. The muzzle flashed. It was a good kill. They needed to die or things would've gotten out of control."

"Keep holding the gun. Feel the warm metal in your hand. The smell of gunpowder in your nostrils. Close your eyes." He paused for a second. "And then open them. Tell me what's around you."

"A brick wall, and a dumpster."

The biker bar? He'd just mentioned getting a splinter from the siding. Given how many people Stuart had likely killed in his career as an officer for the CIA, Dean had no idea where his mind was right now. He noted these details on his pad to remind him to look through the reports contained in Stuart's file—the one they'd obtained by hacking into the Government's database of covert action.

"Tell me where you go next." Landmarks may help him remember, given a lot of cities had unique locales particular to that location.

"To the car." Stuart pulled his blindfold off. "It was a rental."

Dean figured he likely needed to check behind the biker bar anyway. Stuart had been in possession of a gun last night. Could he have killed a man?

Not something he wanted to deal with when it involved a friend. The last thing he wanted to believe was that Stuart, as a result of his trauma, had murdered a man in cold blood. But it was possible, which meant it needed to be followed up on.

"A rental."

Stuart shrugged, removing the blindfold to shoot him a sardonic look. "Dude, it's always a rental."

"I'd have thought the CIA had a garage of cars in each city."

"But the criminals would keep seeing the same car. You can't keep thirty different cars just in case." He stood, lifting his arms over his head. Then he bent to the left, and to the right, stretching his sides. "What's for dinner?"

Dean needed to go check behind the biker bar to assure himself there wasn't a dead body back there. "You should just order a pizza."

"What? You're going out? It's barely lunchtime. I'm thinking crock-pot. Or baked mac and cheese with veggies and bacon. Something that requires forethought. And chopping."

Dean pushed out a breath and set the chairs back at the table. "I have a few things to do."

"Wouldn't have anything to do with that librarian-looking woman you were with, would it?"

"She was wearing workout clothes."

"Nah, not then. But that was a good trick she pulled. I have that voice-changer app, too."

"I know, you used it to pull a prank on all of us."

Stuart grinned, all traces of his earlier stress gone now. "Classic. When are the boys due back?"

The four men they shared a huge house in the foothills with were off on an op. The six of them usually shared chores. When the team was away, Stuart, Dean and Ted had to split them up. And there were four full bathrooms.

"Check your email. See if they're headed home."

Stuart glanced over. "No contact?"

"Client's request." Dean didn't even know who the client was. Just that the team was on a high-priority security mission. They'd been gone two weeks already. "I'll be back for whatever you've chopped up for dinner. Just text me."

"No problem, dear."

"It's *Dean*, actually. But I could see how you'd be confused." He pulled his coat on while Stuart busted a gut laughing, and then locked his notes in the file cabinet in his office.

He drove toward the highway, and called Tate at the stop sign. With the phone on speaker in the cup holder, he listened to it ring as he pulled onto the blacktop and headed toward town.

"Hey, Brother."

"Hey." Dean didn't get any more out before Tate cut in.

"That doesn't sound good."

"Meet me at O'Dowd's in ten minutes."

"Sure thing. Glock, or the shotgun with the Taser rounds I want to try out?"

"You bought a shotgun and Taser rounds?"

"Uh, *yeah*."

"Don't hit me by mistake."

Tate chuckled. "I could see how you might think I'd make a mistake, Mr. Navy SEAL. But don't worry. I've been practicing."

The man was a former FBI agent according to town rumor, and currently a PI, dating Detective Wilcox at Last Chance Police Department. That made two new relationships for cops. Dean might've met a woman he was seriously attracted to, but that didn't mean this would become a thing. Let alone a *thing*.

He shook his head. "Don't be late." And then he hung up before Tate could say anything else.

Dean had been taught to shoot who he was told. To breach the door in front of him, and save the lives he was sent in to save. He'd traded that in for the sake of helping people. Patching up injuries and working with Stuart to keep moving through his trauma. Stuart couldn't afford to get stuck and, if he did, he wouldn't get over it. All Stuart had to do was keep moving—probably the toughest thing for him to attempt right now.

Tate would interrogate him, and then Dean would have to admit he pretty much had a thing for Ellie Ridgeman.

Not that he'd ever see her again.

Tate pulled in just as Dean climbed out the front seat of his car. "Around back."

Dean led the way.

"You planning on telling me what this is, or you just need a witness to what you're about to do?"

"I'm just looking." He saw the dumpster, and at the back corner of the building, he saw the rear was set up with picnic tables and a fire pit. "For that."

Tate moved to stand next to him. "Ah."

A man's body lay on the ground, one leg across the fire pit. Jeans and a leather jacket. Curly red hair. Blood covered the front of his shirt.

Tate sighed. "I'll call Savannah."

Seven

They'd driven as far as they could. Ellie's sister now led the way up a mountain trail. Once in a while she saw a boot print in the dirt, one that caused a hitch in her breath that had nothing to do with how much her hip hurt.

Back in New York, she walked every day and took a stretch and tone class every once in a while. Ellie wasn't out of shape. It was just from hitting the ground the way she did yesterday, diving out of the way of that car. She saw another print. They couldn't be one of her grandfather's boot prints. He hadn't been up this way in months, right? He'd been sick a while.

"So I was looking into hit and runs," Jess began.

Ellie glanced up from watching the ground in front of her—as everyone knows you are supposed to do while hiking—to her sister up ahead. Strawberry blonde hair worn loose, jeans that were frayed with slits in places high on her thighs that Ellie would *never* have the guts to reveal. But Jess didn't care. She did what she wanted, living her life in a way her older sister didn't always approve of. This was also something she didn't care about.

It occurred to Ellie just then that maybe Jess did care about her opinion but didn't want to let Ellie know that. Maybe it hurt her feelings that her big sister didn't approve of her choices.

She huffed out another exhale, sounding like she was out of breath. This always happened when she hung out with her sister. Why did relationships have to be so complicated, anyway?

"Are you okay?"

"My hip hurts." She held up her hands, too. Still bandaged from skidding on the asphalt.

"We can stop if you want."

Ellie shook her head. "When we get there, I'll sit down. How much farther is it anyway?"

Jess chuckled. "He liked his space, didn't he?"

Ellie laughed as well. It sounded nice, but the stitch in her chest didn't go anywhere. "Are we still on the safe side of the mountains?"

"I think so." Jess said, "Why would he build a cabin where it's practically inaccessible? That doesn't seem practical."

"I've just been thinking about it." She tried to sound like she'd reached some intelligent conclusions already, which of course wasn't true. "I was looking at the Founders' Map in the coffee shop."

"And thinking about hiking all over, through all those uncharted and inaccessible non-trails."

"I'm not into extreme sports."

Jess chuckled. "Yes. I do know that."

"I was just curious."

"This is a mystery you can leave alone." Jess quieted a second before she said, "If there's a reason the Founders didn't want us over there, we should just trust them. The last person I heard who took a wrong turn hunting, wound up getting torn apart by mountain lions."

"Huh." Ellie swallowed. That was pretty gruesome.

Still. Surely someone had explored it. Or even flown a drone over there with a GoPro attached to it. Some people saw it as a challenge to skirt the no trespassing order that had been drilled into them since grade school.

"Do you want to hear about hit and runs?" Jess started up the trail, this time walking by Ellie's side. "I forget that not everyone wants to hear about cop stuff."

"It's fine. But why would you look into hit-and-runs? Is there such a thing as a serial hit-and-runner…or something?"

"Not as such." Jess grinned. "Though, it's not unheard of. Just not like a serial killer, you know?"

Ellie swallowed. "Yes."

Jess eyed her. "I checked all the reports from the last few years. To see if the details of any of those incidents matched the vehicle in your hit-and-run. Also, the why of it, you know?"

"Or the location." Ellie pressed her lips together while she thought it through. "Could be there's that one spot, and it's just more prone to out-of-control cars. Or they've polled hit and run drivers for the best places to do some damage and get away with it."

"Wow. You sound like the city council crime stat report."

Ellie shrugged. "Just thinking it through."

"People do crazy stuff that makes no sense for a whole lot of reasons. How can that be boiled down into a pie chart?"

"Quite easily actually."

"Agree to disagree. Especially if the person doing those calculations has never walked a beat."

Ellie let that go. Her grandfather had been a cop, now her sister. She knew how they felt about their brotherhood—which, by the way, had never made sense to her because Jess was a girl—and *the code*. She could never be a part of that. Because she wasn't one of them and had no plan to be.

Plus, she mostly thought that everyone considered their own situation to be unique. Everyone formed bonds with the people around them—whether they liked it or not. There was solidarity when others shared your life situation.

After all, she'd found that with her support group, hadn't she? She just hadn't stuck around long. What was the point in dredging up the past and laying it out so everyone else could feel your pain as it was reflected in their own pain? That hadn't sounded like healing to her.

Eventually she broke the silence. "So, did you find out anything about champagne-colored cars?"

"No." Jess pouted. A look Ellie had seen many times during elementary school. She'd been a much more mature middle schooler at the time. Jess said, "No champagne-colored cars have been used in any crimes around town in the last five years."

Wow, she'd gone that deep looking into it? Ellie said, "You know I'm fine, right?"

Jess shot her a look.

"What does that look mean?"

"People aren't fine. Literally no one is fine, even though we all tell each other that we are. We're *fine*."

"I am, though."

Jess shook her head. "You're probably the least fine person I've ever met."

"It was an accident. I'm a little sore, but no harm no foul. Right?"

"That's not what I meant and you know it."

Ellie opened her mouth to ask her what she did mean then, if it wasn't that, when Jess stopped. "Good gravy, it's a trash heap."

Ellie looked at the dilapidated cabin in the middle of nowhere, tucked under the trees at the end of a gravel path not even wide enough for an ATV. "The entire roof is covered in pine needles."

"Don't get up there and clean them off. They're probably stopping up all the leaks." Jess sighed. "I get the house, and this is what he leaves you?"

Ellie touched her sister's shoulder. "I don't need the house."

Jess's eyes widened. "Ah-ha! But you *want* the house."

"No, I don't. I don't live here. I just think it's worthless to tell you again that I don't want it." She paused. "I have no interest in it."

Jess narrowed her eyes. "Huh. I don't get you." She shook her head and strode to the cabin porch.

Ellie studied it a few minutes more. A cabin. Her cabin. Did she want a cabin? It occurred to her that she could work here just as easily as she could work anywhere else in the world. Most everything she needed was online, or it was already packed and ready to ship wherever she wanted to go to take her sabbatical and write her next book. Though, this was very remote. Quiet and private for sure, but was there even internet up here?

"Watch your step."

Ellie entered right behind her sister.

"Whoa."

She practically shoved Jess aside to see the place. Thick blankets. Bare walls on which hung tack and bear traps. Western art. An animal skin, white with a brown line down the center. Wood furniture. A beat-up wood table and chairs. The kitchen looked like a nightmare from the forties and the whole place smelled like—

"Mothballs."

Ellie nodded. "That's exactly what I was thinking."

This was what her grandfather had given her, along with those cryptic words. But what was his truth? The story she needed to uncover. The secret she needed to finally reveal about him.

Tears pricked her eyes. Hot tears that threatened to fall down her cheeks. He'd given her something to do, a mission that stirred every part of her.

Jess turned. "Oh, no." The empathy was clear in her tone. "I'm sorry. I'd be crying too if I got—" She waved her hand around. "—this as a gift. Shame you can't send it back. What was he thinking?"

"Jess."

"What?"

"I love it."

Her sister stared, eyes wide. Completely silent. She opened her mouth. Closed it. Opened it again and said, "What do you—what?"

Ellie tugged her sister to her and gave her a quick hug. Then she looked more at the living area. "I could stare at all this for hours. It's like a museum." She couldn't help grinning at her sister. Then she spotted a loaded bookcase of battered books and practically squealed as she raced to look at the titles. "Smells like old man."

Jess shook her head, a smile tugging at her lips. "If you mean it's a random collection of old stuff, then yes. Museum." She lifted one brow.

"I like it."

Rundown. In need of a little love. But that would come after she tackled the mammoth job of cataloging everything in here and figuring out where it had come from. Learning the history of each piece.

Sure, a lot of it was probably junk. But if she didn't go through it piece by piece, how could she be sure she would find whatever it was her grandfather had wanted her to find.

"Uh-oh, you have that look on your face."

"What look?"

Jess said, "Like it's Christmas morning and you got a brand…new…book."

Ellie laughed. "I do enjoy Christmas." She looked around some more.

The pang in her chest was still there, but different now. She wasn't seeing someplace her grandfather had been and feeling the loss. She was hearing him speak loud and clear. He would talk to her through all of these things. His collection. His secrets, and his truth.

"Well, at least going through all this old stuff might give you some inspiration for your book."

"Exactly!"

"Wow."

Ellie said, "What?"

"Christmas." Jess added, "If you're looking for inspiration, maybe sticking around isn't an awful idea."

"I never thought it was awful."

"Sure, but it's easier to run from your feelings when you're going somewhere else. To hide. Which is basically all a sabbatical is. Hiding from your life, pretending to 'write another book,' or whatever."

"There's a lot there in what you're saying." Ellie folded her arms. "I'm not sure where to start unpacking all your angst wrapped up in your words. So I'll start with work. Are things not going well with you at the police department?"

"This isn't about me." Jess lifted her hands, then let them fall back to her sides. "Just look around. Maybe you'll find this secret quickly so we won't have to be here until three weeks from now. There's probably nothing in the fridge."

"Why don't you go check if there's coffee?" Ellie figured it didn't matter that there wasn't milk. She could drink it black, and Jess would probably deal with it for some caffeine right now.

Jess pretty much stomped to the kitchen. There was only so much stomping that could be done effectively in tennis shoes. Heels or boots were always better for that. Ellie had found it made students and faculty all take notice when they could hear her coming down the hallway.

She pushed her glasses up her nose and crouched in front of the tiny end table and the stack of books tucked under the drawer, in the shelf between the four legs.

A few old classics and a leather-bound book—his journal. Her grandfather was the one who'd taught her to get those thoughts spinning around in her head down on paper. *You've got to exorcise those things you can't let go of.* When she'd asked him what he needed to get out on paper, he'd confessed it bothered him that he couldn't save everyone. She'd never thought of police work like that.

As she glanced at her sister now, banging around in the kitchen with what looked like a camping coffee pot that Ellie would have no clue how to operate, it occurred to her that Jess might be dealing with the same thing.

The icing on that cake? An unsolved crime involving her own sister.

A tear rolled down Ellie's face. She didn't want to be the source of her sister's spinning thoughts. Perhaps she should stick around for a while. Keep her company and make sure she was all right while Ellie did the research for her book. Here.

After that, she could leave.

She was mulling over the idea when the glass of the front window cracked. She jerked her head up and looked at the brand new circle, no bigger than a silver dollar, smack dab in the center of the window at eye level. The fractures in the glass splintered across the pane.

Jess screamed, "Ellie, get down!"

She looked at her sister, her thoughts frozen to nothingness.

"Gun!"

Eight

Dean frowned. A gunshot? It had been seriously faint, a good distance away so that the rapport of it was muffled. He stared at the land he now owned and leaned back against his car.

This was what Alan Ridgeman had given him. A place to set up his therapy center, assuming he could get the backing to fund the building project. Acres, set into a mountainside. A beautiful, peaceful place with nothing but quiet. The rustle of the trees.

He'd have to make sure hunters didn't use the area, or it could set back some of his patients if they heard sudden gunfire.

Dean's phone buzzed. He looked down to see the notification light up his messaging app—Savannah had sent him a short audio message.

He tapped the button.

"Ever heard of Karl Tenor? I'm sending you his picture."

An image loaded. "This is the dead man from the alley?" Dean hadn't moved around to look at the man's face—he'd have contaminated the crime scene with his footprints.

Her message came back. "That's him."

Dean held the record button down with his thumb and said, "Never heard of him, and I've never met that guy. Local biker?"

"How'd you know he would be there?"

Of course she hadn't answered his question about whether Karl Tenor was a local guy or not. He could see how an argument with a guy from out of town could get out of hand. But an argument with a local guy might be a more significant conflict, and could spur an ongoing investigation. Not that anyone had told him about any of that.

His only concern was whether Stuart had only witnessed the crime, or whether his trauma pushed him to the point of perpetrator.

Before he left, Dean had locked the gun in his safe which no one else had access to. Just in case.

He pressed the button to record his voice and said into his phone, "If it comes down to it, I have a gun you might want to compare against any ballistics you found. Just to rule it out."

She wasn't the only one who could avoid answering a direct question.

The new message popped up a few seconds later. "Of course." She made a frustrated sound. "Don't leave town."

She knew he was protecting someone. If he did his job, she wouldn't find out who. Unless it became a necessary part of the investigation. Stuart had to stay below the radar. He didn't need a paper trail uploaded to the cloud with his name on it—even if it was a fake name.

If it ended up looking like he might've been the killer, Dean would talk to Savannah. He would take her to him. He had no doubt Stuart would want to do the right thing. He'd known the guy a while now, and while it would tear him up inside to have to turn him in, he knew Stuart would do the right thing and face the consequences of his actions.

Dean didn't want to do the right thing, but he would. He just hoped—and prayed as well, now that he was thinking about it—that someone else killed Karl. That Stuart had just witnessed the crime. Which, if that was the case, it was bad enough it had sent him spiraling.

He again pressed record and said, "Of course I—" Another shot went off. This time it was followed by two answering shots. "Shots fired." He gave his location. "A rifle and a pistol. Sounds like there's a battle going on."

Dean pocketed the phone and went to his trunk. He pulled off his jacket and tugged on a vest, then set a ball cap on his head, backward. He slid a wide band of elastic up his arm, settled over his bicep. On the front was a clear pocket into which he stuffed his cell phone. The touch screen mostly worked through the plastic.

A couple of the team guys who were away on their mission had radios that could connect to the police band, but Dean didn't. He grabbed Bluetooth earbuds and turned them on, which connected them to his phone, sticking one in his ear for when Savannah called him.

The signal wasn't great up here, but he'd make it work.

Dean slid a holstered pistol on his belt and grabbed a rifle, pulling the strap over his head and under one arm. He secured it to the clip on his vest.

Locked the car.

Started running.

He took the trail headed in the same direction the shots had come from. That wasn't friendly fire, and it wasn't a hunter taking down his prey. It had been hostile gunfire. A rifle shot, answered by a pistol. Attacker and defender.

His phone rang.

He slid his thumb across the screen, answering the call. "Wilcox?"

Of course it was Savannah, but there was no time to look at the screen.

She said, "What have we got?" her voice breathy, sounding like she was moving fast. Assembling backup and heading over here.

He explained the gunshots.

"What's up there? Isn't it just forest? It could be a hunter, right?"

"Chief Ridgeman's cabin is up there. His granddaughter is in town for the reading of the will. If I was a betting man," he paused, breathy from sprinting. "I'd put money on that being Jessica up there. Probably with her sister."

"The one from the hit and run?"

Dean frowned but didn't answer.

"This isn't good." He heard a shuffle and she said, "Possible officer down situation. Civilians involved." She paused a second. "We have no idea."

"We." Dean didn't feel like he was part of a team much anymore. Not in the eat/sleep/breathe/brotherhood of war he'd been immersed in before. It was nice to feel that camaraderie now, even in a small way. He wasn't part of the police department or emergency services. Though a lot of people did classify him as a first responder. Neither was he part of the team he lived with. They had their own company, and their own missions.

Starting this therapy center was supposed to be his new team. Something he could build himself.

Savannah said, "I'm on my way."

"Copy that." Dean heard the tone as Savannah hung up on her end.

He ran faster, knowing he would get there first. Were the two Ridgeman women safe? Were they hurt? He'd seen Ellie right after nearly getting hit by a car. She'd weathered that like a champ—someone really stubborn. But he'd seen the hurt in her eyes. Something that made him run faster now than he normally did, even when at the sprint part of interval training.

If either of them were hurt, he had his backpack of medical supplies.

All he needed was to get there.

A shot slammed into a tree in front of him. Bark sprayed out, along with the smell of cordite. The shards of wood stung his cheek. Dean kept going, changing direction so he was an erratically moving target and not just a sitting duck. Any rifleman worth his salt could fire ahead of a fast-moving human or animal and hit them. Dean could pass any weapons test he was given, but he wasn't above average in skill level.

When no more shots came, he figured it was a warning only. The shooter wasn't trying to kill him. He just wanted to encourage Dean to turn back without helping the two women he assumed were in their grandfather's cabin—Ellie's cabin now.

Dean continued, heading through the woods, going in the right direction. He'd looked at a map earlier and had a rough idea where it was.

And then he saw it. The cabin, through the trees.

Jess was out front. She turned, gun up, then realized it was him. "I'm going after him. You stay here with her."

"She hurt?" Never mind that he had far more training hunting someone through rough terrain than she did.

"No."

"You?"

"I'm gone." She ran from the cabin.

Dean headed for the stairs. "Ellie? It's Dean." He walked in slowly, just in case she had a weapon. "Your sister told me to stay with you."

As if he would feel pressure to follow her order.

"I don't need a babysitter." Her voice wobbled.

Dean glanced around the cabin. "Where are you?"

"It doesn't matter. Go help Jess find whoever that was." She sounded breathy, her voice thick. "They shot at us."

He saw the bullet hole in the front window. "I see that. She said you were okay. Are you?"

"Yep. Fine."

He didn't believe it for one second. He kept looking and found her beside the couch, sitting on the floor with her back to the wall. Knees bent. He shifted his rifle behind him and crouched in front of her. She hugged a book to her chest.

"What's that you've got there?"

Her eyes were wide. Why did they seem bigger than before? She sniffed. "My g-grandfather's journal." She blinked and he saw the sheen of tears. "He shot at the cabin."

"Did you get hurt?"

She shook her head. "Your cheek is bleeding."

He swiped at the wet there, and his fingertips came away bloody, so he wiped his face on the shoulder of his T-shirt. "Thanks. Probably stings like your hands, right?"

She looked at her palms. Raw and red, with a bandage on each palm. "You should help Jess."

"I need to make sure you are all right before I do that."

"I'm fine. So, go."

Dean frowned. "You don't need to shove me out of here." He looked around. Was that it? She was trying to protect what was hers, which meant he needed to get out. He had no business here.

He stood. "I'll leave you to your cabin full of busted-up junk."

She huffed.

Dean turned back. "Sorry. That was uncalled for."

He was supposed to be helping her like he helped everyone. Why did she bring out this reaction in him, where stubbornness irritated him into firing back? He was trying to be the good guy, the former-SEAL-turned-EMT he was respectfully known as in this town. "Stand up, please. I'd like to see for myself that you're all right."

"How could I be all right?" She shifted and stood, though it seemed to be painful for her. "The place has been shot up. He *destroyed* some of my grandfather's things. Now I might never figure out what he wanted me to know."

Dean shook his head. Not understanding.

Ellie said, "Nothing. It's just part of what he left me." A single tear fell from her eye and rolled down her cheek.

Dean moved closer to her and looked down into those wide eyes. He wanted to wipe the tear from her cheek but knew it wasn't his place to do that. She didn't want his comfort. "I'm sorry for your loss."

"That's been said before." She glanced at the kitchen and winced. Because of the damage, or the train wreck their relationship was becoming?

Not that they had a relationship. Or would. But he'd prefer to actually be friends instead of this standoffish acquaintance thing they had going on. Besides, it was possible she needed his help.

Dean said, "I should go check on Jess."

Another tear rolled down her cheek.

He softened his tone. "If you're all right."

She sniffed again, still clutching that book to her front. "Of course it's all hitting me now." She shook her head.

Dean had to wonder if she was even talking to him.

"I really hate adrenaline."

"It can save your life."

She glanced at him. "I hate it."

"Because you're upset?" He moved an inch closer, still talking softly. "It's okay to be upset. You were shot at, and the shooter destroyed some things that are important to you."

She shook her head. "I don't like it. I need to have control of myself."

"And feelings make you lose control?"

"Can you just go help my sister?"

Irritation was a common fallback in people using avoidance to skirt a painful topic. Dean had to wonder if this was about the loss of her grandfather…or something else.

"I knew I should never have come back. I hate Last Chance County."

Dean's chest tightened as it dawned on him that there was something deeper going on than he'd realized. More than a difficult incident. Had she experienced trauma? "What happened to you here?"

She gasped.

The door slammed against the wall. He spun to see Jess stride in. "I didn't find him. There's no one out there." The young officer stuck one hand on her hip. "But one thing is for sure. Someone is trying to hurt you, Ellie."

Nine

Dean turned to her sister. "Savannah is on her way."

"Who?" Ellie glanced between them.

"She's a police detective." Jess turned back to Dean. "I know she's on her way. I called her."

"So did I."

Ellie left them to their showdown. She picked up a shard of pottery that used to be a mug or some sort of knickknack he'd had on a shelf. Blown to pieces by a bullet that could have instead hit her head.

More tears threatened. Ellie sniffed a big breath through her nose. *You didn't even know this place existed yesterday. No point getting all emotional about it now.*

She decided to just be angry that her thoughts wanted to go there. That her emotions chose now of all times to show up and make her all weepy. Angry was way better than crying. Which meant angry crying was entirely acceptable. Like when she'd been passed over for that last promotion and not given the job of department chair. As if that idiot Professor Tumbleweed knew more than she did about the job because he'd been there longer than her. College politics changed slower than melting glaciers.

"Don't touch too much, El. This is a crime scene."

She whirled around. "A crime scene?"

Her sister said, "You know, so we can figure out who shot at you."

Ellie shook her head. "I don't want a million cops in here, touching everything."

"We don't have a million cops, so that's fine." Jess didn't back down. "An investigation *will* be done. With no arguments from you."

"This cabin belongs to me." What if they touched something that had been left a specific way, just for her to find? "I can't have a bunch of you people stomping around, making a mess."

"You really don't have any faith in me," Jess said. "Since you don't think I'd make sure this place was respected by every person who walked through the door, I'll say it now, we *are* capable of being respectful with people's property."

"I know…" She knew that. Ellie shoved her glasses up her nose and realized she was still holding her grandfather's journal. Like a tether while the world around her swirled out of control. "I don't think otherwise."

"No, you just insinuated it. Which is worse."

Ellie didn't know what that meant.

"Because it means you don't trust cops—in particular, ones that are your family."

"That's not true."

Her grandfather had been there for her when she needed someone. Since then, she'd tried to stay away from cops in general. There was nothing in her life that warranted a police officer. She didn't allow herself to get into any dangerous situations.

"Besides," Ellie argued. "How do you even know the shooter was trying to hurt us, or break any of these things? Could have been a hunter who missed."

"I returned fire in his direction. Then he shot at you *again.*"

"Or he shot at you because you scared him."

"Let us investigate this, and I'll ask him when I arrest him."

Ellie pressed her lips together.

"I'll make sure they're careful, El. Maybe you could start trusting me right now, with this."

Dean shifted his stance, and she realized he could hear everything. Of course, he was standing right here while they argued deeply personal things in front of him.

She turned to face her sister. "Fine."

Ellie moved to the kitchen where Jess had been when the first shot came through. There was an itch between her shoulder blades, and she didn't know where it had come from. Like she was being watched. Or there was way too much scrutiny in this small cabin. She didn't like other people judging her, even if it was harmless assessment.

Dean had found her right when she'd been losing her cool. Maybe he didn't even care. Or he thought she should've been stronger, more like her sister. Or he felt sorry for her now. She didn't know which the better option was. Or why she even cared what he thought of her.

Ellie had two reasons to still be here now that the will was done. One was to help her sister pack up their grandfather's things, and the other was to solve this mystery. There was no room in that for her to be dealing with possible death threats. The last thing she needed was to be targeted by someone. And it wasn't something Ellie would let bother her.

Whoever they were, she wasn't going to waste energy being scared.

Ellie slapped the journal down on the counter. It *definitely* hadn't tumbled out of her hands as she lost her grip on it—and her cool. Again. She gritted her teeth, grabbed the edge of the counter, and bent forward putting her head between her elbows.

No one was trying to kill her.

And if they did, why would she be scared of them?

She wasn't being targeted by anyone, least of all the subject of her nightmares. She'd read the newspaper article. He'd been jailed. Now he was dead. What else was there to know? She'd moved on.

It had been *years* ago. Ellie wasn't a naïve high schooler any longer. She was a grown woman with a master's degree and a career.

"El."

She straightened and saw her sister had neared. "I'm fine."

"Sure." Jess leaned against the counter at a right angle to her, keeping her distance. Like Ellie was a skittish animal about to lash out. "This is probably a good time to remind you of something. That fear you're feeling? It's good instinct. You should be careful, and for the time being, not go anywhere alone. It's worth staying safe. Being protected."

"Because you have no idea what's going on. Which means I could have no reason to be scared. And *that* means I don't intend to waste time being scared." She folded her arms. "At least until I have a reason to be."

Which she planned on being…never.

She said, "After all, you don't know if they were shooting at me or you. Or just trying to destroy the cabin. Could be that the hit and run was an attempt on *your* life."

"Don't tell my chief that, okay? He'll put me on house arrest."

Ellie shot her a look.

"That's not my goal," Jess told her. "I just need you to work with me."

"She's right that you do need protection." He leaned against the opposite edge of the counter, arms folded across his chest. The man looked built for war. Ready to do serious business. It scared her, about as much as it reassured her, that he would do battle on her behalf.

Jess said, "Two near misses isn't something you can brush off."

"Being too busy to be scared isn't brushing it off. I just don't need to get dragged down by emotion that doesn't serve anything. It would just make me ineffectual, which won't help when I have work to do and a mystery to—"

"What'd I miss?" A blonde woman strode in, wearing a red coat over a black shirt and dark blue skinny jeans.

Ellie got a drink of water while she fought to tamp down her reactions to everything. Her sister, the handsome warrior across the counter, the new lady detective who clearly had more style than Ellie would ever have, her grandfather's death, her grief, the will, the cabin and—

"Ellie." Dean's warm voice interrupted her reverie.

She glanced up and then realized water was flowing over her hand. Over the rim of the glass. She shut off the faucet and tipped some out before taking a sip like everything was fine.

These people were all trained to deal with stress. She'd spent almost a decade trying to get over hers while making strides to become an invaluable member of the faculty at her university.

Jess acted like there was something wrong with being that focused.

"Hi, Ellie." The blonde stuck her hand out. "I'm Detective Wilcox. You can seriously call me Savannah, though. As Jess's sister, that makes you family to the police department."

Her grandfather had been the chief, so Ellie knew how that worked. Cops looked out for other cops and their family. People they cared about.

Ellie shook her hand, quickly realizing she hadn't dried it off since she overfilled the glass. "Sorry."

Great. Now the fabulous detective knew she was a distracted super nerd. Not something that normally bothered her, except that right now Dean was staring again.

She lifted her chin and shot him a look like, *What?* He only smiled.

"Any idea why someone might be trying to hurt you?"

Ellie turned to her. "No."

Jess sighed.

Savannah said, "I'm going to need you to think a little more before answering." She glanced at Jess like she needed an answer to a question. Or Jess should do something.

"You asked why. I don't know why. I have no enemies here. I don't live here, and I haven't for years."

"But it's possible," Jess said.

"Sure. In the sense that multiple things can be true, or plausible. Like the fact that either time you could have been the one being targeted. Right?"

Her sister couldn't argue with that.

Savannah said, "I'm looking into that. But Jess is trained to take care of herself."

"I'm not helpless. I've taken self-defense classes enough that I started teaching it two years ago. I was raised by a cop who took me to the range and showed me my way around all kinds of guns."

"But you don't own a weapon, right?"

"Why would I?"

Jess lifted her hands and turned to pace away from the kitchen. "Maybe because someone is targeting you."

"Don't yell at me. I'm not helpless, and I'm not a child that needs to be managed." She turned to Savannah. "I had planned to leave town by now, so this wouldn't have even been an issue, but I need to find what my grandfather left for me."

The detective frowned. "I thought he left you this cabin?"

Dean shifted his stance. Whatever he wanted to ask or was thinking right now, she was determined not to care. So she didn't look at him.

"He did, along with a secret that I'm supposed to uncover. Because he trusts me to do the right thing with 'what was buried' and this story. Finally."

Which meant it was old. Something he'd done when he was younger? She knew he'd been in Vietnam, and she'd studied that decades-long conflict extensively. Though, not his unit's specific role in what had happened.

After he'd come home from the war, her grandfather had been one of the earliest residents of Last Chance.

Dean unfolded his arms and braced his palms on the edge of the counter. Like that made him any less imposing. "Could it be that someone is trying to keep you from finding out whatever this is?"

She opened her mouth to speak but discovered she had no answer.

"That's what I'm wondering," Savannah said. "And Jess needs to be at work in an hour."

"You haven't even slept."

Jess shrugged. "I'm covering for Donaldson."

Savannah pinned Ellie with a stare. "That means you're going to be alone."

"She needs protection."

Ellie whirled to Dean, swallowing the gasp. "Someone give me a gun, then."

One side of his mouth curled up. "Nope."

"My grandfather taught me how to use them. We've covered this."

Dean said, "You're busy, and you don't have the time or the skills to watch your back." Before she could argue, he turned to Savannah. "I'll stay with her while Jess is at work." Then he turned fully around to face her sister. "That okay with you, Jessica?"

Ellie couldn't even speak. Dean was going to stay with her? And worse, now they were talking about her like she was the "subject" they needed to keep safe. While they argued, Ellie slipped down the hall and headed for the back door.

Some protection detail. They didn't even—

Dean grasped her elbow and spun her back. "Not gonna happen. You stay where I tell you to."

"Not gonna happen," she parroted back.

He grinned at her. "At least this isn't going to be boring. Now get to work looking for this secret." He waved at the living area. "Because we're headed back to town before dark."

Ten

Even three hours later, he still hadn't figured her out. The cops were gone and she was looking through her grandfather's things. He'd boarded up the broken windows so it was secure. About fifteen minutes ago, she'd settled on the armchair with a book and had barely blinked since. She read the way his younger brother—the tech genius—would fall into a computer program. The kid would forget to eat, among other things.

"We should head out soon." He waited for a response. "It's gonna get dark."

Ellie nodded without looking up. He was pretty sure she had no idea what he'd just said.

"Good book, I guess."

Dean's phone buzzed. He shifted the armband phone holder to look at the screen and then stepped outside, remaining on the porch where he could still see her. Front door open.

Stuart came into view a minute later and made his way to the porch, a backpack over one shoulder. He looked relaxed, not lethal, which was the difference between a SEAL and a CIA officer.

Stuart didn't look like what he was, or the extent of what he was capable of. It was all about subterfuge. With Dean, you could see at first glance precisely what he was made of. And the extent he would go to in order to complete the mission.

In this case: to protect Ellie.

In the past few hours, he'd seen so many facets of her, he couldn't sort through them all. But he knew one thing. She was in danger, and he was going to protect her. Her grandfather's death had hit her with—of all things—the lot of his belongings which might be the answer to this mystery she'd told them about. The reason why she'd been given the cabin. It wasn't until she faced their loss that her grief then hit her.

In all of it, Dean had seen her pain, vulnerability, determination, strength, need, weakness and fear. She'd fought hard to stay standing, but the truth here was that she needed him.

He wondered if that might be why he'd been given the land surrounding the cabin—literally a circle around it. As though for some reason, her grandfather had decided Ellie needed Dean's protection.

Stuart stepped onto the porch. "Ted showed up. I left him to eat and then put the leftovers in the fridge for us."

"He'll eat all of it the way that kid puts down food." Dean stuck his hand out. "Thanks for coming."

Stuart grabbed it and turned the handshake into a hug. "Least I can do."

"We need to talk about that." He checked that Ellie was where he'd left her and motioned for Stuart to walk out of earshot. Not that she was eavesdropping. But she didn't need to inadvertently hear something that wasn't relevant, just to get scared all over again.

"What is it?"

Dean didn't want to say it, but he had to. "I think I know what set you off last night." He scratched at the afternoon stubble on his jaw. "I actually think you *witnessed* a murder."

"The biker guy?" Stuart blinked. "I thought I killed him. I figured it was a buried memory, something I'd forgotten doing."

Dean didn't know what it would feel like to believe there were people he'd killed whose faces he could not remember. He could recall each one, and the second he saw them in his mind, realize they were dead. There was no coming back.

Stuart rubbed both hands through his hair, then scrubbed them down his face. "Whoa. I thought I did that."

"Could you have? Really? I mean, until Detective Wilcox arrests someone else, it could be possible. But I just don't think so. A cold-blooded killer, taking life with no reason? That's not you."

"Way to front-load the good news." Stuart shoved his shoulder, but there was no malice in it. "Now you're saying I might've done it? No. Dude, that kind of runaround is not cool." He swung the backpack off his shoulder. "Here's the surveillance stuff you asked for."

"Thanks." There was a reason he gave Stuart the good news first. And he wouldn't apologize for giving Stuart the relevant information in a way that didn't trigger another post-traumatic episode. He didn't even like the word "episode" let alone want to cause one in his friend and patient.

Stuart had stood up and was about to head out again when someone spoke up from behind.

"Surveillance? Like, for watching people?"

Dean turned to answer Ellie's question. "In this case, it's for securing the cabin and making sure anyone who shows up gets their face on a camera, so that they can't get in without us knowing it."

"Oh." She directed her smile at Stuart. "Thank you."

"His idea." But Dean's friend stepped closer to her and held his hand out. "Stuart Leland. I don't believe we met last night under the best of circumstances. Sorry if I scared you. And thank you for your help."

"There's nothing to be sorry for."

Dean recognized the sympathy on her face and realized that was it, again. She'd been through something that, in the face of trauma-induced PTSD, meant she had a deep understanding of it. The fear, the guilt. The shame Stuart felt. She'd been there. In his shoes.

Dean needed to get the team on a full background check of this woman. If he was going to effectively protect her, that meant he had to know everything about her.

"Are you doing okay? I heard you had an eventful day today as well."

Ellie blew out a breath and nodded. "I did. But I'm all right."

Dean shot his friend a look. Seriously? Now he was flirting with her. Coming on like Mr. Charming. Ellie blushed under Stuart's attention. Dean wanted to shove the guy back, and narrowly resisted the urge to mouth, *Bro code,* to his friend. Everyone knew you backed off when your buddy was clearly interested in a woman.

Everyone knew that.

Stuart glanced at him. Humor lit in his blue eyes. "Okay, then. I'm heading out now. Call if you need anything?"

"Yep." Dean folded his arms across his chest and watched his friend disappear back into the trees.

"Doesn't he know the path back to the parking area is that way?" Ellie pointed west.

Dean gently turned her like a giant sundial. "It's actually that way."

"Wow, I was way off." She frowned and shook her head. "When do you want to leave?"

"Thirty minutes." That was all the time he figured she needed to gather a few things. And it was conveniently how long he needed to set up the system and check that it was running. "Do you need a backpack for anything you want to take?"

"Oh. Yes, it would be wonderful to bring some things with me back to the house."

He wondered how she would feel when she found out he intended to sleep on the couch when Jessica wasn't there to keep watch.

She disappeared into the house. He tracked her down in the bedroom, sorting through drawers, and then he got to work setting up the cameras. Front door. Back door—the one she'd been about to leave out of before he cut her off. As if he was going to let her leave and risk putting herself in the line of fire? Yeah, right. He was more skilled than that.

By the time he was done, and he'd bolted the back door from the inside, Dean found her with a stack of books and a music box on the coffee table. She was bent over looking at that storage space under the drawer on the end table.

He went to look at the image that had been painted on the top of the music box. "Don't forget the book on the kitchen counter."

She started, slamming her head on the underside of the drawer. "Ouch." She straightened and saw the lamp falling toward her. She shifted out of the way and let it fall rather than hit her.

He righted the lamp, then held out his hand. "Okay." When she took his hand, he helped her to her feet.

She pushed her glasses up her nose and looked up at him. The woman barely came to his nose, and he wasn't a big man. Her huge brown eyes peered up at him. Blinking.

"Good?"

"Um…yes. I'm good. Thanks." She shook her head. "I'm not usually this out of it."

"You're doing fine. It's been a lot the past couple of days." He added, "Not many people can deal with finding out their life could be in danger the way you are."

"Oh, well, I'm not really thinking about it, to be honest with you. I tend to unpack things slowly and mull them over. You know?"

He didn't know. "Can't do that in my line of work. You have to react and trust your instincts completely."

"I don't." She seemed convinced of it.

"Haven't we all got built-in responses? Things our brains do without us even thinking about it. Like when you drive and take a turn without thinking about it, and you suddenly realize you're headed to your old job. Or the last place you lived. Automatic things."

"Hmm."

Dean grinned, happy to have given her something to think about instead of what was actually happening. He planned to keep her safe while she was working it out. And while she was trying to figure out this "secret" that her grandfather had left for her.

He pointed at the music box. "All this needs to go?"

"Yes, please."

Dean packed the backpack he'd emptied of surveillance equipment.

"It's all up and running?" She was looking at the camera up in the eaves of the porch. Not super conspicuous, but you couldn't see it until it could see you. So it worked for now. Until they could get something better installed.

Which meant the team would then be back, and he'd get some solid backup helping him keep Ellie safe. If things escalated, anyway. It might not come down to that. In fact, he hoped it wouldn't because that would mean Ellie was in serious danger.

He secured her front door and used a small cordless drill Stuart had brought in the backpack to affix a deadbolt to keep it shut. He handed Ellie the key. "This belongs to you."

"Thank you."

They started walking.

"And thank Stuart for me, as well. Please?" When Dean nodded, she continued, "Was he okay, after last night?"

"With what you did, using that app—that was fast thinking, and I'm grateful—he came out of it because of you. But it's what happened before that I'm worried about." He scanned around them, watching for indications someone was out there. A someone with the same rifle that had been used to shoot out the windows. "It seems Stuart might have witnessed a murder, if not, he possibly participated in a man's death."

"You think he could've hurt someone?"

"He's had serious training. Not like me, but he's deadly when he needs to be. Lately, that hasn't been necessary, and yet it's not something you forget. So I'd say it's definitely possible. He might've been in the wrong place at the wrong time. Or he did something he's going to have to answer for—whether he remembers it or not."

"A wrong is a wrong, no matter if it was committed unknowingly," she said. "But it seemed like post-traumatic stress to me."

"That's right. It is, and I've been helping him work through it." Dean needed to tread cautiously. "Is that something you have experience with?"

She started to speak, but his phone rang.

"This is Dean." He studied her while he listened.

"It's Bill at dispatch. There's been a traffic accident on Hill Road, half a mile west of mile marker seven."

"Copy that." He started to walk faster but saw Ellie wince when she tried to do the same. "I'm on my way."

"Has something happened?"

"Car accident. Sounds like I'm closest."

Eleven

The couple of pain pills she'd taken from her grandfather's medicine cabinet had started to work by the time they pulled up at the scene of the accident.

On the highway, headed back toward town, a truck had turned over. Two other vehicles—a car and a delivery van—had collided with it. Or each other. It was hard to tell what had happened.

Dean pulled up the parking brake. "Stay here."

He pushed out the door and slammed it behind him before grabbing a duffel from the trunk and sprinting to the overturned truck. All while Ellie sat there.

A police car was parked on the far side as though it had come from town. Blue and red lights flashed. Where was the ambulance? Surely someone had been hurt. She couldn't believe there were no injuries. Shattered headlights and debris lay across the asphalt.

She was a college professor. She might be trained in self-defense, but she'd never taken first aid classes. She didn't know what to do.

Ellie gripped the backpack of her grandfather's things between her shins. Inside was the journal she'd been reading. The one where he'd written frequently of his regrets. The dishonor he had buried. She'd skimmed through weeks and weeks of sporadic entries. He hadn't penned his thoughts often, but when he did, it was about "what they'd done" and how he'd been complicit in it. Much to his shame.

Her grandfather had been a proud man, dedicated in his role as a police officer. When she'd been hurt in high school and there was nothing he could do about it, he'd been torn up. She'd buried her feelings. He'd written down his in the journal.

Most of the entries she'd read were from before she'd even been born, though. So what she was supposed to discover hadn't had anything to do with what had happened to her.

It was a truth buried decades before that.

Possibly even as far back as his time serving in Vietnam.

Could the secret have to do with war crimes? She'd done plenty of research and had plenty more books to read in order to prepare to write her own. What she'd found wasn't pleasant. War never was. It wasn't heroic, or noble. It was ugly and often horrific—in a way that destroyed people. War changed everyone—those who were there, and those who stayed home. The home front was going to be the focus of her book. How culture shifted for women while so many men were away.

But it would seem that, given her grandfather's will, she might be looking more at the war itself to find out what he had done.

Not a pleasant prospect. But if he wanted the truth to come out, she would find it. After all, he'd even said in his will that he trusted her to do the right thing with the information. The story he wanted to tell her. His written words about the matter—however vague—dripped with brokenness.

Ellie glanced around, looking for the ambulance that was surely on its way. Unless it was tied up somewhere else and unable to get here, and that was why they'd called Dean. He moved around, fast but not frantic. Looking capable as he helped people out of vehicles and spoke with the officers there. As long as she stayed in the car as he'd told her to, she was safe. She might be able to help. But she also could be putting herself in the line of fire again. Or distracting him from what he needed to do, forcing him to watch out for her as well. That could endanger someone else needing care if only she'd have stayed in the car.

So Ellie stayed put.

She kept glancing around, half looking for a guy with a rifle trying to kill her. Or that champagne-colored car hurtling toward her. Ellie shivered. Her gaze snagged on a man standing over to her right. Dark jeans and a blue hoodie, the hood pulled up so his face was shadowed. But she was pretty sure he was staring at her.

Just the line of his body language intimidated her into another shiver. Who was this guy? As she watched, he lifted one hand, pointing his pinkie toward his mouth while his thumb angled to his ear. A phone? What did…

Hers rang. Tucked in her back pocket, it began to vibrate. Ellie just stared at him.

He lowered his hand slightly, then moved it back to his face.

Ellie shifted enough to slide the phone from the back pocket of her jeans. Cold washed over her. She looked at Dean, a cry for help. But he was helping someone else. She couldn't bother him when the ambulance still hadn't arrived, and there were hurt people here.

Ellie looked back at the man, still standing there with his hand up. Indicating she should answer her phone.

The ringing stopped. She'd taken too long.

On the screen, another incoming call from the same number flashed as her phone vibrated in her hand. Ellie's thumb shook as she swiped it across the screen, then put the call on speaker. "Y-yes?"

The voice that replied was distorted. "You've been looking into the past."

The voice hadn't been altered in the same way her app changed a voice. This was different, like a mask. Or a computer program.

She shook her head. That didn't matter right now. She had to focus on what was going on here and what to say to this guy.

"Stop looking." The voice was hard, inviting no argument. "The past will stay where it's buried. Quit digging it up."

Hoodie guy had lowered his arm, both hands now by his sides. He looked ready to attack. Poised. But he wasn't on the phone. His mouth was closed, and it didn't move when the caller spoke again.

"If you don't, you and those you care about will suffer."

Ellie fought back that drowning feeling. The one that threatened to rise up into her throat and choke her until she couldn't breathe. Until she died from being swallowed by fear.

The man in the hoodie turned then, and she watched him walk casually down the highway. He hopped a cement barricade and disappeared around the corner of a warehouse building.

Someone passed the window of her car, right by where she was sitting.

Ellie squealed. The phone dropped between the backpack and the seat. She realized it was just an EMT, finally here.

She fought to steady her breathing, one hand to her chest. *You're smarter than this fear. Don't let him get to you.* If she panicked, it would all be over. She might as well give up and quit. Instead, she needed to act as smart as she was. Think this through. Use all those methods she'd learned to control her emotional reaction to fear. Put the physical reactions aside, and focus on the here and now.

What was real.

What was true.

Those were the things she was supposed to focus on. Like the fact people were hurt. She might be in danger, but others were putting their own safety on the line to save people. Ellie had good reason to be here in the car. However, looking at Dean up ahead helping those who needed it made her want to do the same.

To fight for someone else, even when she couldn't fight for herself. Maybe because she couldn't.

She lifted the phone from the floor by her feet and saw it was still connected. "You don't scare me. My grandfather had something he wanted me to know, and I'm going to figure out what it is. If that's a threat to you for whatever reason, that's your problem. Not mine."

Whoever this was, they knew about the secret. If the story got out, they would have a problem. That had to be why they were prepared to scare her. But were they prepared to do worse than that? Ellie couldn't help but think she was gambling with her life, or at least until she found out for sure whether or not they were capable of taking a life.

A low chuckle came through the phone. So distorted it almost sounded comical, and she had to hold back laughter of her own. That wasn't going to go down well.

Whoever it was on the other end of the line said, "You'll risk your life for something, and you don't even know what it is? I'll tell you."

Ellie braced, waiting for what he would tell her. She assumed it was a man, anyway, given the coordination and planning that had gone into it. A man determined to stay anonymous. Women didn't usually react in the same way men did. Mostly, she guessed a female would hit hard and fast in the heat of anger. Ellie would have known there was a problem and that she should leave it alone. Men always thought they could threaten a woman into doing what they wanted.

Not Ellie. She wouldn't give in to fear this time.

"It's destruction. You'll ruin good people's lives if the truth gets out. So I'll do everything in my power to stop you."

"It won't be so easy," she told him. After all, her grandfather had given her this task for a reason. This man thought he could try and hit her with a car, and he thought he could shoot at her. Well, neither time had she known she was in danger. He hadn't hurt her. So what would happen now that she had world-class, former-Navy-SEAL protection on her side, and she knew to be careful?

She would be watching out for danger. Ready for the next attack.

Ellie didn't have more to say, so she hung up the phone. Her hand still shook, but she wasn't going to let it stop her.

She'd overcome a lot in her life. No way would she give up now because of this.

Ellie sent her sister a long text and a bunch of screenshots of her call history. Jess would insist on investigating. That was fine if they could figure out who had threatened her. Who had tried to kill her.

Then she pulled the backpack up and onto one shoulder and got out. She kept her head down as she moved, watching for a shooter hiding on a roof. Or behind another vehicle. There was help everywhere, so if he did take a shot at her and she did get hurt, then she would have aid quickly.

Fear can't stop me.

It wasn't gone, but that didn't mean she wasn't able to work through it. Acknowledge it and set it aside.

The way she'd done with every resurgence of her panic over the years since her life had irrevocably changed.

"Everything okay?"

She nodded to Dean, sliding the backpack on both arms so she'd have her hands free. "How can I help?"

His eyebrows lifted. "You shouldn't be out here. I asked you to wait in the car because it's not safe."

She explained about the phone call, which he didn't like. Ellie wanted to see a different emotion on his face. Not just obligation or disappointment. She wanted the warmth she'd seen from him. Some indication he was as affected by her as she was by him.

But, then again, maybe he wasn't attracted to her. Could be he was only doing this because he helped people and that was the man he was.

"You should go and get back in—"

"I'm not going to hide." She lifted her chin, determined to make him see she was strong. "I let Jess know about the call, and now I'm going to be smart. But I'm not backing down."

The gloves on his hands were stained with blood. He nodded, looking like he was impressed with her. "Okay, let's get to work."

Twelve

Dean shoved the ambulance door shut and rapped his palm twice on the back door. As it pulled away, he turned to Ellie. "Okay, now spill."

She'd been on edge since she got out of the car. Where he'd told her to stay put so she would be safe. Now she was sticking to him like glue.

"What happened?"

Her eyes widened, but she didn't say anything yet. Dean had time. The cops and now the paramedics were gone. People had disbursed. She was looking at her shoes, the line of her shoulders extremely tense.

With no apparent explanation.

He wondered if this was more than just fear over the couple of near misses she'd suffered so far. Already he'd seen indication she had suffered some kind of trauma. He had no idea what it was. But with Dean's primary function being helping people—whether that was physically or mentally—he didn't think it was too much to ask what someone he wanted to start a relationship with might need emotionally from him.

Dean wanted a place to go—someone to be with—where he didn't have to work with them. To not feel like he had to "fix" them, as well as everyone else.

He liked Ellie. Dean had a vested interest in keeping her safe because it was the right thing to do. But if he was going to start a relationship with her, it would be because it was a sanctuary for him, a peace he found with her. Not more work he felt like he had to do.

"Ellie." He touched her elbow gently. "I need you to tell me if I'm going to keep you safe."

Before she could answer, a black and white police car pulled up and Jessica hopped out dressed in her police uniform but with a jacket over the shirt and a hat over her blond hair.

Ellie groaned. Dean figured out why when he saw the thunderous look on her sister's face. He turned to the officer and nodded a greeting. "Officer Ridgeman."

Ellie shifted behind him. Using him as cover?

He folded his arms across his chest, enjoying the stretch to counter the fatigue he felt from the work he'd just done at the accident scene. "How can we help you?"

"You can't." She pointed at Ellie, who now clutched the back of his shirt. "She can."

He looked over his shoulder and kept his voice low. "Ellie."

She lifted her gaze, her face close to hers. Fear stark in her eyes. "I told Jess about the phone call right before I got out of the car. So she could do some technical stuff that police do and figure out who he is."

"I'm guessing you left your phone in the car," her sister said. "After you sent me *a text*."

"Did you get anything from it?"

Jess said, "Ted is looking into it, but he needs the phone you got the call on."

Dean turned to Ellie. "What did he tell you?"

"Leave it alone, or else. That kind of thing."

His gaze tracked the movement of her lips as she spoke. However it was her grip on his shirt, the other hand on his arm, that told the real story. She was scared. "We're leaving now. Time to get somewhere safe."

"Good." She nodded. "I want to go through the backpack and see what there is to find in what I brought from the cabin."

"Okay."

"Hold up." Jessica lifted a hand. She squared up on Dean. "You left her in the car. Alone. And got out to assist the accident?"

"We were closest, so Bill called me. We were first on scene." Not that he needed to explain himself to her. "We helped, and now we're leaving."

He would talk to Ellie later about getting out of the car, even after that phone call. Though he understood fear driving a person's actions. He'd seen it plenty of times in countries where people saw no rest from war, no refuge from a life in danger. Hunted every second of the day.

He just hadn't thought he would see it at home where the world around him wasn't at war. Which was the reason he hadn't taken the boys up on their offer of joining their team. Dean was done with that. But personal protection detail for a woman he was drawn to? That was exactly what he wanted to do.

Physical protection. If he had to help her get a footing mentally, the way he had to do with Stuart—and a few others—that would only color what was between them. He wanted to be a boyfriend to her, not a therapist.

"You put her at risk. You're done." Jessica lifted her chin. "Ellie can come with me, and she'll be safe at the police department while I finish out my shift."

"And when you need sleep?"

"I'll get a protection detail."

"So do it." His suggestion was a good one. If she thought she could do a better job protecting her sister, that was fine by him. Dean would step aside, but would probably remain part of the rotating detail she was likely to schedule. Conroy, who was the current chief of police, was a friend. Dean would at least be able to convince him.

There was no reason why he shouldn't let Jessica take over her sister's safety.

Except that tiny flex of Ellie's fingers when he'd made that last comment. The thought of him handing her off to her sister made her nervous. Concerned. Scared. All of the above, or something else. Maybe he could get her to tell him. Or she would continue to keep it a secret from him. Either way, Dean realized he wanted the chance to prove it to her. She could trust him. No matter what, he was determined not to let her down.

Jessica pressed her lips together.

"You're too busy," he surmised aloud. "You don't have time."

The lip press curled slightly.

"It's fine, Jess." Ellie shifted to peer around Dean's arm. "I'll go with Dean, and it'll be okay. I know you're in the middle of a case."

Dean nodded. "I've got this."

Jessica sighed. "I know."

She'd rather be the one protecting her sister. He didn't blame her for that, and it was nice to know she felt about her sister the way he felt toward his little brother. Ted was his whole family, as far as Dean was concerned.

He wanted to know if the case was about Stuart, though. If she would tell him. "Big investigation?"

"This guy we've been trying to identify for months now." She ran a hand back over her hair. "Or, at least, it feels like months. First, it was Summers. Then his uncle. Now we're farther up the chain but… Ellie?"

He'd felt the change in her as well.

She'd let go of him.

Dean turned. Her face was pale, so much he wondered if he was going to have to catch her. "Are you—"

She lifted her hand, palm facing him. Dean stopped walking toward her. She bent double, hands on her thighs, and sucked in breaths. "I'm okay. I'm fine. He's dead. Right?"

"Summers, or his uncle?"

Ellie whipped up straight with a gasp.

Jessica said, "I *knew* something happened to you. I've been thinking about who, and what. What did they do to you?"

Ellie shook her head. "They're dead. It doesn't matter." She lifted her chin like that would convince either of them.

Dean glanced at Jessica. She was about to argue when her radio crackled and he heard Bill's voice, though he couldn't make out the specific words. Jessica twisted the radio to her face and pressed the button. "Lima Charlie six. Show me responding."

She took two steps backward and pointed at her sister. "We are going to talk about this."

The look on Ellie's face said differently. She watched Jessica leave, even after the car had disappeared around a turn, and didn't look at him.

"She's right, you know."

Ellie whipped around to face him.

"We should get somewhere safe."

"Fine." Ellie headed first to the car with that backpack still on her shoulders. Head high.

Dean followed, scanning the area. "I'll need to know everything about the phone call you told your sister about." Back when it had been fresh in her mind.

"I'll forward it to you." She turned, standing by the door.

He opened it. "I'll give you my cell number."

"Fine." She didn't move to get in the car.

He smiled. "Fine."

She didn't want to tell him what the problem was. Nor did she want to talk about how it made her feel. That might come, when or if she decided to trust him. But right now he appreciated realizing that she avoided it with banter. Ellie was determined to be strong, and that meant not giving in when she'd been blindsided.

About a mention of Ed Summers and his uncle.

"That's why you didn't want to come back to Last Chance. Because something happened to you here."

She glanced away, not meeting his gaze.

Both men were dead now. And yet the fear was still as real for her as it had been when they were alive. Whatever it was had been serious.

"Let's get out of here."

She slid into the car, looking relieved. Dean shut the door then circled the hood. There was no way to find out what had happened to her without invading her privacy, which meant he had to wait until she was ready to tell him what happened.

A tow truck headed up the highway toward him. They were close to town, but it had come from the other direction. Another job. Or where the driver lived. Dean pointed in the direction of the wrecked car the police had cleared off the road.

The passing semi ahead of it ruffled Dean's hair. He huddled against the driver's door as it passed, going full speed.

He decided to wait until the tow truck did the same before getting into his vehicle, as the police had rolled the wrecked car to a spot in front of him on the shoulder. Then he would get in and drive Ellie to safety.

So far she hadn't been targeted at her home. But that could change at any time. This guy—whoever he was, warning her to stay away—had found her in three different locations. He could even be tracking her. After all, he had her number.

Did he need a safe house situation? No cell phone. No internet. Just around the clock protection from a team of highly-trained security experts.

Something to think about, at least. Worth sending an email so when the team reconnected after their op, they would see he needed help. Hopefully it wouldn't drag into weeks, and months, and Dean could get back up.

Unlike the semi, the tow truck slowed, and the driver lifted a hand to wave. Dean returned it. The side had huge red letters. *Larry's Towing.*

If he hadn't read the words, he'd never have seen the boom start to swing in his direction. It took a second to realize it was about to hit him.

Dean ducked to a crouch. The hook for the winch on the back of the tow truck slammed into the roof of his car. Metal screeched as it tore. Ellie screamed.

Dean felt the impact as it slammed into the back of his shoulder.

He hit the ground and everything started to spin.

Thirteen

Ellie flung the car door open. "Dean!"

She'd heard that awful crunch, and had seen him go down. Was he hurt? The second she caught sight of him, Ellie cried out. "No!"

He lay on his side but she could see his back shoulder from where she was because he was partially rolled to his front. There wasn't any blood.

"Dean?"

Here he was, suited up for battle with layers and a protective vest and it still hadn't prevented him from being hurt. Though, it may have saved his life.

"Dean." She touched his shoulder but dared not roll him to his back. Her voice whimpered as tears worked their way up her throat. Kneeling on the street wailing wasn't going to get him help.

"Is he okay?" The man approaching was younger than her, and she'd seen him before. He wore cargo pants, running shoes, and a tank-style T-shirt that showed off huge shoulders and biceps. "The whole winch arm came loose. It should have been secure."

Ellie went cold with fear. He'd hurt Dean. Was he going to hurt her too? This might be the person from the phone call. Or on the street.

The man moved to her and then reached out with his hand. As though he intended to *touch* her.

Ellie slid Dean's gun from the holster on his hip. The one he'd brought to protect her. She thumbed off the safety and pointed it at the man. "Back off."

This weapon was going to be used to protect him now.

The man reared back, lost balance, and landed on the seat of his cargoes on the asphalt. "Whoa, lady. I'm only trying to help."

"Don't come near me. Or him." Her grip on the gun wavered, and it shook in the air. But Ellie locked her elbows and held it up. No way would she allow weakness to fail her now.

The younger man stared at her, wide eyed. She'd seen him before.

Ellie said, "Don't come near us."

"Yeah, you already said that." The man shook his head. "Don't shoot me."

"Then back off."

He lifted both hands and scooted back, then hopped to his feet. "I'm gonna get on my radio. Call this in."

He moved away from her.

Ellie didn't lower her gun but aimed it at him, just in case he planned to do something.

When he moved around to the driver's side of his tow truck and out of her view, she looked around. No one was here, and it was fully dark now. She shivered. Anyone could sneak up on her, so she had to be vigilant.

She got her phone out and saw a text from Jess. A repeat of her parting words. Instead of calling her back, Ellie moved to dial 911.

No.

If the guy who'd called to threaten her somehow had access to her phone, he could listen in. He would know Dean was hurt, and she was vulnerable. Ellie had to protect both of them single-handedly since he couldn't help her right now. She tossed her phone on the ground and rummaged through Dean's pockets for his.

"Sorry. Excuse me."

He moaned.

"I'm sorry." A tear rolled down her face. "This is my fault. You got caught in the middle trying to protect me."

There was no way this wasn't by design. She didn't believe in accidents. Happy, or little, or whatever. No way did she think Dean had been hurt randomly. That man had warned her that the people around her would be hurt, and this had to be a direct retaliation because she hadn't backed off. She'd left the car and waded right into the situation.

"Please wake up." She whispered the words to him, wanting desperately to get out of there. But she had to call 911. It seemed like forever before someone picked up.

"Last Chance Emergency. This is Bill."

"Dean is hurt."

On the ground, he moaned and shifted his legs.

"Don't try to move. I'm getting help." Into the phone, she said, "I need an ambulance. And more cops. They were just here, so you can just tell them to turn around and come back."

"Why are you using Dean's phone?" The man sounded older. And suspicious.

"Because he's hurt!" She practically wailed the words, subconsciously drawing on the fact that if you pretended to be helpless, men would want to rescue you. Every woman knew that. "Dean was hit by the tow truck winch thing. We need help!"

"Ellie." Dean shifted.

She touched his hair. "Don't move. I'm okay, but you're not." To Bill, she said, "We need help. Dean needs help."

"Put him on the phone."

"He's barely conscious. He can't talk to you."

The young man said, "Dispatch is calling it in." The tow truck driver trotted back around the front end of the truck this time.

She lifted the gun.

"Whoa, lady. Don't shoot me."

Dean shifted. "Ellie."

"Try to not move." She patted his hair, trying to reassure him.

On the phone, Bill said, "Ellie. It is Ellie, right?"

"What?" She realized what he'd said. "Yes."

"Put Dean on the phone."

"He's in no condition to—"

Dean lifted his hand. "Give me the phone."

She handed it to him.

"Yeah?" He took a breath. She could see how much it hurt for him to breathe in the way he moved as his back expanded and then contracted. In the dim light of the tow truck lights, she could see his face pale. "Uh-huh. Yes."

She needed to do something, but he wasn't bleeding and she had no idea about medical treatment. When he shivered, Ellie unzipped her jacket and pulled it off. She shifted the gun as she moved. The tow truck driver must've thought she was distracted because he reached for it.

"Don't!" She may have yelled it a little too loudly, bringing the gun up again.

The tow truck driver yelped and skittered back.

She hadn't thought he could move that fast.

Ellie gritted her teeth. "Just give me some space, okay?"

"Yes, it's right. Same place." Dean paused. "Copy that." He set the phone on the asphalt and lifted to sit up, the call on the screen still connected.

He didn't even sway, though she saw a flash of teeth as he righted himself. "Give me the gun, Ellie."

"You're hurt. I don't think you should be sitting up."

"Ellie."

"He tried to…" She didn't know what, but that wasn't the point. She wanted to explain. "I don't know him, and he's acting weird. Which means I don't trust him."

He held out his palm. "Pass me the gun, please."

She did it right away, giving Dean control of the weapon while Ellie swiped up the phone and held it to her ear. "You're sending someone, right?" If he sent a lot of someone's, that would be fine with her.

"This is unprecedented."

"Because Dean got hurt?"

"Help is on the way." Bill, the dispatcher, sounded taken aback.

"Any idea when they plan on being here?" She could tell Dean was pushing himself. Determined to protect her when he was the one that was hurt.

He shifted toward her. "Ellie."

She had no idea why he felt that he had to move right now. But it looked like it hurt when he moved, so she knew it wasn't a good idea. No matter what he wanted to say. "You should lie back down."

"This is Bill again," the caller said. "Stay on the phone, so I know everything is all right."

"The vest took most of the force."

She didn't look at him. If she did, she would lose it even more. Ellie was about to snap. And if she did, she'd either be wailing for the sky like she was already tempted to do, or she would start ordering everyone around.

Dean grunted.

She laid a hand on his arm. "Maybe you should lie down." Why did she have to keep repeating herself?

"I'm okay, El. I've been hurt worse than this."

"Is that supposed to make me feel better?"

"El." He did it again.

She squeezed her eyes shut, one hand still on his forearm. She could feel his strength under her fingers. With the other hand, she held the phone. Dean had been hurt because of her. She wasn't about to run off on her own, half-cocked, trying to do the right thing. Things would only end up turning out worse than this if she put herself in even more danger.

"Hang in there, girlie."

She shifted the phone and said, "I don't need your help, Bill. I'm fine."

"Sure you are. Thought we wouldn't protect you? Jess's big sister. The chief's granddaughter. Probably thought I didn't remember, neither. I was on duty the night they raided that party." He barely paused before saying, "I'll never forget it. He lost his mind finding you there."

Ellie hung up on him.

"Hey—"

She cut off Dean before he could ask what that was about, lifted her face, and tried to smile. "They're on their way."

"I know." He glanced at the tow truck driver. "Mark. Hey."

Ellie said, "You guys know each other?"

"Mark is the reception guy at the gym we were at the other night."

"Oh." That had to be where she'd seen him before.

"Don't go anywhere," Dean said. "The police are going to want an explanation."

The guy looked Dean over. "What are you, some kind of undercover commando or something?"

"He was a Navy SEAL."

Dean winced. She didn't know why.

Mark said, "So how'd you get saddled with the crazy chick?"

Ellie gasped. Dean's chest shook. Was he laughing at her? If he thought Mark was funny, then she was looking forward to him getting help…all the way to the hospital.

While she looked for approaching police cars and wondered how many more hours she'd have to sit on the side of this highway he said, "She needed help. That's why I'm with her."

Ouch. If Ellie cared what either of them thought, she might've been offended by that. But it was true, wasn't it? Dean was only here to keep her safe.

Too bad he hadn't been able to keep her safe.

"Huh." Mark eyed her. "Guess that's probably true. I still don't know what happened to the winch."

Ellie pressed her lips together. This guy didn't want a piece of her mind. It wouldn't make her feel better anyway, and he would only end up referring to her as a "shrew."

He eyed her. She didn't like his stare. It made her want to move closer to Dean, farther away from him.

Instead of doing that she said, "I'm Eleanor Ridgeman, Professor of Modern History at Furrowbridge College in New York. I'd say it's nice to meet you, but under the circumstances…" She shrugged.

"I figured you for a librarian."

"Sorry to disabuse you of that notion."

He chuckled.

Dean squeezed her knee. "Basuto is here."

The sergeant she'd met after her almost hit-and-run, along with his partner, climbed out of their car. Then another cop car showed up, and two more officers. Savannah Wilcox, the detective, pulled up in a muscle car. She asked Ellie half a million questions about what happened.

Afterward, Savannah went to Dean and crouched in front of him while the EMT prodded his shoulder and made him wince. She wanted to scream at the guy. No wonder, when everyone needed medical help, they called Dean instead.

"Hey."

She spun around.

"Whoa." A young cop stuck his hand out. "Donaldson. You're Jess's sister, right?"

She nodded. "I don't think I've met you. I'm Ellie."

"Everything okay? You seem a little on edge."

"It's been a very long day, and I didn't sleep last night."

"My partner and I are just leaving. Did you…want a ride home?"

The invitation confirmed to Ellie that Jess hadn't filled him in on the day's events, otherwise he'd be more about protection detail and less about doing her a favor. Ellie started to shake her head, then saw Dean arguing with the EMT.

"He's going to the hospital. Pretty much whether he likes it or not, though that's only what the sarge said. I don't think he actually would go so far as to hit Dean with his stun gun just to get him to go get an X-ray."

Several people shifted, and she lost sight of him. He needed to be seen by a doctor, and not with her in tow.

"You can drive me back to Jess's house?"

"Sure thing. We're actually on lunch break in a minute, anyway. You're not out of our way."

Ellie bit her lip. She still had Dean's phone and the backpack. Her phone was somewhere on the ground. She didn't even want to know where.

If they were tracking her with her phone, they wouldn't know where she'd gone until it was too late. By then Dean would have found her—to get his phone back.

Ellie would be safe at home in the meantime.

Getting to the bottom of this mess.

Fourteen

A cop car was parked outside the Ridgeman residence. Dean lifted his hand, and the officer inside waved back. When Dean started up the driveway, the car engine turned over and the guy drove away. Before he went inside, Dean installed sensors and cameras like he had at the cabin. No sense being caught unaware.

Jessica's house keys were in his pocket. That had been a fun conversation.

"You're supposed to be protecting her."

He'd nearly leaned against the wall at the reception area in the police station. Bad idea, considering his wound. "Sorry. I had to get an X-ray of my shoulder. I didn't know she was gonna leave with Donaldson."

"Thank goodness he let me know he was taking her home."

He'd steered the conversation away from his failure, mostly so he could get her keys and get out of there. So he could get back to protecting Ellie.

Jess had said, "Go put that obsessively overprotective nature of yours to good use and make sure my sister doesn't get hurt."

Her parting comment had rolled around in his head since. And even more so when his younger brother Ted, the police department's technical specialist, appeared at the end of the hallway. He'd seen his brother wince. He hadn't even stuck around to ask if Detective Wilcox was there so he could get an update on the dead biker.

Dean tried not to move his shoulders too much when he walked. The bruise on the back of his shoulder marked the spot of his cracked shoulder blade, but he'd turned down the offer of a sling. He hadn't wanted his movement restricted that much. Now he had his gun in its holster on the left side, on his belt. Just because he *could* move his right arm didn't mean he planned to.

Unless absolutely necessary.

Why had Jessica said that anyway? His "obsessively overprotective nature" wanted an answer. Given how close Ted and Jessica were, he figured Ted must've told her how Dean had abandoned him for years, leaving him alone with their father.

Now he thanked God every day since that Chief Ridgeman had taken one look at Ted and seen something in him. The chief had turned what could've been a stint in juvie into an internship that gave Ted the support he needed through college. Now he worked there full time and was thriving.

Dean decided, as he unlocked their front door, that it was entirely possible he and Jessica had similar personalities and were destined to clash about everything. What Dean didn't like was how it bothered his brother that they were at odds.

But that was a problem he couldn't deal with right now when he needed to instead find out what possessed Ellie to leave the scene and go home where she was now alone.

"Ellie? It's Dean."

He got no response, so he pulled his gun and swept the first couple of rooms for her. He cleared the kitchen and living room. The dining room. When he saw her in the study reading like nothing was wrong, he cleared the upstairs rooms as well. Just to prove to himself no one else was here.

When he went back, she was in the exact same position. The phrase "nose in a book" came to mind as he watched her study pages of handwriting in what looked like an old, yellowed journal. It looked a lot like the kind he used to use to write notes and record his thoughts.

"Anything good?"

Ellie screamed, dropped the book, and whirled around. Her legs seemed to get tangled. She'd never have been able to get up in time if she had been in real danger.

"You'd be dead right now if I was the person trying to hurt you. Whatever it was you've found would be gone." He holstered his gun instead of what he really wanted to do—throttle her for being caught unaware.

She finally untangled her crossed legs and stood, pushing her glasses up her nose. "You're here. You look…good for someone battered halfway unconscious."

"Being cute isn't going to get you out of trouble."

Her eyes widened. "I'm not being *cute.* I was scared to death."

"So instead of going with me to the hospital, which was what I wanted you to do, you left with Officer Donaldson and came here alone?"

"I thought there was an officer outside, watching the house."

"There was." He wanted to cross his arms, but that would hurt right now. A lot. "And if someone snuck up to the back door while he was out front?"

She gasped. "Did they?"

"No." He sighed. "Did you at least find something to justify putting yourself in danger?"

Ellie frowned. "Jess said you might be like this. She said you're the kind that has to be the one who takes care of whoever you think needs it."

"And you don't? After a hit-and-run attempt, getting shot at, and with what happened on the road with the winch." He was still mad at himself that he hadn't ducked far enough, fast enough to avoid getting hurt.

She started to say something, caught herself, and pressed her lips together.

If Dean had to be honest with himself—which he usually tried to be—it was pretty distracting. "I plan on being as protective as I need to be in order to keep you alive."

"Okay." She said, "I do appreciate it, you know."

He nodded and crossed to the couch her grandfather had stashed in his office after he bought new ones a few years back. Dean eased down onto it. The groan slipped out.

Ellie came over. "Are you okay? Can I get you anything?"

"I'd rather you weren't out of my sight for a little while. Okay?" He'd had enough out-of-the-blue adrenaline rushes for today. Not "scares" as such, because he tended to ignore fear in favor of logic. But he figured she got what he meant. Even if she just thought he was being overprotective the way they all said he was with Ted.

Ellie moved to the spot where she'd been when he first walked in, which meant he didn't have to strain to look up at her from his prone position. She picked up a book her grandfather had read, one about the Navy in Vietnam.

"Do you think your grandfather's secret is all about something that happened back then?"

She shrugged one shoulder, lifted the book, and shook it. Nothing fell out.

"Outwardly he was all about his service. It's in everything he had around him, a celebration of the time he gave to this country. Then in his journal, it's all about how ashamed he was. How guilty he felt."

Dean nodded. He knew the pride that could be found in service, though he had to balance that with what the Bible said about the same thing. And he knew that outward display could mask a deep shame. Orders were orders. Servicemen and women carried the weight of what they'd seen differently. How it stayed with them in the long term was as individual as the person. Horrors aplenty. And yet they were supposed to let it wash over them? Bleed off. *Just give it time.*

It was why he had gone into counseling and therapy. To help those who had been discharged—discarded—and find a way for them to regain their lives.

Ellie said, "What he'd seen and done in Vietnam was nearly all he wrote about. Even years later there are still regular entries. Dreams he had. Memories. A smell that brought up an image he'd forgotten. Some were good, but most were bad." She looked up. "I'm sorry. Maybe this isn't good for you. If you've been through a lot of the same things."

"Not the same." He shook his head. "Everyone's journey is different. And while we can't presume to know what they went through, it is possible to understand one another. To give respect and love to our neighbors."

He'd talked through a lot with her grandfather when he first got sick. It sounded like the old man had used his journal to process what life had left inside him.

"It's easier to try and forget my journey." She flashed a smile he didn't believe and never met his gaze. "I didn't want to remember any of it. My grandfather persuaded me to find a group, and I went a few times. Then I met with the leader one on one. All it did was make the dreams start up again. So I quit."

Dean wanted to ask what had happened to her but knew this wasn't the time. He said, "It's not a bad thing to see a resurgence. Sometimes it's how we face enough of it that we can move on."

Ellie made a face then. "She wanted to get me into a therapy program where they use LSD to make you confront what happened so you can work through the fear."

Dean could see on her face how she felt about that. He had to admit it was a drastic therapy and wondered if that was something she might've needed.

"I've heard of it." Dean decided he needed to tread carefully considering she was shuddering. "I've done it once, with someone I was helping. But I don't think it's for everyone."

She blew out a breath. "I thought she was crazy until I looked it up and found out it's an actual method professionals use for trauma therapy. Sending them on an LSD trip." She shook her head. "That's crazy."

He nodded. "We have a lot of tools at our disposal. It's not a one-size-fits-all cure."

"You probably think I should've been through treatment."

There was another minefield he needed to navigate. Dean said, "What matters is whether you're content."

When she said nothing, just waited, he continued. "If you stay as you are in this moment for the rest of your life, will you be satisfied with it? Or, do you want to change something? Because we all have room to grow, and things we want to do differently. Sometimes it's diet. Or a new exercise program. Sometimes it's a need to exorcise demons we can't live with any longer." He decided then that he wanted to tell her. "Like my father."

When she just waited and listened, he said, "He's basically a con man. I couldn't stand being around him, so I left and joined the Navy as soon as I could so he wouldn't be able to manipulate me in any way any longer. Except that he did try to manipulate me even after that, by using Ted to do it. When he tried that, I cut off Ted as well. I explained to him what Dad would do and how to fight against it. But I just couldn't do it anymore. It was destroying me."

"What happened?"

"I might've saved myself from being dragged into his schemes, but he nearly destroyed Ted in the process." And that was something Dean would always have to live with.

"Now you're here, though. And Ted is great."

Dean said, "I drove my father to the county line and kicked him out of the truck. I told him never to come back."

"Wow." She said, "There are a few people I'd have liked to do that to. But I just ran away instead. And not to find strength in myself, the way you did. I was scared."

That was really what she thought, that he'd found strength? It had been trained into him to survive— like most of the tools he drew on now to get done what he needed to.

If she had to live with the fear, he had to live with the guilt.

She settled back on the floor. "I found his service history. He was in Vietnam for several years." She frowned. "Are you sure you're all right?"

"You don't have to worry. I'm going to keep you safe."

"I'm not worried about *me*, or even about your ability to do your job." She bit her lip, the journal clutched on her lap. "Right now I'm just worried about you."

"It scared you."

"You were hurt." She squeezed her eyes shut.

"The vest took the brunt of the force. I cracked my shoulder blade, and I'll be uncomfortable for a couple of weeks. But that's all." He said, "You know I was a Navy SEAL. And your grandfather was in a similar unit."

"That doesn't make me feel any better." She shot him a glance. "Not after reading about some of the things he got up to."

Dean chuckled. It shook his chest so much his bruise hurt. "Ouch."

"I knew you weren't okay!"

"I'm fine, Ellie." He caught her gaze with his, wondering what she would do if he told her he could show her just how "fine" he felt. How would she react to a kiss? No, it was much too soon for that. But a guy could dream.

"Thank you."

He wanted to look at her some more, but his eyes didn't seem to be able to stay open. "For what?"

"Telling me about you."

"So you can tell Jessica she has me all wrong?" Or all right, since he'd abandoned Ted.

"I'm not sure that's exactly true. She's just got her skewed vision glasses on, like always." Ellie rolled her eyes. "One of these days, that's going to get her in trouble."

Dean heard an audible gasp and sat up.

"What? What is it?" He rubbed his eyes, brushing off a bad dream about his father.

"He looks so young." She got up and crossed to him, handing over a picture. Dean checked the wall clock and realized he'd been asleep nearly twenty minutes. *Not good.* Before he could chastise himself, she shoved an old photo at him.

Dean stared at the group of six men in fatigues, standing around a military Jeep. He was still dreaming.

"Look at him."

He didn't move his gaze to where she pointed. It was snagged on a man on the other end of the photo.

No. It couldn't be.

Fifteen

"What is it?"

He covered it well, she had to give him that credit at least. Looking exhausted and pale from what was probably a huge amount of pain he didn't want her to know about.

And yet, she didn't think there was a single helpless thing about him. There was no doubt in her mind that he would protect her. Injured or not.

But he wasn't well enough to hide his reaction to the photo.

"Nothing. Just memories."

"Of these guys?"

He scrubbed his hands down his face. "I think I nodded off for a minute there. I was dreaming, about everything we were just talking about."

He had fallen asleep? She'd been reading and hadn't noticed. Her grandfather had snored like a black bear in hibernation. If Dean had been asleep, then he rested completely silently.

He said, "I'm going to put on a pot of coffee. Want some?"

She backed up to give him room to stand, not making it too obvious she was watching him move. It didn't work.

He said, "I'm fine. Remember?"

"Yeah." She drawled the word. "The only problem with that is I don't actually believe you." She shook her head. "But then I have so much of all this swirling around in my head that I feel like I'm going to miss what's right in front of my face."

"You'll figure it out." He moved close enough to touch his lips to her forehead.

Ellie blinked. Such a small touch, and yet it was like having peace wash over her. Head to toe he just…calmed her. She'd never met anyone like him.

Who she *had* met were guys who routinely tried to get whatever they wanted from her and didn't have any qualms about lying to her face. Which meant she knew what being lied to felt like, and she was more than sure Dean was lying to her about the photo. She studied the image. Six men. How many were still alive? Her grandfather was the oldest out of them, a Lieutenant according to his shirt sleeves. The rest wore tank tops. Rifles and dog tags. Lounging against the Jeep in the Vietnamese sun.

She turned it over to read what had been written on the back. *Last Chance Boys.*

The first time she read the words, it sounded in her head like a threat. Like, "This is your last chance." She shook her head. No, it was more likely that each of them had been local. Guys who grew up together and found themselves on the other side of the world fighting a war side by side.

But the town hadn't been founded until *after* Vietnam.

It didn't make sense.

One looked to be barely out of high school. The rest were college age. One had a cocky smile. None of them, save her grandfather, was familiar. Had Dean recognized someone in the photo or was it simply a reaction to the memory of being at war?

Dean was so low key about his path as a Navy SEAL that she wouldn't even have known he'd been one. Not if several other people hadn't told her. She didn't think that was about shame. More that he was simply the kind of person who didn't need anyone's approval or their thanks.

He just did the right thing. On his terms.

Ellie took the photo to the desk and turned on her grandfather's computer. His printer scanned in the image. She watched it load and tried to figure out how she would get the names of these men. Through local means or some kind of military information service. There had to be a way to find the history, the way people looked up who their ancestors were.

She saw him in the doorway. "Maybe you should knock, or at least announce yourself."

He frowned.

She didn't want him to think she was mad at being disturbed, so she said, "Because mere mortals usually make noise when we move. So if you're going to go all superhero on me, maybe you could let me know you're in the room somehow."

"The coffee is doing its thing."

"Great. Thanks."

He sat back on the couch while she did some web searches. He pulled out a tablet from the backpack he'd brought in.

Despite what she'd said about him needing to let her know he was standing there, she was now completely aware of him. In an elemental sort of way, he was completely distracting to her concentration.

If Ellie was going to figure this out, she really did need someone to watch her back. But did it have to be a hot guy she had a crush on?

That got you in trouble before.

She bit her lip hard enough to make it hurt. Ellie had to find out what her grandfather wanted her to know, and she had to stay alive and healthy enough to do that. Dean's presence couldn't and shouldn't be a distraction. After all, getting swept up in her feelings had resulted in her being hurt before. Every single time.

What was the point in going through that all over again?

Not that she thought he was the kind of guy who would even think about assaulting a woman. No like the other one had done. She even shook her head, though she said nothing. Of course Dean wouldn't do that. But she wasn't ever going to stop being careful. Ellie would never again let her feelings compromise her judgment.

"You okay?"

She glanced at him. "Huh?"

"Is everything all right?"

"Oh, yes. Lots to do, that's all." She tried to smile, but the past had come too close. All that stuff she'd moved on from and put away? It was a lot closer now. Near enough she could feel it crawl up her throat.

She stared at the monitor until her eyes burned, trying to remember what she was going to do online.

"Nothing happening at the cabin."

"Oh?" She looked over, blinking away the sting. "You can tell from your tablet?"

"Jessica gave me the Wi-Fi password." It beeped in his hand. He swiped the screen, then said, "I have to make a call."

But he didn't leave her. And she was grateful for it.

Ellie could pretend for a moment that she was working, when what she was actually doing was reassuring herself that someone capable was here to watch out for her. *You took self-defense.* But that didn't protect her from rifle bullets. SEAL training hadn't even protected Dean from that winch.

"Yeah, hey." His gaze was on her, despite the fact he was on the phone with someone else.

She ignored his frown and dragged the journal over, flipping through pages. She'd tucked a receipt in where she left off reading. While she stared unseeing at the pages, she listened to the sound of his voice.

"I got an update from Savannah. There's a guy, the biker's closest associate. He's in the wind, PD has got a BOLO out on him. When they track him down, they'll get the story on what happened last night. At least according to him."

She didn't understand what half those words meant, or what he was even talking about. But she knew Savannah was the detective she'd just met. The one with more style in one finger than Ellie had in her whole body. Honestly, she was trying not to hold it against the woman.

For years, Professor Eleanor Ridgeman had been a bestselling author and respected lecturer. Why, now that she was back in her hometown, did she feel like that scared girl who'd been pushed around and hurt? Ellie had read enough memoirs to know most people regressed when faced with their childhood. Old habits, old patterns of behavior.

Right now her life was in danger. She needed to be Professor Ridgeman. And yet here she was, little Ellie who couldn't protect herself.

She pushed the chair back and stood. Left the room, brave and capable. Just to pour two cups of coffee. Lame, but it was still a start. Baby steps and all that.

Not that she was prepared to face down whoever was after her to make sure she didn't fulfill her grandfather's will. At least not right now.

They'd tried to scare her off. Professor Ridgeman wasn't going to accept that. History was there to be uncovered, no matter how ugly. It showed humanity what it was made of. Strength. Bravery. Selfishness. Pride. All of it. The past didn't pull any punches. But it also couldn't hurt her. Not the way that the present always seemed to be able to.

Ellie's instincts told her to run and hide again. She was the one who always got hurt.

Dean touched her shoulder. "Hey. You okay?"

"I feel like I'm losing it." She didn't care if he thought she was crazy. "Thinking about myself like I'm two different people. Ellie, who is currently back at home and sleeping in her childhood bed. And Professor Ridgeman, who is determined to publish another book and make her department chair—with his sticky hands—eat his words about how I'm a 'one hit wonder.'"

How did Tumbleweed know she couldn't do it? He hadn't even seen her try.

"Do you have any idea how cute you are right now?"

She pushed her glasses up her nose. "Ellie, or Professor Ridgeman."

He chuckled. "Both."

"Well…I don't know what to say about that. But—"

"Let me guess," he said. "There's a lot of work to do, and you should get back to it."

She frowned. "How did you know that?"

"I'm aware of what a brush-off sounds like."

"Who gave you the brush-off?" Ellie gaped. "Was she crazy?"

Why would anyone do that to a guy like him? Such a good guy. Strong, brave, and handsome. It was like he wasn't even real. As if her dreams had conjured him into being, just so she would have her dream guy there to protect her.

He started to laugh.

"Are you real? Maybe I've lost my mind."

"If you have, it's possible I have too."

She said, "Why?"

"Because I've never in my life seen anyone as beautiful as you."

Ellie blinked. It wasn't eye strain this time. She didn't know what to do…or what to say. He thought she was beautiful? She wanted to believe it, but the last time someone had said those words to her, it had been a trick.

His tablet started ringing.

Ellie jumped on the change of subject. "Is that for cabin security?"

"No." Dean frowned at the screen. "This is for here."

"What?" The word came out squeaky and barely discernible. "You have cameras here?"

"Of course." He stared at the screen. "There's someone in the backyard, headed for the house." He angled the tablet to her so she could see the image. "It's pretty fuzzy. I don't have the budget for high-quality stuff since I'm saving for my therapy center."

Ellie looked at the screen.

He said, "Is this the guy you saw by the car?"

She studied the moving image. Dean's body was warm. Even though she wasn't touching him, she still felt the heat radiate. More comfort he offered her without even knowing it. "Dark clothes and his hood pulled up. I'd have to say it's possible. But it's also not possible for me to say for sure."

"Unless I catch him." His eyebrows lifted, and she realized he looked happy at the challenge. "Do me a favor? Get in the tub and stay there until I come to get you. You do *not* leave it."

"I…what?"

"The bathtub, Ellie." He pulled a second gun from his backpack and handed it to her. "Take this. It's loaded, so try not to shoot me after I catch this guy, yeah?"

"Uh…"

"And call Savannah. You have your phone?"

She nodded.

"Call it in. Get in the bathtub."

He strode to the front door. "I wanna see you go in there."

Ellie pulled her phone from her back pocket and hustled to the bottom of the stairs. She glanced back at him. Her hero. "Dean." She didn't know what to say.

He nodded. "Be safe, okay?"

"You too."

She raced up the stairs, dialing the police department's emergency number as she went. In her other hand she held a loaded gun.

While Dean went outside and tried to catch a bad guy.

Sixteen

Dean sprinted around the house. He reached over the gate and unlatched it, then pulled it open barely an inch.

A man in blue jeans and a heavy sweater with the hood pulled up made his way across the backyard. He was similar to the description Ellie had given him of the man she'd seen. Could be the same guy. Dean would find out either way. When he caught the man.

He holstered his gun and pulled a stun weapon he'd brought.

His footsteps were silent as he rounded the corner and moved toward the man, not about to allow him to even reach the back door—let alone get inside.

This was no career criminal. And neither did he have any formal training. The man didn't even notice as Dean approached. Kind of like the way Ellie had been, sitting on the study floor reading, completely oblivious. But for a completely different reason, this guy never even saw Dean.

"Hey."

The man flinched and turned. Twitchy was the word that came to mind.

Dean held the stun gun aimed at his torso. "You're trespassing."

The man's gaze darted around. After a second deliberation, which Dean saw in his expression, he reached to the back of his waistband. Going for a gun?

"Hands where I can see them."

In the distance, Dean heard police sirens. Good. Ellie had called for help, and the cops were responding fast to the family member of one of their own.

The man heard the sound as well. He continued to pull out what had to be a gun.

Dean fired before he even got the thing up.

The man's body jerked, and he made the muffled outcry of someone reacting to a high-voltage electrical charge surging through his body. The gun fell to the ground.

Dean kicked it onto the grass. The guy flailed. His hand caught Dean's chin.

For a second, stars sparked across his vision. Dean grabbed the wrist, spun the guy around, and slammed him against the wall of the house.

He pocketed the stun gun and used a zip tie he'd brought with him to secure the guy, hands behind his back.

"Cartwright?"

"Clear!" Dean followed that up by calling out. "Suspect apprehended." He wasn't a cop, but he spoke the lingo. In the SEALs, this would be a checkpoint. The time to radio in, mission completion.

But he was no longer a SEAL, at least not on paper.

He didn't often miss it. Except when adrenaline rolled through him like this, and he felt that rush of mission success.

"Hey." Basuto holstered his gun and came over. "Nice job."

Dean hauled the guy toward the sergeant, who took custody of him.

"Weapon in the grass." Dean wasn't going to touch it. Instead he moved to the back door and used the spare key he'd pocketed to unlock it and let himself inside so he could tell Ellie it was all clear.

His hands shook. Dean turned back to Basuto and told the big man, "I want to talk to him before you take him away."

"Detective Wilcox is on her way. Any questions you have, she'll do the asking."

"Copy that." As long as Dean got to be there, he wasn't going to argue. He took the stairs two at a time and knocked on the bathroom door. "Ellie, it's Dean."

He heard a movement and muttering, then she opened the door. "You caught him?"

Dean nodded. "It's all clear." He took the gun from her hand and tucked it back in his holster. He needed to unload all his weapons now that tonight's operation was complete. The smell of sweat and the rush of adrenaline brought with it too many memories to let it linger around him.

Ellie stepped into his personal space and slid her arms around his waist.

Dean's brain had to catch up with the fact she was giving him a hug, and then he slid his arms around her. "It's okay."

"You're not hurt." She looked up at him, her face close. "I mean, aside from your shoulder."

He didn't mind admitting, "It does *not* feel good."

She moved around him. "I don't see any blood on the back of your shirt."

Her hands lifted his shirt, and he stilled. "Ellie—"

"Whoa."

He swallowed, not able to speak. And not for a pleasant reason, like a rush of attraction. That was there underneath it. But she was seeing the…damage was a good word. New and old. He figured none of it looked pretty.

"Dean." Her warm palm touched the center of his back.

He had to clear his throat. "I twisted while I was securing the guy."

She lifted his shirt past his shoulder blades. "Ouch. Though it occurs to me that I'm not the one here who is a medical professional, it might be good to have one look at it. Because if my back looked this bruised, I would either be passed out or curled up in a ball, crying."

"I'll call the doc when I get a minute." She lowered his shirt. He turned around, saying, "Usually people call *me* for stuff like this, so they don't bother him."

"Well, I'm bothered. So you should call."

Dean studied the slight smile curling her lips. "I'm okay, Ellie. The guy is in police hands now. He won't be hurting you."

"Dean! Ellie!"

He said, "That's Wilcox."

Ellie nodded. "I guess we should go downstairs."

Dean couldn't resist. He touched his lips to her forehead again. He just needed to—for a number of reasons he didn't have time to list. Then he headed downstairs first, wondering if she knew why he'd done it. He wasn't trying to start a relationship with her. But he cared about her and was here to make her safe. It was about solidarity. Shared fear. Shared relief. The fact she seemed to care about him as well.

Detective Wilcox stood in the foyer.

"Basuto has him outside?"

Savannah nodded. "You guys okay?"

Ellie said, "Dean had me hide in the bathtub with his gun."

The detective glanced at him.

"One of them, anyway." He shrugged.

Savannah said, "Is that the point here?"

Ellie said, "Am I missing something? Was Dean not supposed to do that?"

Wilcox said to her, "I'm just glad you're both safe. Dean caught the guy, and I can close this case."

Dean wasn't so sure it was that cut and dry. "We should talk to him. I'm thinking he's not the mastermind, and we already have a theory this involves more than one person."

"I don't think it's a theory," Ellie said. "It's a fact. I was threatened by one person on the phone while another stood on the side of the street and did the in-person threatening. And that man wasn't the same one talking on the phone. I didn't even see his phone. That means I was threatened by two people."

"Then we definitely need to talk to him."

Wilcox said, "Because the two of you are working my case?"

Dean shrugged. "Just being helpful citizens."

"He's threatening me," Ellie pointed out. "I would like to know who is behind it, since I've nearly died a couple of times now. And this guy hurt Dean's shoulder."

She was right. No way had that been an accident.

Ellie cared about him. Dean glanced at her, wondering if he'd ever felt such pleasurable satisfaction from such simple words said by a woman he cared for. He didn't think he had. Because right now he wanted to hold on to Ellie Ridgeman and not let go.

If he'd had this kind of feeling before, he would probably be married right now.

"Does Jess know about this?" Wilcox waved a finger between them.

Dean pretended he didn't know what she was talking about. "We really should talk to that guy."

Wilcox looked like she wanted to laugh.

Ellie said, "My sister is busy with a case. And I'm a grown woman. I'm not required to explain myself or my life to her."

Wilcox held up both hands. "Okay. I hit a nerve. Sorry."

Ellie held her chin up, but he spotted a tremble in her mouth. As much as he had to admit he was falling fast and hard for her, she had to be the one who made the move with him. He couldn't keep pushing things with her, or he would be persuading her around to his way of thinking instead of allowing her to make up her mind about him and what she wanted.

"It's been a long day." Dean said, "If we get a chance to talk to that guy, we'll be able to relax. Get some sleep."

Wilcox led them outside into the nighttime chill. It was cold enough he shivered, even while sweat rolled down his forehead. Dean swiped it away.

He felt Ellie's fingers brush his other hand and looked over. She mouthed, "Thank you," which confused him since she'd said that already. It was becoming harder and harder to keep his feelings in check with her, but he needed to.

Not only did he want Ellie to take a step toward him, but he also had to keep his focus. He would protect her, but he was also working on the therapy center. A new venture like that wouldn't leave time for a relationship.

This was getting more complicated the longer he stuck with it—and her. Now he'd seen that Vietnam era photo, he knew he needed to find his father, and quick. He had to find out from his old man, pictured in that photo with her grandfather, what he might know about all this. There was nothing else he wanted from the man. Just information that would help him keep Ellie safe.

He didn't care that his father had been a Marine.

Dean gritted his teeth. *It doesn't matter.* All he wanted was information. His dad didn't mean anything to him.

Basuto held on to the suspect. Dean stopped at a greater distance than he would have otherwise, knowing Ellie would stop beside him. He didn't want her close to the guy.

Wilcox said, "So what was the plan, huh? Wave that gun you had around and scare her, or something else?"

The guy only smirked.

"Either way, it didn't work. Guess it's all over."

"I still paid my debt."

"This was a favor? Someone you owed?"

"Farmed out like every other thug in this town, right? That's what you guys think." His teeth flashed in the light spilling from the house. "Just another 'boy' West has, out doing his bidding. Keeping you all scrambling."

"So you owed him, and he sent you here? What does West want with Ellie?"

Dean's whole body tensed. A local crime lord, and Ellie had his attention? That couldn't be good.

The guy blew out a breath. "Nothin' 'cept another favor owed. She gets roughed up, told to leave it alone. Whatever happens, you guys see my sweater they told me to wear and think I'm it." He chuckled. "He thought that was a good touch. Getting a hoodie for me to wear. He thought you especially would like that. Old times, or something?"

Dean said, "What is he talking about?"

"It doesn't matter." Wilcox folded her arms. "This isn't the top of the food chain. Ellie is still in danger because this guy—" She motioned to the suspect. "—is nothing to us."

"Ouch." The guy sniffed. "I'm someone."

"Yeah, someone who is going to tell me who West is."

The name clicked with Dean. Something Stuart had said, the argument those two bikers had. Could Karl Tenor's death behind the biker bar have something to do with the police department's hunt for a local bad guy? This "West" person?

"Now." Wilcox's tone invited no argument.

The guy said, "You think I know?" He laughed. "No one knows who he is."

"Get him out of here."

Basuto walked the guy to his cop car. Wilcox turned. "I'll get something from him."

She looked mad. About the hoodie thing? He didn't get that, but it was clear Wilcox didn't like to be manipulated any more than anyone else did.

"At least we know not to relax right now but to stay vigilant." Dean said, "That much is for sure. Like how this is getting more complicated by the second. And it doesn't originate with whoever this West person is."

Savannah nodded. "We're working on that."

"I want to talk to my grandfather's lawyer again." Ellie said, "He's…older, and they were friends. Maybe he knows what this is about."

"That's going to be hard," Wilcox said. "His assistant filed a missing persons this morning."

Seventeen

Ellie saw her sister climb out of her car on the drive. She met her at the door, opening it before Jess could knock. She pressed her index finger to her lips. "He's asleep."

"He's supposed to be protecting you." Jess dumped her backpack on the entryway floor and took off her jacket.

"He is, that's why he's injured and exhausted." She waved her sister into the kitchen, where she'd mixed up a batch of blueberry muffins. Not scratch, but neither of them knew how to bake aside from watching people do it on TV.

"How long have you been unprotected?"

Ellie slid the muffin tray in the oven. Thankfully the beeping or the sound of her moving around in the kitchen and mixing it up with a bowl and wooden spoon old-school style hadn't woken him. The guy had to be exhausted. In pain, because he hadn't wanted anything more than regular pain meds.

"I'm not unprotected." She set a timer on her phone so it wouldn't beep, just vibrate. The microwave timer was loud enough she'd be able to hear it upstairs. "Besides, someone tried to break in last night. Now whoever is behind this knows Dean is here to protect me."

He'd been amazing. Heroic. Considerate, and strong. What kind of man was like that? She couldn't say she'd met *anyone* like him her whole life.

She was half tempted to fall in love with him right now. Except that this wasn't where she lived and long distance relationships weren't how you built a future.

All her feelings for him proved was that her judgment could still be compromised by her emotions.

The last thing she needed was to fall for Dean. Even as tempting as it was, she had to trust her own mind. Logic said a guy who lived across the country from her wasn't the guy for her.

Jess said, "Sleeping is not protecting you."

"That's why I called. As soon as he fell asleep, I had you ask the cops outside to walk around the house regularly." Then Dean's tablet had started beeping, sensing the motion of the officers on patrol. He'd stirred. Before he could wake up, she'd turned off the notification sound. The last thing he needed was to be woken up by nothing but cops looking out for both of them by giving him a much needed break.

"You like him."

Ellie lifted her chin. "Why do you say that like you're accusing me of some kind of heinous crime?"

"He's different than I thought at first." Jess poured herself a cup of coffee. "But that doesn't mean I think you should crush on a man who is only here to make sure you're safe."

"Just a hero?" That was fine with her. "All business, nothing else." Too bad her sister hadn't seen the way he looked at her. But that was for the best. She didn't need Jess making it harder to do what needed to be done when all this was over.

She might be planning on staying longer than she'd thought, but that was about honoring her grandfather. Not about having more opportunities to be around Dean. Feeling this unrequited thing that was happening. Making her want to let him sleep all day, make him muffins so he had something good to eat when he woke up and…no.

Stop it. She had to focus.

Ellie slid the phone into her back pocket and went to the office where she sat reading while Dean got his rest. "I've been going through grandfather's things."

"What did Pop leave you?"

He'd hated when Jess called him that. Ellie smiled now, thinking of how even though it had irritated him, he'd never said anything to her sister. Which, to Ellie, meant he'd secretly loved that Jess called him that instead of "Chief."

Her sister pushed books around on the coffee table and then picked up the music box.

"I still can't figure out what this is about."

Jess turned it in her hands. "A trinket from Vietnam? Have you tried translating the writing on it?"

"How am I supposed to do that?" Ellie said, "From what I've found, that's old Vietnamese script. Like Chinese symbols, they represent words. But none of the ones that came up on Google matched any of those."

"And you tried just uploading an image of it to search?"

Ellie nodded. "Nothing. Except that I know they're Chu-Nom characters. With the little accent over the 'o' that looks like a hat. I sent the photo to the head of Asian studies at the university. When she gets back to me, I'll tell you what she said."

"Okay." Jess set the box down. "What else?"

"Other than something big had gone down at some time in Grandpa's past?" Ellie shook her head. "I know he went through crazy war experiences. But in his mind, one superseded everything, and he *never* let it go."

"It's somewhere in here, or in the stuff at the cabin, otherwise how could you be expected to find it?"

She had to concede that point to her sister.

"Maybe Mom has seen this box. She might know where it's from, or if it'll help."

Ellie swallowed. "Do you…speak to her?"

"You don't?" Jess took a photo of the music box with her phone and tapped and swiped the screen.

"Not often. No." She'd been far closer to her grandfather than her mother who followed her own whims. Which often made zero logical sense to Ellie's rational thought processes. Did she think her mom might help? It was possible. If Jess wanted to ask, she was entirely at liberty to do so.

"Huh."

Ellie shrugged. "We don't get along."

That was the story she'd always told. The truth was more painful and part of the cache of things in her mind purposely labeled "the past," and Ellie was determined to not allow it to seep into the here and now.

But was that better?

A driver and a shooter had both targeted her. Someone was trying to warn her off this. Meanwhile, Dean was doing his best to protect her and had wound up with a breathtakingly awful bruise across the back of his shoulder. Another injury to add to the road map of scars on his back. She wondered briefly if the rest of him was the same, but brushed the thought aside, realizing that wasn't a helpful line of thinking. Still, it was clear he'd been through war.

He was still a good guy, prepared to wade in when the damsel in distress was in jeopardy. Only she'd added to his scars, and now he was wrung out. Like her. Instead of a physical challenge, this was like a mental challenge she was failing at. A problem she couldn't solve, the unanswerable question. Ellie felt like her brain was coming up short. Along came her emotions, determined to take over.

Which left her freaking out, unable to concentrate like she normally could. Imagining that every creak of the house was that man or another from her past. Coming back to hurt her for good this time.

"I don't like being scared."

"Who does?"

Her sister worked undercover a lot. "How do you do it?"

"I use the fear as part of the role I'm playing. Whatever the person I'm pretending to be would be freaked about, I embrace it."

Jess said, "Which doesn't help you at all."

"Since this is very real."

"I'm sorry I wasn't here. When the call came in, I was two counties over with Frees, picking up this biker dude from the sheriff's department. By the time we got back to Last Chance, the drama was over."

"It was five minutes."

"Yeah, but you were scared, and I wasn't here."

Ellie didn't know what to say. Her eyes filled with burning hot tears, but she didn't let them fall. She checked the timer on her phone—five minutes left—and blinked at the view out the window for a while.

Dean had taken care of her in his capable way, like it was all no big deal. Maybe it was no big deal to a former Navy SEAL. She was a professor. She'd grown up around guns, but all this was decidedly not her normal life.

"Morning."

She glanced up to find Jess's attention on the doorway. Dean stood there, hair mussed from sleeping. T-shirt wrinkled.

He lifted two fingers and disappeared in the direction of the bathroom.

Ellie stood. "I'm going to check on the muffins."

That way they would be ready when he was out. She would have something tangible to give him when she said thank you for the thousandth time, and also sorry that she'd put his life in danger. That he'd been hurt. All because that guy on the phone, and his friend, and the man someone named West had sent here last night, were trying to get to her.

Frightening her was working. Enough her hands shook, and she nearly dropped the muffins along with the pot holders. The oven door shut too fast, slamming in a way that made her wince.

"Smells good."

She turned, trying not to look too pleased that he appreciated her efforts. "Coffee?"

His attention was on his tablet. "Who…" He looked up. "Did you turn off the sound?"

Ellie stammered. "The cops were walking around the house. I didn't want it to wake you." She smiled. "I made muffins. Have a seat."

"Someone entered the cabin." He looked at the watch on his wrist. "Three hours ago."

He tapped and swiped the screen, muttering to himself. Ellie winced. She hadn't known it would be a problem. After all, a man had approached this house last night. Who would go up to the cabin as well?

Jess strode in, headed for the coffee pot. She glanced at Dean, then stilled. "What is it?"

"The cabin was broken into." He looked up. "I think they're still there."

Ellie started to speak but Jess cut her off saying, "Coat and shoes."

"I'll make a call." Dean disappeared.

"What's happening?"

Jess pulled out three hot cups. "The muffins just became to-go breakfast. Let's move."

Two minutes later she was shuffled into the backseat of the car and handed a muffin, along with a full hot cup of coffee. Even the logo for her favorite coffee chain didn't reassure her.

"Don't you need to sleep?"

Jess twisted in the front seat. "We have a chance to catch whoever is trying to stop you from finding out what Pop wanted you to know. There's no way I'm being out of the loop on this one."

In the driver's seat, Dean glanced at her sister.

Ellie took a bite of her muffin. Too big, it got stuck and she had to sip scalding hot coffee—with no sugar—just to swallow it down.

Dean headed for the parking lot where his friend waited, leaning against an off-road vehicle with no doors and four seats. She was shuffled from one vehicle to another and had to grip the safety bar to keep from swaying out while Stuart drove them up the path. Dean sat beside him in the front, clearly super mad at her. Jess was quiet in the seat beside her, checking her gun first and then her email.

"I'm sorry I turned off the volume."

Dean shifted to glance back at her. "Huh?"

She saw when his shoulder injury registered. He couldn't talk to her from the front seat. What was she thinking? He would only hurt himself more just to hear her. "Nothing. Don't worry about it."

Stuart glanced at her but said nothing. Then they were at the cabin and what else was there to say? What was there to do except sit in the vehicle and wait while they went in. Jess kicked the door open.

Dean said, "Hold on."

Jess nodded. "I smell it too."

Even Stuart was over there, gun out, ready to do battle on her behalf while Ellie sat in the vehicle where it was safe, and she couldn't do any more harm.

Stuart said, "Gas leak."

They all raced from the porch. A second later the cabin exploded in a fireball, flinging her sister and two good men through the air.

Ellie screamed.

Eighteen

Dean blinked up at the sun. Clouds. Wind rushed through his ears, the sound like a tornado approaching. No. It was a long time since he'd been anywhere near an impending weather system like that. They normally didn't happen in Last Chance, or even close by it.

He rolled over, cataloging aches and pains even as he ignored them. Or tried to. He held his arm against his waist, wincing at the pain in his shoulder. After he'd secured the area, he could worry about himself.

Ten feet away, Jess lay as though she'd been flung like a ragdoll and left where she landed. He moved to her, rolled her to her back one handed, and saw that she'd received a nasty blow to the head. Breathing. Heartbeat strong. Unconscious.

He moved to Stuart next. His friend mumbled, eyes glassy.

Dean patted his cheek. "Hey, buddy. How're you doing?" Dean checked him for injuries and found nothing pressing. But that didn't mean all of them wouldn't feel it tomorrow. He'd been nearly blown up before. Couple days and he'd be laid up like he'd been hit by a truck.

Where is Ellie?

He needed to get to her, wherever she was lying. The all-terrain vehicle had fallen on its side. Was she crushed under it? He moved around, but there was only grass. Nothing else. No sign of her.

Dean checked inside, looking everywhere—even places she wouldn't be able to hide in. "Ellie! Where are you?"

He saw a discarded cell phone on the grass. Probably tossed there like the rest of them had been. He scrambled to it and saw it was Ellie's phone. The screen illuminated her call history.

She'd dialed 911…he checked his watch. A couple of minutes ago.

That meant help was on its way.

He glanced around. Where was she? "Ellie!"

The cabin trailed smoke into the sky. What was left of it, at least. The whole structure was a pile of wood and debris that flickered with flames dying down now. Serious destruction. A gas leak, somehow ignited, had torn it to pieces.

There was nothing left.

Dean turned, scanning. Had someone taken her? Dread settled in his gut like the knowledge of that incoming tornado. It was possible whoever did this had stuck around and dragged her off.

But which way had they…

A gunshot rang out.

Dean was sprinting toward the source before he'd even registered what the sound was. He wanted to thank God for SEAL training, and the reflexes that had given him, but he needed to find Ellie first. That had to be a priority.

He winced. That wasn't right. *God…* He couldn't think past that. He just ran toward where he hoped Ellie would be. After he saved her, he'd have all the time in the world to get his life aligned with how God wanted it.

Grunts reached his ears before he saw them.

Ellie and another man wrestled for control of a gun. Dean came in from the flank, though he was still a quarter mile from them. Getting shot would do none of them any good, but he had to save her.

He reached for his holster.

His hands came up empty. No gun.

The man stumbled back, but neither of them let go of the weapon. The man kicked her thigh, and she cried out.

She balled her fist. Ellie hit her attacker with a vicious right hook he would be seriously proud of if he'd had the time to be.

Dean looked for an opening and kept running toward them, this time not desperate. He needed to keep a cool head if he was going to get them both out of this without either one of them getting hurt.

The man twisted and his free hand came up. His elbow nailed her in the head and she went down.

Dean yelled, "Ellie!"

The gunman swung his arm around and fired.

Dean dove to the ground, behind a fallen tree, and landed hard. Air expelled from his lungs in a rush. He tried to inhale but nothing happened. *Winded.* Breathe. He had to breathe.

Black spots blinked in front of his eyes. It took another agonizingly long second listening for the shot that would end Ellie's life. End his life. Finally Dean managed to take a breath.

As soon as his body had enough oxygen, he lifted up and looked. The man was nowhere to be seen.

"Ellie!" He scrambled to her, nearly falling a couple of times. He landed on his knees beside her and touched her shoulder.

When she rolled, he saw her wide eyes, full of fear. "Dean."

Ellie hugged him around the waist, pressing her face to the skin of his neck. He was gritty, sweaty. He probably smelled. But it was the sweetest hug of his life.

Too bad he couldn't enjoy it. "Where is he? Where did he go?"

"He ran off." She moved, groaning as she did.

"Okay?"

"Are you okay?" She shifted to sit, and he lifted to a crouch. Her eyes filled with tears. "You flew through the air. And Stuart. Jess!" She scrambled to her feet so fast he nearly toppled over doing the same. Then she grabbed his good hand and took off, tugging him behind her. "We have to help them."

"They're okay." He slowed her to a jog and stuck his hand in his pocket. His shoulder didn't feel good, and she didn't need to risk tripping and hurting herself more. As they moved, he told her how he'd found Jess and Stuart. They made it back in little more time than it had taken him to run to her after the blast. Dean touched his forehead.

"You're not okay."

He didn't want to talk about it. "You called 911."

"And then I saw him."

"So you chased him?" He didn't think that had been smart.

She shook her head, her words now breathy from their easy run back toward the cabin. "That's not the point. Come on, I want to see her."

"Just be careful, okay?" He wanted to know what had happened. "So you took my gun and chased after him. I saw you guys fighting over it. You got in some good licks."

She winced. "Not good enough."

"You're alive, aren't you? So am I. Jess and Stuart are banged up, but they'll be good." He squeezed her hand that he was still holding. "You did good."

Never mind that she should never have put herself in danger like that, taking off after a guy who'd just blown up a cabin—or so he assumed—even if she did have a gun.

"Why does that not sound like a compliment?"

He sighed. "I thought he'd taken you."

He'd never been so scared. Not even in SEAL training or during some of their most intense missions. Even when his teammates' lives had been in danger. When innocents had been caught in the crossfire.

"Ellie!"

As they jogged over, Dean called back to Jess, "Don't get up. Stay there."

But she sat up. Ellie hugged her sister, a tangle of limbs until she realized the blood on her sister's head. She looked at him. "Is she…"

"She needs to be as still as possible until—"

"Dean!"

He turned to see two firefighters, two EMTs, and a uniformed police officer sprint toward them. He waved. "Over here!" And then looked around. "Where is Stuart? He was lying over there." Dean pointed to the spot.

Jess nearly shook her head, and winced. "He was standing when I woke up. Said he was going to walk it off."

Dean found his phone in the grass. While the EMTs worked on Jess's head injury, he texted Stuart asking what he was thinking walking off like that. If he got back a reply quickly, one that made sense, then he'd know Stuart really was okay.

Then he sat back on his heels and took a long inhale.

His phone buzzed in his hand a second later.

It's only two miles home. I have a headache, and my legs still work fine.

Dean replied that Stuart had better text again when he got home, or he'd be doing all the chores for a week. It was an empty threat, and Stuart would know that, but he wanted to know his friend and roommate got back safely.

"This place is a mess."

The two firefighters had no equipment. No truck. Thankfully the blaze had calmed to smoldering. Still, it gave off a considerable amount of heat.

He'd really been standing on the porch? He probably should be dead, but then he could honestly say that about so many of the dark days in his life. He'd lost count of the number of times he'd had a near miss. Alive still, for a reason.

He looked at Ellie. They shared a relieved smile.

Was she the reason he was still here? *Thank You, God.* Spending time with her, even if it was only as her protector, was a gift he recognized.

As he watched, she took in the burned-out ruins of her grandfather's cabin, her cabin. What was left of it. Tears rolled down her face.

When he had first met her, she'd needed help but hadn't wanted him to help her. Now that he was there to help her there was nothing he could do or say to lessen the pain she felt over this loss. So fresh on the heels of losing her grandfather. Now she'd lost what he had left her.

And there was nothing Dean could do.

Except be there for her.

"Dean!" Conroy trotted over, followed by Ted.

Dean's kid brother looked like he wanted to be sick. "What—"

Ted slammed into him. His thinner arms wrapped around Dean's chest like a vice.

Dean winced. "Easy on the shoulder, yeah?" He tried to sound light and breezy, but he wanted to throw up.

"No." Ted moved his arms to Dean's waist, but arguably squeezed him harder. "I thought you were dead. You got *blown up*."

"Wasn't the first time."

Ted reared back to thump him in the chest. "Not funny."

Dean grabbed his wrist. His brother was really shaken up about this. "I've been in danger before." He glanced at Ellie, who was staring at them. "I'm fine. Why don't you go check on Jess?"

He pressed his lips together and shook his head. "The EMTs will do more than I can, and she has her sister."

Okay, so there was more to this. Dean would have to ask him about it later.

"We're all good. Even Stuart, who told Jess he was going to *walk it off*. He's probably already home by now." Dean checked his phone and found the text. He showed Ted. "See? All good." He squeezed his brother, the tendon between his neck and shoulder. "But I do need to ask you something real quick."

"What?" The fear on his brother's face was starting to settle. Dean wasn't used to having his brother here, needing to be reassured. He usually came home weeks or sometimes months later off one Navy mission or another. Not less than an hour after, where Ted got an eyeful of the repercussions. Like now. It looked like a war zone up here.

"Do you know where Dad is?"

Dean still had a hold on his brother's shoulder, so he felt Ted flinch. "Why would I know where he is?"

Dean wasn't sure that was the truth. "I gotta ask him something. It's important, and it might help keep Ellie safe."

Conroy said, "What makes you think that?"

"A photo." Dean figured the truth would come out soon enough. "Chief Ridgeman served in Vietnam with a group of guys from Last Chance."

Conroy said, "The town was founded right after the war ended."

Dean shrugged. There was a lot he'd never known about his dad, apparently. "I think our father might know why someone is so desperate to keep Ellie from finding out the truth." If this was all about something that had happened back then.

"Was your dad one of the founders?"

Ted glanced at Dean, who tipped his head to the side in a shrug. "I know he liked it here, but I have no idea. If those guys in Ridgeman's picture from Vietnam were the town's first residents, I've never heard about it. We moved around a lot, but I know my dad favored Last Chance." Dean turned to his brother. "Can you find him?"

Ted started to speak. From the look on his face, he was going to be cagey.

Ellie spoke first, "Your father was one of the men in that picture?"

He spun to find her right behind him, the tracks from tears on her cheeks. How did he explain this? "I—"

"You knew one of those men, and you lied to me."

Okay, so that was true. "El—"

"We need some help!" one firefighter yelled. The other was crouched in the center of the destruction. "There's a body down here!"

Nineteen

Dean took a step toward the cabin wreckage. Ellie stepped in front of him. "Not so fast."

If he was going to play dumb, that was fine for him. As for her, she wasn't going to just ignore it.

Ellie folded her arms. "Your father was in that photo with my grandfather? Who else did you recognize and not tell me about?"

Anger surged through her, hot like a roaring fire. Like the one consuming her inheritance. Any chance she might have at figuring out what her grandfather intended was rapidly turning into a colossal mess.

No. She couldn't think about that right now. What she needed to do was focus on Dean and the breach of trust. He was supposed to have been sticking close to protect her. The truth said more about his character—he'd been there to protect himself only.

"I don't recognize any of the others. I barely recognized your grandfather."

"But you knew one of them was your dad," she shot back.

Dean said, "That's my business."

He wasn't even going to defend the fact he'd lied to her. Lying by omission was still lying. Ellie's heart squeezed in her chest. How much more loss was she going to have to feel today? It was enough to make her want to squeeze up in a ball and ugly cry.

She hadn't done that in a long time.

Dean tried to move around her, but she got in front of him again. He shook his head. "I need to help them."

"They've got it. They're trained, certified first responders. You need to tell me the truth right now."

She didn't like what all this was doing to her. She sounded like a shrew, a heartless one at that. But the truth was, what *could* she do? Ellie's skills didn't extend to fighting off attackers, saving people from exploding cabins, or digging someone out of wreckage.

If she sounded like a horrible person, then at least that would keep her and Dean from getting any closer. She was just guarding her heart, right? And apparently there was reason to do so.

Dean shrugged. "There's nothing to tell. He was in the photo, so I asked Ted if he could find him for us."

There was no us.

She looked at Ted, not wanting to make herself sound worse than she already had in her exchange with Dean. It would only come out desperate. A sad, lonely woman's attempt to make something out of nothing. He'd know she liked him. That she was nursing a monster crush.

One that had distracted her in a serious way from seeing what was right in front of her face. Best not to say anything.

She turned to the side. "Fine. Whatever."

Ugh, now she sounded like a juvenile shrew. Why was this whole trip home bringing out the worst in her? She wasn't like this. If her coworkers or students ever saw her acting this way, they would think she'd lost her mind.

Maybe she had.

"Our father is none of your business."

She turned to face Ted, and the frown creasing his thick, dark brows. Ellie said, "Until someone gets hurt *worse* than they already are. Like your brother."

Ted worked his mouth back and forth. "It's still none of your business."

"Hey." Jess shoved the EMT's hand away. "Quit hassling her, Ted."

"She's the one accusing my brother of lying."

Ellie tried to interject, but Jess cut her off. "Because he did lie. He knowingly withheld information. And it could have gotten one of us killed."

Hurt flashed on Ted's face for a second before he shook his head. "Everyone is fine."

"Except the guy in the cabin when it blew up." Conroy hopped off the debris and strode over. "I'm tempted to sit all of you down and make you walk me through everything that's happened, and what you all know about this."

Dean followed after Conroy. He'd gone up to the cabin with him, despite his injury. Now all his focus was on his brother when he said, "It's not Dad." Then he glanced at Ellie. "It's the missing lawyer."

"I wanted to talk to him." The words came out before she even realized how self-centered that sounded. A man had suffered, and she was only worried about the information she could have gotten out of him?

Dean said, "He's not dead. You may still get your chance."

"He's alive?"

Conroy nodded. "He was beaten pretty badly and appears to have been restrained at some point. He was in the big chest freezer in the cellar."

Ellie blinked. She hadn't even known her grandfather's cabin had a cellar. "How long was he in there for?"

"We don't know."

He could have been tied up in the freezer when they'd come here yesterday. Ellie shuddered.

Dean said, "The cameras showed a break in just after five this morning." As though he knew what she was thinking.

Ellie didn't want sympathy from him right now. Not only did she not think she deserved it, but she also didn't trust anything coming from him. Nor did she plan to anytime soon.

Conroy said, "So either he was dumped here and whoever set the explosion thought he'd die in the blast, or he was conscious and knew what was about to happen so he climbed into the freezer thinking it could save him."

"Which it did," she said.

He nodded. "He's in rough shape and unconscious, but we'll get him to the hospital."

"Along with Dean and Jess."

All of them bristled.

She didn't back down. "They both need to be seen by doctors. Jess probably has a concussion."

The EMT by her sister said, "I'm thinking the same."

"See." Ellie waved at her sister.

"Officer Ridgeman will be taken to the hospital."

"Dean should get checked out as well."

Ted nodded. "I agree."

Dean started to grin. "Et tu—"

"Shut it."

Dean pointed at his brother. "Don't tell me to shut it."

"Make me."

Ellie said, "Is this necessary?" Sure, she bantered plenty with her sister. It was a great stress reliever. But they all needed to focus right now.

Conroy turned his compassionate gaze on her.

It didn't help. Kind of actually made it worse, since apparently he thought she wasn't okay. Ellie said, "What does the lawyer have to do with whatever I'm supposed to find? And, like me, does he know something he isn't supposed to? Because if he was meant to die here to keep him from saying something, that means he represents a threat."

"Exactly." Conroy nodded, his expression turning to one of approval.

"I'm glad he's alive."

"It may be a while before he can say anything at all, but we can all be thankful his heart is still beating."

"Along with the rest of ours." Ellie was tempted to thank God that they'd all survived. No one else could have pulled that off. The second the cabin exploded she'd thought for sure they were all dead, and she would be up here alone with three bodies and nothing left of her grandfather's gift.

They'd come through it unscathed, for the most part. Only the thought that this wasn't over kept her from celebrating. She still intended to find out what her grandfather's guilty secret had been. Another temptation to pray. A tiny whisper that she should, in order to ask that no one else get hurt while she finished this.

The still small voice that called her to those childish things, where she thought of God like a papa-daddy who sat on His throne up in heaven waiting for her to ask Him for what she needed. Now that she had grown out of that fantasy belief, she needed to leave the temptation to talk to Him again alone. More proof being home was messing her up. Making her want to pray, of all things.

"Whoever brought him here, they beat him pretty badly," Conroy said. "I'd guess they carried him, because I'm not sure he'd have made it under his own steam. Though, it's possible. We'll have to see what the doctor says about his state."

While he spoke, the EMTs carried the lawyer past them, headed away and down the path at a steady clip that was almost a run.

"Jess needs to go too."

"I'll take her in a second." Conroy watched Jess make her way over.

"Are you okay?"

Ellie's sister snuggled up to her side. "My head's going to hurt like a mother tomorrow."

She frowned at Jess's use of language.

Her sister chuckled. "Other than that, I feel like I've been blown up, and I want to hurl."

"Great." She didn't like how many people were getting hurt. But it felt good to hug her little sister right now.

"We need to get this guy." Jess said, "If my head didn't hurt, I'd probably have an idea how to do that. I'm sure I would."

Conroy nodded. "I'm sure, too."

"I have to figure this out." She asked Dean, "The house is okay, right? Because all the things of my grandfather's that I collected are there."

Assuming what she'd taken would even help her now. Maybe she'd missed the solution that was right in front of her, and now it was blown up. Everything he'd given her that she'd left behind was now smoldering rubble.

Dean went to retrieve his backpack. Maybe that had been blown up as well.

Ellie couldn't lose it. Even if she wanted to, nothing would come of grieving this loss. Not right now. Maybe later, when she was alone in the bathtub like before. Or not, since it would be much better to actually take a bath to just relax.

But how could she do that when there was so much going on? A man was in the hospital. The mystery was still a mystery, and now it wasn't just her that was at risk. The lives of people she cared about were in danger.

"Okay, let go." Jess shifted away from her.

Ellie realized she'd been squeezing her sister way too hard. "Sorry."

Dean finally looked up from his tablet. "The house is good, Ellie. For now."

"So what's next?" Ted glanced between them.

Dean answered, "Ellie saw his face."

"You did?"

She nodded in response to Conroy's question. Jess looked about ready to blow. Ellie said, "I saw him, so I grabbed Dean's gun and chased after him. But he got away."

"With the gun."

Ellie pressed her lips together.

"Sorry," Dean said. "I was just remembering aloud what happened to it."

Conroy tapped on the screen of his phone, then said, "If I get you to look at mug shots, Ellie, do you think you'd be able to ID him?"

"Maybe." She thought about it. "I've seen him twice, but I've never gotten a good look at his face."

Jess squeezed her hand. "It's worth a try, right? He nearly killed the lawyer, just for doing his job reading us the will."

Conroy said, "Maybe."

Her sister whirled on him. "What?"

Ellie had no idea what "cop" thing was transpiring between them. "Someone should probably explain this to me, as well."

"It's like you said." Conroy nodded to her. "He might be in the same position as you, and knowing too much makes him a threat to whoever wants to keep their secret." Conroy turned his phone so she could see the screen. "I took this photo of his shoulder when they were taking him out of here. I've never seen it before, so I snapped a picture. Considering everything, I didn't want to take a chance."

"So you *do* know what's been happening."

"Only what has Jess told me."

Ellie was about to argue with him when her sister said, "Pop had one of those."

"What?" She turned to her sister, then looked at the screen of the phone. "He did?"

"I saw it when he was sick. I had to help him dress a few times." Jess's eyes were dark, full of grief. "It was on his shoulder. He said it was an old Navy tattoo."

"So maybe they got the tattoos at the same time." Ellie shrugged. "What does it mean?"

"They served together." Dean's expression darkened. "Holmford, Ridgeman, and my father."

She swallowed. "Mr. Holmford was one of the men in the photo as well?"

Dean said, "We really do need to find my father then."

Conroy said, "What if all those military guys in that photo of yours are the founders of Last Chance?"

Ellie gritted her teeth. "They buried a secret, and then built a town on top of it."

Twenty

Conroy perched on the edge of an unoccupied desk. No papers, no computer. "Everyone sit down."

Dean folded his arms carefully, trying to do it despite the pull in his shoulder. Savannah was here, as was Mia—the police lieutenant, and Conroy's fiancé.

Ellie turned an office chair toward the police chief and folded her hands in her lap. Dean wanted to make a crack about the teacher's pet, but he didn't. How dare she get mad at him for withholding that information about his father? This was *his* father. Why was it any of her business if he kept it to himself, or not? Until he chose to talk about his past, or his parentage, it wasn't anything she needed to know.

And until he was sure it was relevant here, he had a right to privacy.

Apparently she didn't think so.

Jessica and Dean's brother stared at each other longer than he thought was necessary. It was like looking at Juliet and Romeo, only, if he had to guess, it seemed they were taking a break from the whole relationship thing.

He needed to go back to working on setting up his therapy center. If it wasn't for the fact he'd been injured in this as well, he'd be out the door.

This wasn't just about a woman he respected and was attracted to being in danger anymore.

This was now personal.

Dean dropped his arms, sticking his thumbs in his pockets. It didn't hurt that much less than folding his arms.

Conroy said, "First of all, is everyone all right?"

That wasn't where Dean had thought Conroy would start. He nodded. Jess tugged a chair toward her sister and sat. "I'm better now."

"You're on medical leave until further notice."

"But—"

Conroy held up his hand, and she closed her mouth.

Dean said, "Good idea."

Conroy twisted to face him. "If you were one of my people, you'd be on the bench too."

"But I'm not."

"From now on, everything that happens gets run by me."

Dean saw Jess's smug smile. He ignored it. "Fine. My backup is OUTCONUS right now anyway, so we could use the help."

Conroy said, "That is becoming apparent."

Ellie raised her hand. "I have a question." Conroy waved her on, and she said, "What does OUTCONUS mean?"

"Outside the continental US." By way of explanation, Dean said, "I live with a private security team. They'd come in handy right about now if they weren't on a job."

"Oh. Yes, I'd imagine they would."

Conroy said, "This is beyond what each of you can handle, so we're going to work this together."

Dean nodded. "If we ID each of the men from the photo, we can interview them. Find out which one keeps trying to attack us. And why."

He, for one, was tired of getting a new injury each time he went somewhere. Now Ellie's cabin had been destroyed. Would she even be able to figure out her grandfather's secret? It was a good thing they could at least investigate and hope to find the perpetrator. She could solve her little mystery on her own time, finally safe.

Then he could go back to his work knowing he'd done everything he needed to. A good woman would be safe again, and he'd get on with his life's work. *Keep moving forward.* Dean needed to be in motion or bad things happened. He didn't need a resurgence of the nightmares or his other issues.

"And your friend who left?" Ellie said, "Is he okay?"

Dean pulled out his phone. "He got home."

"Who is he anyway?" Jess threw the question at him like an accusation.

"Someone you've never met yet." Dean shrugged but saw Ted eying him out the edge of what he was seeing. Dean said, "Which is his business."

Jess grabbed a paper from the desk closest. "What's his last name?"

Dean didn't answer.

She looked at him. "And his date of birth."

Dean kept his lips pressed together.

"Is he part of that security team? Someone you picked up on the side of the road?" Jess waved a pen as she gesticulated. "A criminal you're hiding up there at that huge house?"

"His. Business."

"So you are covering for him." Jess glared at Dean. "Keeping his secrets and protecting him."

Beyond Jess, Savannah eyed Dean in a way he didn't like while Ted fidgeted. The kid had never been able to keep a secret and apparently that hadn't changed. None of the cops needed to know that Stuart lived in their house.

"Lying about this, like you lied about that photo."

Beside her sister, Ellie shifted. Uncomfortable even though she'd called him on the same thing.

"Privacy and lying are two different things," Dean said. "Stuart's business is his own, and under the legal strictures that bind me in the work I've done with him, I'm unable to divulge anything about him."

Jess's eyes narrowed. "He's one of your patients."

Dean said, "Stuart lives at the house with us." He motioned toward his brother. "But that doesn't mean you can grill Ted about him either."

His brother lifted both hands. "I know nothing."

"Stuart is a referral. A friend of a friend." Dean said, "More than that, you'll have to ask him."

"I will," Jess said.

Savannah leaned back in her chair. "Is he the reason you went to look behind that biker bar the other night? I heard about what happened at the gym."

"You think his needing my help at the gym is related to a murder you're investigating?"

"How did you know there would be a body there?"

Dean said, "If you want to interrogate me, then arrest me as a suspect. Because this conversation is over."

He was legally required to keep Stuart's confidence, as his therapist and trauma counselor. Even a court order couldn't force him to break it.

Savannah started to speak. Conroy lifted his hand, "Back to the topic we're supposed to be on. Which are the repeated attempts of harm directed at the two of you." He moved a finger back and forth between Ellie and Dean.

He wanted to be tied to her, but not like this.

"Based on the phone call Ellie received, we know these attempts on her life are because she's been looking into her grandfather's history ever since his will was read." Conroy glanced at her.

Ellie said, "I know something happened, and he was deeply ashamed of it. But I don't know what. Yet."

He liked the hope in her voice. "Conroy, did the former chief ever divulge any secrets to you?"

Conroy said, "Pretty sure I'd remember."

Mia shot him a compassionate glance, but she appeared to be busy with paperwork. Half her attention on their conversation and half on her own business.

"But you think the town's founders are who we should be looking at?" Ellie shook her head. "Because of a connection between my grandfather, Dean and Ted's father, and the lawyer?"

Conroy nodded. "It's the first connection I've seen."

Dean wasn't so sure. "A photo and matching tattoos doesn't necessarily link these men to what's been happening. But history aside, someone right *now* is trying to hurt us. To keep Ellie from finding out this secret. That's the most current issue, right?"

She shifted in her seat. "But if we find out what happened, then we know what this is all about."

"Can't do that if you're in the hospital, like Holmford. Or dead."

Ellie swallowed, as though everything that was going on hit her all over again and she wanted to be sick. What was with her? It was like she ignored reality in favor of…something else…and then had to face it when reality smacked her in the face. She didn't need to get hit with it like that, so suddenly, if she was willing to see what was right in front of her.

Jess laid a hand on her arm. "No one is going to get to you. So far Dean's done a passable job of protecting you while he gets hurt himself. Now the whole police department is going to pitch in. We'll keep you safe."

"Dean is the reason your sister is alive, Jess." Ted's face reddened. "And talking about him like he's not even here is rude."

Dean said, "Maybe you could go see if you can locate Dad."

Ted shot him a look. "I thought you said he wasn't part of this?"

"Doesn't mean we shouldn't know where he is."

"And you want me to use police resources for my personal business like that?"

Conroy said, "Ted, I'd like you to identify and locate each of the founders of Last Chance." Before anyone could voice an objection, he continued, glancing around at the group as he spoke,

"First of all, I'm the chief so I can use police resources however I deem. Second, it may just be a theory, but it's also the best lead we've got. A connection between Chief Ridgeman, Mr. Holmford, and Last Chance County. Add in Dean and Ted's father—who I've never even met, by the way—and I'm even more sure it could be less of a theory and more an actual lead."

Savannah said, "I'm out to chase a lead of my own."

As she walked to the hall that led to the back exit and the parking lot, he pulled his phone out and sent Stuart a text. The guy didn't need to be blindsided.

"I'm going to do some work of my own," Ellie said. "See if I can dig up a newspaper series about the founders. Find out as much as I can about them. After that, I'll go through what I have of my grandfather's again. If I find anything that might point to what might've happened, I'll let you know, Chief."

"I'd appreciate that, Professor."

She smiled up at him, as though he'd given her an "A" for her extra credit assignment.

"That'll help you with the will. It doesn't ensure no one attacks again." Dean said, "Whoever it is, they know their way around a hunting rifle. They can rig gas to leak and cause an explosion. I'd be willing to bet they're connected locally."

"He's right." Jess didn't seem to like that, though. "The guy who tried to break into my house owed West a favor, and that was how he was repaying it."

"Who hired him?"

She turned to Dean then. "If I knew that, I'd know who was doing this, wouldn't I?"

"I meant, did he say?" Dean said, "I'm not a cop, nor was I one in the Navy. I've never interrogated anyone. But I can imagine what it feels like." He smiled at her, but none of this was amusing.

Conroy said, "If this is connected to West, we need to know. The person targeting Ellie could know West's identity, and that could put us one step closer to taking him down." He lifted a hand, palm out, and Dean saw that Ellie had raised hers to ask a question.

"That's a different case. If it relates, and we get intel, that's one thing. Your safety is the priority here, though. Nothing else."

He glanced at Dean. "Not even your issues with your father."

Dean said nothing.

Conroy continued, "Which may very well play into all this."

"Why is that?" Ellie glanced around.

Dean said, "The photo you found, of that group of Vietnam vets?"

"The one with your father and my grandfather in it?" One eyebrow lifted, her opinion of what she saw as his deception still clear.

Dean nodded as though he hadn't seen all that in her expression. "My guess is, those are the town's founders. I need Conroy to confirm if it's even true. But if it is, then my father might know the answer to what you're looking for."

She pressed her lips together. Taking the thoughtful approach while Jess huffed beside her, venting her opinion of him aloud.

Dean wanted to ask Ellie what she thought about that and maybe discuss it further. But how would that get answers? They should work this. Like all the cops were doing.

He'd go back to protection detail.

She could do her history professor thing and find out what someone wanted to remain buried. He would watch her back while she did so. Jess and Conroy could do the cop stuff, since that was what the city paid them for.

She finally spoke. "I'd like the chance to uncover this by myself."

"As long as that's the safest course of action, I have no problem with it." Dean figured it was best to get that out up front. "But this has escalated to someone being hospitalized, and we don't know yet if Holmford is going to make it. Which means, as of right now, you're in protective custody."

Jess rose to her feet. "You may not—"

"You put me in charge of her safety, and I've more than proven myself." Why were some people never satisfied? "But if I'm going to continue to put my life at risk, we're going to do things my way."

Ellie laid a hand on her sister's forearm. "It's fine, Jess. You have a job to do."

"She's right. You do."

Jess narrowed her eyes.

Dean said, "Interview the remaining founders and figure out who is doing this."

"While you stand there and look pretty?" Jess said, "Sure. I'll do my job. The one I've been doing this entire time."

Ted interrupted. "Jess—"

She said, "I don't need him insinuating I'm lapse in my duty."

"Like you insinuated I'm not worth anything more than standing around to get in the way of whatever comes flying at your sister?"

Ted tried again. "Guys—"

"Ding ding ding." Conroy sighed. "Everyone back to your corners."

"I'm taking Ellie back to the Ridgeman residence," Dean told Conroy. "Though given all that's happened, I'm thinking she should pack her things, and I'll find a safe place where she won't be found until she's figured this out."

"Just one stop on the way."

He turned to Ellie, not liking how guarded her tone was. "Where?"

She lifted her chin. "I want to look at Mr. Holmford's house."

Twenty-One

"This is kind of creepy." Ellie looked around Holmford's entryway. "While he's in the hospital, we're in his house without him knowing."

"Welcome to my job." Jess shrugged. "Creepin' on other people's lives. Usually on the worst day of their life."

Ellie turned to her sister. "That's…"

"Yeah, don't worry about it." Jess said, "Where's Dean?"

"He said he was going to walk around outside."

"Guess that means I'm clearing the house." Jess held up a hand. "Stay here and don't move until I get back."

Her sister wandered off, not relaxed. With those strong lines of tension in her shoulders and legs. Gun out, ready to face down whoever might be here.

While Ellie stood around uselessly.

She pressed her lips together and studied the entryway. Peter Holmford had lived alone for years. No wife, not even a girlfriend. His house smelled a little musty, not something she wanted to dwell on. The décor was utilitarian. Card table in the entryway, on which was a collection of keys and mail. On the floor underneath was a pile of shoes—boots and tennis shoes.

Life, set up in a way that meant he did what was convenient with no concern for aesthetics. Because if no one came over, then there was no one he needed to impress. Right?

Her own apartment was comfortable. Her decoration consisted of periodically adding another bookcase until they all overflowed. It was set up for comfort, the way Holmford's was set up for function.

She didn't have time to think about what that meant before Jess was back. "It's all clear."

Ellie nodded. They walked through the sparse living room and reasonably clean kitchen—though it was hard to leave a mess when there wasn't much food in the house beyond a couple of condiment bottles in the fridge and a box of pasta in the cupboard. No sauce.

"I'm trying to marry this—" She waved her hand around wildly. "—with the put-together man we met."

Ellie agreed, "He clearly saw no need to impress anyone with his home."

"Probably put all his money into sprucing up the office and didn't have any left for a house he never invited anyone over to anyway."

"So it's an appearances thing?" Ellie was stuck on what her home and office said about her. Was she superficial, or did she not care what other people thought as she'd always told herself?

"Maybe." They found the bedroom. Not difficult, considering there were only two and the house was one story. Jess opened the dresser drawers but didn't move his things around.

Ellie slid the mirrored closet door aside. Rows of suits hung on the rail, two suitcases and a duffel on the floor. One pair of sneakers, one pair of work boots. Enough suits to get through the work week while the dry cleaners took care of the ones he needed cleaning.

Above the clothes, a shelf had been packed tight.

Jess moved to stand by her side. "Grab that one."

Ellie looked at her.

"You're taller than me. You can probably reach it."

"I'll get it." Dean was suddenly there, pulling down the shoe box Jess had indicated with one hand. "I'll put it on the bed. Anything else?"

Ellie moved to the shoe box and flipped the lid off. Inside was a collection of memorabilia she recognized as being from the Vietnam War. "Do we know if he was in that photo?"

Jess said, "Conroy thinks so, but I believe he's confirming it with Department of Defense records."

Dean moved beside her. "Anything we should know?"

"There's nothing in the rest of the house about his service." Ellie said, "It's all here in one place, tucked in a shoebox he had stuffed in a closet." She shifted some of it. "Uniform. His discharge papers and service record. A Vietnam service medal and a Purple heart—so he had to have been injured somehow."

Jess folded her arms. "But he hid it because he didn't want anyone to know. Instead of being proud of what he did, serving his country, he never told anyone."

"It was a tough time," Ellie said. "There was a lot of public outcry. Those who did serve were drafted, so many of them never would have enlisted if they'd been given the choice."

Jess made a face.

"Not everyone will jump to fight—and possibly die—for their country." She said, "It takes a certain kind of person."

"I know that." Jess frowned. "I put my life on the line every day for the people of Last Chance."

Ellie nodded. She knew that, but if she said as much then she would just be repeating what Jess had said. She didn't know what they thought of her, considering Ellie had never done anything like it. Her grandfather had served in Vietnam. He'd come here after and served for years as a cop. Now Jess was a cop as well. Dean had been military and still gave all his energy to help others. Meanwhile, Ellie still had her nose in a book, pretending the world didn't affect her.

That living didn't hurt.

She looked over at Dean. He'd served for years—she didn't know how many—as a Navy SEAL. He knew what it meant to fight and bleed for his country. "What do you think?"

He glanced at her.

"Why would someone who'd served hide everything from that time away in a closet? Why not just throw it out?"

"He wants to be proud. But he can't be."

"Why not?"

"Everything he saw," Dean said. "Everything he did. It's still all there in his head, and he just can't smile and nod and pretend it's all fine. Because it isn't." He turned and walked out of the room.

"Did he seem okay to you?"

Jess swung around. "Are you serious?"

"He looked overly flushed. Was he sweating?" Maybe his injury was worsening. Like an infection, or maybe being flung around when the cabin exploded had made it worse. Did she need to worry that Dean might need to go to the hospital again?

"Oh," Jess said, "you mean like he might be sick or something?"

Ellie said, "What do you think I meant? I'm just worried that's all. What's the big deal?"

"Wow. For someone so smart, you can be obtuse about what's right in front of your nose. And I'm not talking about whatever book you're reading right now." Jess glanced at the door. "I almost feel sorry for the guy. Or, I would if I liked him."

"Don't be mean to him, Jess. He's a nice guy."

"Now you're defending him. After he lied to you?"

Ellie realized she was. "He's exhausted and injured. He's been protecting me this whole time, and I'm the only one involved in this who is so far unscathed. And I'm the target."

She needed to get back to her research so she could figure this out. But that only brought to light what someone wanted hidden. So it didn't get her out of danger. It arguably would put all of them in even more danger.

Did she want to give this up? Not really. She felt like she was racing the clock, needing to figure out what the secret was. If that was even possible after the cabin had been destroyed. And she had to do it before what she still had was destroyed as well.

She found Dean in the second bedroom, which was more of a storage room, given the boxes. But on the wall hung a framed picture. A map of Last Chance.

"The house is okay, right? Your surveillance stuff is still up and running, and no one else has tried to break in?"

He turned to her. Sweating and flushed, he definitely wasn't all right. "The surveillance is still running, yes. Nothing has triggered it."

Yet.

She heard that unspoken word. "I'd like to get back there as soon as possible."

Did he have a fever? Maybe one of the other injuries he had was infected now. She didn't know a lot about medicine, but her study of history told her exactly how dangerous things could be if left untreated.

And he was exactly the kind of man to try and convince them all that he was fine. Even when he needed at least to sit down and rest.

He reached up and swiped at his forehead with his sleeve.

Ellie bit back what she wanted to say. "Let's head out soon." She started to turn, but something about the map snagged her attention.

She moved to it. "Huh."

Dean said nothing.

She stared at the lines and swirls. The town, and the area surrounding it. She found the spot where her grandfather's cabin was located. "This is…"

"What?"

"I saw a map exactly like this on the wall in the coffee shop. But it seems…off somehow." She shook her head. "It was probably made by a different person."

"You have a photographic memory?"

"No, but I retain nearly everything that I hear or see. It's more like I get a sense of the overall picture, and not every line and detail like someone with an eidetic memory."

"So you're just super smart."

"As are you." She turned then, determined to make peace. "To have all the medical training you do. The emergency medical work you do, and the therapy. That's a lot of very different kinds of knowledge, and skills."

Even though she wanted peace, there was no hope of a relationship between them. She could accept that now.

Everyone had a right to privacy, and she knew how it felt to want to keep something to yourself. No one had the right to any part of her life that she didn't want to give them. If Dean didn't want to share with her about his father, that was his right. Which made it none of her business.

He'd been right to act as though they had separate lives. Their lives were separate, and there was no way they'd be able to mesh them. There were things they would never know about each other. Even if she stayed for a while. Long term, they lived across the country from each other. They both had busy schedules, and that precluded time that a relationship would need. It just wouldn't work between them.

And then there was Jess. Ellie didn't want to complicate what was going on between Jess and Ted—though she was pretty sure her sister was in love with him—by complicating things with herself and Dean. That was far too much drama for her liking, especially because she just wanted to get to the place where she could work on her book.

Her career had to be her focus right now, or what had her work all these years been for?

Jess stood in the doorway. "Anything?"

Ellie shrugged. "Not that I can find."

"I didn't think so, but it was worth a look."

"So there wasn't any point in coming here?"

It was Jess's turn to shrug. "If I had covered something up, I wouldn't leave any evidence pointing to what it is. Or where I buried it."

"But you're a cop, so you know about evidence."

"So was grandpa. Which means if he was involved, then he made sure nothing could be found that would leave a trail back to him. It could've ruined his whole life and his career."

"So he was a dirty cop?"

Jess bristled. "It depends on what happened. And what his part in it was. And if anyone other than you had made that accusation, I'd probably punch them. So you're going to want to be careful who you say stuff like that around. Especially at the police station."

Ellie sighed. She lowered her voice to say, "If we can't convince Dean he needs to see a doctor, then we need to get him somewhere he can rest."

Jess glanced down the hall, even though Dean wasn't there anymore. Hopefully he was out of earshot. Her sister said, "I'll call the sergeant. He can have someone watch the house while you research and Dean gets some sleep."

"Can you call a doctor, too? See if they'll make a house call." She was banking on the town's appreciation of everything Dean did, and that it would induce someone to help him out when he needed it.

Jess yelled, "Time to go!"

Ellie winced. "You didn't need to yell in my ear. I'm standing right here."

Before they left she took a photo of the map with her phone. Later she could figure out what it was about it that she couldn't put her finger on.

Twenty-Two

Dean blinked awake. He sat up on the couch and groaned as his shoulder protested the movement. His whole body felt feverish, and he'd sweat through his shirt. Since there was no one in view, he pulled a clean shirt from his bag and switched it out. Someone behind him cleared their throat.

When he spun around, Ellie stood on the other side of the couch.

He couldn't read the look on her face. "Everything okay?"

She swallowed. "I'm calling the doctor about your shoulder." She turned away, cheeks flushed. "There's coffee, and my breakfast casserole is almost ready."

"Copy that." Except for the doctor part. "I'll call the doc myself, though."

"If I believed you, I might agree."

He trailed after her instead of going for the coffee. While she sat back down at her computer set on her grandfather's desk, Dean pulled out his phone and called the doctor, leaving a voicemail while Ellie watched him. He couldn't help but smirk even though he felt awful. The ache in his shoulder was persistent enough he needed someone to look at it. But only because he couldn't treat the back of his shoulder.

When he was done, he stowed the phone.

"Thank you."

The oven timer let out a long beep. Dean said, "I'll get breakfast dished up so you don't have to stop what you're doing."

"Double thank you."

He smiled to himself as he wandered back to the kitchen, retrieving his gun from the coffee table on his way. Things had been hairy, and it wasn't worth being caught unarmed. Basuto had been replaced by Officer Frees since Dean fell asleep.

He didn't mind the extra backup. It wasn't an assessment of his skills. Not when he was pretty sure he should have taken the prescription the doctor offered him when he'd checked Dean's shoulder for internal injury. In case he got an infection. *Guess I wasn't going to avoid that one.* He could've done without it, probably. But he'd hit the dirt getting blown up. At least, that was what he was going to assume made him feel worse today than he had yesterday.

Dean poured two coffees and served the breakfast casserole, the smell of bacon making his stomach rumble. As he balanced it all in two hands and went to the office, his phone rang in his pocket.

He set it down and pulled his cell, expecting it to be the doctor. Instead it was Savannah.

"Cartwright."

"It's Wilcox. Got a minute?"

"Yep." Dean took his mug and plate to the office couch, watching Ellie eat with one hand while she stared at the computer screen. "What's up, Detective?"

"While Ted is ID-ing everyone in that photo, I went and spoke with your friend Stuart."

"Yeah?" He didn't want to be too eager to ask her if she could clear him, or what she'd found out about that man's death. But he did know they had the second biker, the one he'd been arguing with, in custody. Dean just wasn't sure if that was related to the man's death, or about a separate incident, or even an ongoing argument.

"He may have witnessed what happened and can corroborate the suspect's statement, but that doesn't make him reliable. As much as I'd like it to be otherwise. For his sake and the sake of my case."

"The guy you picked up, that's your suspect?"

"Jess brought him in, but yeah." Savannah said, "He had the murder weapon in his car. Confessed to shooting his friend. I'd love independent evidence to corroborate that, but that's just me. The county prosecutor will take it."

Dean swallowed a bite of cheesy egg. "So Stuart is clear?"

"He said he was going to visit his sister."

"Copy that."

"Does he have a sister?"

Dean said, "He's okay. That's what counts. Right?"

He figured the rest was need-to-know. It might have been a while since Stuart had been a CIA operative, but he'd probably never shake those covert ways of doing things. Visiting his sister meant he was headed out of town for rest. Probably on his own, backpacking through the forests around Last Chance.

Who knew how long he'd be solo camping? Dean figured it would be at least until he finished processing the idea that he might have killed someone in Last Chance and not remembered it.

Savannah made a noncommittal sound and hung up the phone.

Dean saw a missed call from the doctor, which had been followed up with a text. He would come over. Dean sent the address.

He wondered about bringing the doctor—or anyone, really—here to the Ridgeman house. Who knew the identity of the persons targeting Ellie? He needed to keep her safe. But did he really suspect the doctor of having anything to do with it? Unless he was one of the founders, there was no reason he should be on the list of suspects.

He honestly disliked the fact he was suspecting the doctor at all. The man hadn't ever given any impression he wasn't a good guy before. He needed to examine why he suspected the man of bad intent now, but he needed all his focus to keep Ellie safe.

At least he had police backup. Just in case. If the doctor suddenly changed his tune from overwhelming support of Dean's life and work to trying something that put Ellie in danger, help was close by. There were cops outside. More would come within minutes.

"Huh."

Dean needed to stretch his legs again, so he got his coffee and wandered around the desk to look over Ellie's shoulder. "You have something?"

She glanced at him and blinked. "Oh, uh. Maybe."

"What's the maybe?"

"This is the map from Holmford's house." She pointed to the left image with her index finger. "The other is a photo Jess took of the map on the wall in the coffee shop."

He studied them, realizing she was right about this being the same map. "They look identical."

"There are some minor differences, but I don't know if they mean anything." She leaned back in the chair and sighed. "I keep coming back to what Jess said. That if she was the one trying to cover something up, she sure wouldn't leave clues that lead right back to it."

"Unless it was the only way to ensure *someone* found out about everything without alerting the person you're trying to hide your actions from."

She frowned.

"You know there is more than one person involved. From the photo, we can surmise it's at least two, if not more. Could be all of them, but also might be a smaller group."

"Like my grandfather and Mr. Holmford."

Dean nodded. "So if one was the ringleader and pressured the rest into being involved in something…could be one or more of the others left ways for it to be discovered. Like an insurance policy."

"So by mutual agreement, they keep quiet in order to keep them all from getting in trouble for it."

"Except your grandfather got sick and passed away. Leaving the truth to you, so it can finally come out."

She chewed on her lip for a while, then sighed. "While you were asleep, Sergeant Basuto brought a tablet over and I looked through mugshots. But since I didn't get such a good view of that guy in the hoodie, I didn't see anyone in them that I thought was him."

Dean nodded. "It's good that you looked."

"But I could have found him, and I didn't."

"It's not your fault. He doesn't want you to know who he is," Dean said. "So why give you a good glimpse of his face?"

"True." She smoothed down the material of her black skinny pants over her knee. "I don't like being scared." She looked up. "I'm sorry you got hurt because of me."

"Who says I'm hurt?"

"The massive bruise on your shoulder."

He said, "Nah, I've had worse than that as a SEAL. You think a bruise is going to slow me down?"

"Maybe not, but an infection—or whatever it is—has knocked you on your butt. You were out for about eighteen hours. I was getting worried. Bill called like four times to check up on you."

"He did?"

She nodded.

"Huh. I'll have to get him a gift card. There's this diner just outside of town, and they do the best pies."

"I know." She grinned. "The huckleberry with ice cream is my favorite."

"I'm a chocolate peanut butter kind of guy." Dean couldn't resist saying, "A smile looks good on you. When all this is done I hope to see it more."

"I'm supposed to spend the summer in New Hampshire working on my book, but I haven't confirmed anything yet. Then I thought maybe I'd do it in my grandfather's cabin...that's now nothing but rubble." She shook her head. "It's all up in the air. Not that I'm going to tell Professor Tumbleweed that. He'll tell me I'm only making excuses."

"You like what you do?"

"I figure there are good and bad aspects to every job."

Dean nodded. "True."

"I've always been a history buff. One day I'm going to pen an epic historical tome. A tragedy and a romance so all those people who told me I can't write emotion can eat my words. I'm going to write about a monumental battle where nearly everyone dies."

He started to laugh.

She shoved at his knee, grinning. "It's definitely going to be one of those endless literary affairs that's long enough it can double as a door stop because it's as heavy as a brick. And no doubt I'll win numerous awards for it."

"You'll have to sign a copy for me. A first edition."

"Maybe I will." She folded her arms, lifting her chin. "Who knows?"

He liked the idea of that, and nodded. "Who knows."

There was hope there. And maybe a measure of promise of what could be. It meant the book wasn't closed on what might happen between Dean and Ellie. If he could keep her safe, and get them both through this without any more mishaps, then anything could happen.

And that was a wonderful, faith-filled place to be.

Is that what you want, Lord? For me to wonder. To hope and wait.

Ellie scrolled through pages of the website for the local paper. "If the founders' story is as mysterious as this reporter makes it out to be, maybe I'll write the story of Last Chance."

He always figured a mystery meant the reporter had found nothing, so they made it sound like there was this big mystery. Though, in the case of Last Chance it might be close to the truth.

He said, "If you're writing about Last Chance, you'd have to be here. Right? That means staying longer. Maybe rebuilding the cabin?"

She shrugged one shoulder.

"Would you quit the university to stay here?"

She wrinkled her nose. "It's been wonderful being a professor. Right now, thinking about it, I'm having trouble concentrating on the good parts. But that's just the mood I'm in with everything going crazy."

"It's worth thinking on, though. Right? Whether or not you might want a change?"

"That's what I was supposed to be doing while I worked on my book, truth be told. A chance to get away and reassess. There hasn't been much opportunity to do that since I got here."

He got the message and decided he'd pushed too hard. If she decided to stay here, that was one thing. But he didn't want to always wonder if she'd only stuck around because of him.

Right now she was in danger. He had to wonder if she might be better off—safer—staying somewhere other than Last Chance.

Dean's phone chimed. At the same time, Ellie's cell lit up and vibrated across the surface of the desk. She lifted it to see the screen. "The officer outside says the…" She swallowed, looking nervous. "Doctor Gilane is here to see you."

"Guess that's my cue to leave you to it."

She got up, instead. "I'll go with you. To make sure everything is all right."

Dean stared at her while he tried to figure out if she was scared in general, or just scared for him. "Thanks."

She closed the laptop lid and brought it with her, not once meeting his gaze as she gathered her things.

"I'm sorry if I put more on you than you're ready for or more than you can handle right now."

She held the laptop against her with one arm and lifted her coffee mug with the other. On the way past him she leaned up and touched her lips to his cheek. "Thank you for bringing me breakfast."

"El—"

She swept past him. "Come on. The doctor is waiting."

Twenty-Three

The doctor entered the house looking about the same as she remembered. He shook Dean's hand, then saw her standing across the entryway still clutching her laptop. "Eleanor."

"Doctor Gilane." She held her hand out. "It's good to see you again."

He didn't let go of her hand. He set his other on top, the two-handed hold that was supposed to communicate a greater level of care for the person. "It's good to see you also. You look…well."

She tugged her hand from his, and he let her do it.

Dean said, "You guys know each other?"

"Sure do." She tried to smile. "I grew up here, remember?" She swallowed past the lump in her throat, no longer interested in hiding the fact she was keeping something from Dean. She wasn't about to tell all over what happened. But he already knew there had been an incident. She might as well work toward trusting him.

After all, he'd all but asked her to think about staying in town longer. Not even knowing she'd thought the very same thing—before the cabin burned down.

Ellie said, "Actually, I went through something terrible in junior year." She had to take a breath to say, "The doctor helped me afterward."

Compared with that last time they'd had significant interaction, the idea of telling Dean was only slightly less painful.

Ellie pushed the memories aside. The smells. The aching discomfort. She'd seen the doctor since, briefly across the crowd at the funeral. He'd steered clear of her, and she'd been grateful. But now the source of her nightmares was dead.

So what was she still afraid of?

"Let's go into the kitchen." Dean motioned for the doctor to go first.

She could tell from his frown that he knew something was wrong, tied to her need for the doctor's help. But there were more important things happening in the here and now. If she wasn't thinking about the history she taught back at the university, then she was going to only think about the present. Where she stood right now. Much better than allowing her personal history to bleed into this moment.

Her past needed to stay gone, where it belonged.

She offered the doctor a cup of coffee and had to avert her eyes when Dean removed his shirt again. It had been seriously distracting when she'd come upon him changing earlier. This time it was a test of whether the previous glance had simply been about surprise—followed by the realization of how his wound looked around the bandage.

Who knew a man's chest and stomach could look like that?

Ellie hadn't had much opportunity to think about it. She spent summers in the library or traveling. And certainly not to hot beaches where she'd have the occasion to see a former Navy SEAL showing off his maintained physique.

Dean's lips curled up. Then the doctor touched his shoulder with gloved fingers and he winced.

"You need another X-ray, but likely that'll just confirm that you injured it further." The doctor said, "Remember when I recommended the prescription for painkillers?"

"I didn't get the chance to have it filled."

Ellie frowned. She leaned on the edge of the counter reminded of how he'd suffered because of her. Because he'd been determined to keep her safe, to get to her as quickly as possible.

The doctor gathered steam for a lecture. One she'd heard before when she told him she didn't want him calling the police. In the end, she'd acquiesced to him phoning her grandfather—even though she knew he'd have done it anyway without her approval. Even though she'd been seventeen, which was plenty old enough to make her own decisions.

Then she'd had to persuade her grandfather to leave it all alone. Let her heal and not start a one-man war going after the guy who'd hurt her.

She'd left town a few months later with her mom and Jess. Her sister had even been her roommate for a while as Jess went to school to get her criminal justice degree. Their mom drifted in and out of their lives—as reliable then as she'd ever been.

She was getting money from her father, what did she care about her two grown daughters who were doing fine without her help?

"I appreciate your knowledge of medicine and how it gives you some insight into the situation you're in." The doctor took a breath.

Ellie jumped in. "Doctor Gilane, you were one of the founders of Last Chance, weren't you?"

The doctor's inhale got stuck in his throat. He choked and then began coughing, still touching Dean's wound. Her former SEAL protector looked like he wanted to throw up that breakfast casserole.

Shame, since that would be a waste of bacon.

She got the doctor a glass of water and ignored Dean's expression. She knew exactly what she was doing, thank you very much.

Ellie smiled, trying to make it look completely innocent. "I'm sorry, I startled you. It's just that I've been looking into Last Chance history, thinking about my grandfather and his life, you know? Since

I'm here for a few more days. After that, I won't have as ready access to his things."

She said, "I came across a newspaper series that delved into the town's history. It mentioned a doctor who was part of that original group. I just assumed that was you since I remember you being the *only* Last Chance doctor when I was little."

He leaned back and smiled that bleached smile, but she couldn't help thinking it looked strained. "We've come a long way over the years. The town has grown considerably, but I wasn't the doctor who was here when the town first started. That was before my time, I'm afraid."

Ellie wasn't a human lie detector, so she didn't know if he was telling the truth or not. Hopefully Jess and her police department people would figure out fast enough who in town should be next on their list of suspects, and whether it should be the doctor, or not. They needed to get the ball rolling so they could prevent whatever might happen next.

"Do you know who it might've been?" She asked him. "It would help us figure something out."

"You're an investigator now?" The doctor chuckled a humorless laugh.

"No. I'm a history professor. I bring to light the ugly truth people would rather bury." She didn't usually study things that resonated into her present. It was easier to keep her feelings out of it if she didn't know anyone involved.

"I've always thought of humans as inherently good."

While Dean studied her—whatever that was about—and got poked, Ellie said, "No. The Bible has that right, at least. People are inherently selfish liars who do ugly things to each other for sometimes no reason at all."

The doctor peeled off his surgical gloves. "Isn't that why the town was founded? So like-minded people could experience a haven from life? A place to recover from what they'd seen and the things they'd been forced to do, and live in peace."

"I don't know," Ellie said. "Was it?"

She wondered if he was lying. There was no way to tell without a background check to find out how long he'd been here. Ted was ID-ing the men in that photo. But what if the doctor was one of them, right here under their noses, lying to them about how long he'd been here.

That was easy enough to verify.

"Thanks for coming, Doc." Dean shook the older man's hand.

Considering he was tanned and looked like he might've even had some plastic surgery done, there was no way to discern his age from just looking at him. Surely Conroy knew—or could work it out.

Ellie wasn't ready to let him go, though. When the doctor turned away, she mouthed, "Stall him," to Dean, and sent her sister a text to run Gilane's background. Not that she carelessly assumed he was lying, but she didn't believe in coincidences. This was a small town. Had there been a doctor before Gilane?

Her cohort frowned, not liking being dragged into a scheme with someone he respected. "I'm still waiting on Holmford's paralegal to get back to me."

The doctor said, "Right. Peter is in a bad way, I'm afraid. She's probably holding down the fort at the office. No doubt she's swamped covering everything."

"That's understandable." Dean said, "I inherited Chief Ridgeman's land, the area around the cabin." He glanced at Ellie, almost apologetic looking.

She gave him a tiny shrug and for the doctor's benefit said, "We're all pretty surprised by my grandfather's will. But having gotten to know Dean over the last few days, and hearing all about this therapy center he wants to set up...well, from the good he does around town, I can see why my grandfather wanted to support the work."

"As do we all." The doctor smiled. Not the genuine one he'd given her upon realizing she was here. This was different, and it set her on edge.

"Besides," she said. "I don't live in Last Chance. So what do I want with property in the hills above town?"

He looked brittle. As though the façade was about to crack.

The doctor said, "If the town was founded to give people a place to deal with their pasts in peace, then why not a therapy center that treats PTSD and other traumas? Dean is carrying on the legacy of Last Chance. You of all people can understand how important it is to talk through painful experiences and work toward healing, I'm sure. It's noble to want to serve others, and that's the kind of person Dean Cartwright is."

"I'm learning that." She glanced at Dean and saw he wasn't comfortable with the way this conversation was going.

He said, "Doctor, I've been wondering. Have you heard from my father recently?"

"Huh." Gilane scratched at his jaw with a manicured thumbnail. "Can't say as I have. But I get a lot of those robo-calls that I don't answer. He could have left a message, though. You know how it is."

Ellie joined in his chuckle even though all of it sounded fake—his and hers. Dean just looked concerned. She had to wonder about the relationship between Dean's father and the doctor. Evidently they knew each other.

"Well, I should get back to the hospital." Gilane pulled the front door open and Dean ushered Ellie out onto the front porch with him. Why, she had no idea.

"Thank you for coming, Doctor."

"I'll get your prescription called in to the pharmacy. Be sure to pick it up this time, yes?"

"Will do. Thanks." Dean laid his arm across her shoulders and tugged her close to his side. She couldn't tell if his intention was to shield her, or if he was mad and wanted her to stay with him so he could vent after the doctor left.

Ellie wasn't going to let that dampen her mood. Today marked the day she faced down a significant memory brought on by seeing the doctor. One memory in the whole painful catalog that had shadowed her entire life. And it hadn't brought her down. She'd held her chin high through it. Faced him. Thought about it, and then moved on.

There was a ways to go, and maybe there always would be. But one thing was true.

She was healing.

He shifted, and she felt his breath on the shell of her ear. "Are you going to explain to me what that was?"

Ellie glanced up. "You really don't look well. You should probably lie down again."

A muscle flexed in his jaw. "I won't be managed, Ellie. If you—" He frowned, his nostrils shifting. "Do you smell that?"

"What?"

He stepped inside but held one arm out. "No. Stay there." He paused for half a second, in which time she realized what he'd smelled.

"Smoke."

"Call Jess. No, Bill. Use the emergency number—get help here." He crowded so close to her front she thought he was going to hug her. He yelled over her shoulder, down the front walk to where the officer on duty stood.

"Hey! The house is on fire!"

Twenty-Four

Fire.

Ellie blinked and the officer who'd been at the curb raced over. "I already called it in."

Ellie nodded, holding her phone in one hand. The house was on fire. She couldn't believe it. If they'd been inside…

And now more of her grandfather's legacy was being destroyed. Unless they could stop it. She spun to Dean. "Fire extinguisher."

"Where is it?"

"Hall closet." Her grandfather had been adamant about having one, even getting it checked regularly so the tag was up to date. They hadn't been able to stop the cabin from exploding. A man had almost died. *Don't let anyone die here.* There had been enough pain and hurt so far, that was the last thing she wanted to see. *No more.*

Ellie didn't know who she was talking to. That childhood God she'd sang and talked to had never done anything for her. Why call on Him now?

Doctor Gilane held his hand out. "Let's move away from the house, Ellie. We shouldn't be close by."

He seemed genuine. He'd helped her years ago, and he'd come to help Dean today. They seemed to respect each other. Still. She didn't want to go with him.

Dean whirled around, one foot in the entryway. "No." To her he said, "You come with me, or you stay with the cops."

"I'm coming with you."

He hesitated.

She moved around him. "I'll get the fire extinguisher." She could get to it quicker than him, considering how well she knew this house.

The house was *on fire.* Her things. Her grandfather's things. Her sister's things. Memories. Valuables. All of it could go up in flames while they stood around here. Waiting for the firefighters. Or allowing shock to overtake her.

No. No way.

Ellie didn't want to fight the blaze. She wasn't a firefighter, just a professional bookworm. She hauled the fire extinguisher from the highest shelf in the linen closet. It was so heavy it tipped toward her face, and she launched it toward Dean on a reflex.

He caught it with a grunt. "Stay in the hall." But he didn't enter the study.

Ellie whimpered. No, she didn't want to let this overwhelm her. So the fire was concentrated in the study. The quicker they moved, the more they might be able to save.

"Don't come in here." He readied the extinguisher, his stance and the width of his shoulders displaying such strength that even in the midst of a fire she felt safe with him. "This is a serious blaze. I won't be able to do much before the firefighters get here."

"Please try and save it."

He sprayed the flames from the doorway. He was right. Half the room was lit up. Across the room, the window had shattered. Heat blew at her like a summer storm. It ruffled his T-shirt.

Ellie coughed. It wasn't just smoke, though. She could smell a tang. Like some kind of chemical laced the air. She lifted her shirt and breathed through it, but it didn't do much.

She ran to the hall closet and grabbed two hand towels which she soaked in the powder room. She tied one around the lower half of her face, then ran to Dean.

Sweat rolled down his temples. This couldn't be good for the infection he'd gotten from his shoulder wound.

She tugged on his arm, and he backed up to the door. Ellie held the towel up, setting the ends on his shoulders. It wasn't going to hold, but it would get them out of there.

Tears burned her eyes as much as the heat from the flames. The study. It was being destroyed. Targeted as the cabin had been. Now it was rubble. She'd nearly been killed twice. Dean had been hurt.

This had to stop.

"Ellie!"

She spun to find her sister. Behind her, firefighters streamed into the house. Ellie got out of their way. Her sister tugged her out of the house. She heard Dean and the firefighters speaking, low and loud. But she couldn't make out the words. Her ears were ringing.

"Why did you go in there? You could've been hurt."

Ellie pulled the towel down. "Dean told me to stay with him." That was all she could get out before she bent double, coughing. There was nothing else she could have or would have done but remain.

Her sister shook her head. Ellie moved closer to her. She touched her sister's elbows and moved her face close. Hopefully she could get out what she had to say before she started coughing again. "I'm so sorry."

She'd lost the cabin. Now her sister was losing the house. Both of them, their inheritance from their grandfather being torn out of their hands. She hadn't even wanted the cabin. But having it gifted to her had meant so much.

Her grandfather had understood her. He'd known what she needed, and he'd respected and trusted her enough with the darkest part of his life. The thing he had never been able to move on from.

Jess hugged her.

"Are you guys okay?"

They pulled apart to find Ted beside them. "I'm good," Ellie said. "Dean is still inside, though."

She took a moment to study him. Younger than her, his dark hair draped over his right temple. He shoved it back, and she saw the faint outline of a scar there. He'd been hurt before. The last thing she wanted was for him to suffer more now.

Dean had a strong, protective streak with a radar for his brother. From her interactions with Jess, she also knew this wasn't always well received. Ellie's younger sister wouldn't like it at all if she tried to stand between her and danger. Jess had forged her own path, and Ellie—for all intents and purposes—just had to get out of the way. Let her do what she was going to do.

Even when she brought up her worry over her sister's chosen career, Jess told her she knew the drill. They'd had a cop in the family before.

But ever since Jess began working in Last Chance, Ellie had been less worried than when she was an NYPD officer.

Though, given everything that had been happening, maybe she *should* be more concerned.

To give Ted some peace of mind, she said, "I'm sure he'll be fine. The firefighters had already caught up to him when Jess and I came out."

It occurred to her then that she had promised to stay with Dean. The second the situation changed, she'd ditched him. An injured man, in the middle of a fire.

Did the firefighters know he'd hurt his shoulder?

She looked around, trying to find the doctor. Maybe he'd told the first responders of Dean's condition before they went in.

Ellie broke away from her sister. She took two steps toward the door when Dean strode out. She was so relieved her legs nearly gave out. Could she ask him for a hug?

He headed toward them, arms coming up for an embrace.

Ellie took a step. Ted cut her off, moving to hug his brother. Of course. That made sense. They were family, and she was only the person he'd agreed to look out for—to put his life on the line for. Like a bodyguard, or private security. They didn't hug the people they were protecting, right?

He was all right.

She took a deep breath, coughed most of it out, and reassured herself that he was fine. She hoped. If he wasn't, he would recover. Like Mr. Holmford, her being targeted hadn't cost him his life.

She was simply putting everyone around her in danger.

"Ellie, you—"

She stepped back before Dean could finish. He was still hugging his little brother, their care for each other evident.

"I need to go…look at the back yard." She didn't wait around to see how ridiculous they thought she was. Ellie got to the front corner of the house where the trash cans were stowed before she sensed someone following.

Jess was right behind her. "I'm coming, too."

"Why? I'm just looking."

"Because it's better than watching the two of them pretend that nothing happened. That everything is okay."

"Maybe it is." Like in the moment, all the stress washed away, and all that mattered was they were both here. Alive. "Whatever their differences, they still care about each other." She eyed her sister over her shoulder. "Like some other people I know."

Jess gave her a wry smile. "Be careful."

Ellie stopped at the back corner. There was no gate and no fence, which often fueled her sister's frequent complaints about not being able to get a dog. Then she'd complain that she worked too many hours to leave a dog alone.

Obviously she should just train as a K9 police officer, but Jess only complained how hard that was to get into and how long it took.

Jess peered out over the dark of the back yard. "It's probably trashed."

"Trashed isn't destroyed. Maybe we should refer to it as 'salvageable.'"

Jess went first, and Ellie followed her. "You're the last person I ever expect to be an optimist, and it *still* surprises me every time something hopeful comes out of your mouth."

"No one's died yet."

Jess turned.

"I've almost died. Holmford almost died. Dean almost died. You, and Stuart, almost died." Ellie had a lot of reasons to be afraid, grieving the loss of more than just a man she'd adored. "But we're alive. All of us. That's a reason to be grateful."

"So go to church. Sing 'Thank You, Jesus' a few times. But you don't need to try and convince me there's anything to be grateful for." Jess swung her arm out. "The house is destroyed. And it wasn't an accident. You see that?"

Ellie had noticed the broken window. "What about it?"

"Someone threw a Molotov cocktail in the study window. They knew exactly where Pop's belongings were, the ones you were searching through. They probably even tried to harm you in the process."

"I wasn't in there."

Jess said, "They targeted you, specifically. Trying to keep you from finding out what Pop hid."

Her sister's voice had hitched. Ellie said, "He didn't do anything wrong. You think he did? We knew him, and he wasn't the kind of man to be selfish or break the law."

"Maybe the man we knew was because of what he'd done. Because he felt so guilty, he had to live the rest of his life right. Now he's dead, and you're stuck digging it all up." Tears rolled down Jess's face.

"I'll figure it out." She didn't know how, and now all that her grandfather had left her was destroyed. "We'll fix the house. Everything will be okay."

"You don't know that." Jess was about to say more when her phone rang. She answered it, taking a few steps away as she spoke with someone on the police force. Or so Ellie assumed.

Her sister hurt deeply, and in response to that, she got angry. Because things were out of her control.

In the same situation, Ellie denied her feelings. For years she'd hidden in books, deep in the past, pretending the present held no value to her. She'd become a renowned professor. Speaker. Teacher. Soon-to-be author. But at what cost?

Her mom was a stranger to her.

Jess seemed lonely, seeing everything in a negative light.

She tried to find the good now, but it was hard. Ellie was sweat and soot stained. Standing in the scorched backyard of her childhood home.

She let out a long sigh that hitched a couple of times in her scratchy throat. At the end of the breath, arms banded around her.

She gasped but couldn't inhale any air.

He is so strong. I can't get away. Terror rolled through her as he dragged her backward, into the dark of the trees.

One hand clapped painfully over her mouth. She whimpered against it.

His hot breath smelled of alcohol as he said, "Now for some real fun."

Twenty-Five

"Are you sure you're okay?"

His brother's expression was dark, giving off the same impression Dean often registered and had grown accustomed to when it came to matters with his brother. With it came the reminder that his brother had seen and done things Dean couldn't even imagine. That life for him, after Dean left him home alone with their father, hadn't been good at all.

Ted made a face. "Don't lie to me. I can tell when you're lying, trying to placate me because you think I'm a little kid that can't handle the truth."

Dean bit down on his molars. The same frustration that burned in him now because of the adverse events over the last couple of days that he'd had no control over—like the cabin, and now the house—raged hot. His brother had been vulnerable. The truth was, yes Dean did see him as that sad little boy he'd walked away from. But that wasn't who Ted was now, and Dean had to let it all go. The guilt would eat him alive.

Dean slapped both hands down on Ted's shoulders. His brother flinched and pain shot through Dean's shoulder. Okay, bad idea. Still, he said, "I'm fine. Okay?"

Ted sniffed, then nodded. He shoved his hair back like he always did. A nervous tick, not knowing what else to do.

"It takes more than a tow truck, and a fire…and an explosion to get rid of me."

Ted didn't laugh. "You're really doing this protection thing?"

"It's not a job. I'm a licensed counselor, not a security specialist." He gave his brother a squeeze.

"So you're just doing it because of Ellie."

"Honestly?" Dean didn't know why he was asking. They'd made a pact long ago to only tell each other the truth. "Yeah. She's a special woman, and I wanted to get to know her better while she's here."

"Why, if she'll only leave again?" Deep hurt flashed in Ted's eyes.

Dean said, "Sometimes people don't leave. Like me…the last few years."

"She does seem nice."

"I know she's not your type. You don't have to pretend you like her."

"She cares about Jess. Why wouldn't I, just because she's probably smarter than me?"

"You think so?"

Ted shrugged. "Jess told me about her, so I looked up some of the papers she's written about World War 1. She is really smart. I'm surprised she doesn't have a Ph.D. yet."

"Huh." A woman who appreciated military history? He should look them up himself. Get to know her professional side as well as her personal side. Before Ellie and Jessica showed back up, he had to ask his brother a question. "Is everything okay with you and Jess?"

Ted started to roll his eyes.

"You need to talk to me."

"Sure, counselor."

"I'm not a prosecutor. And I don't want to be your therapist, Ted." Dean sighed. "I just want you to open up to *someone*."

He needed to be Ted's brother, not his shrink. Dean wanted their relationship to be normal and not fraught with minefields he was trying to work around.

How's that working for you?

Ted pushed out a breath. "She and I… I thought it was going somewhere, but maybe I was wrong. We have to work together, so there's no point making things harder for both of us by complicating it. Now isn't the time to get personal."

It seemed like the whole police department was working on the case to take down a local bad guy who went by the name, "West." He'd only put those two things together recently, from what Stuart had told him. The dead biker had been working for West. Maybe even trying to get out from under his thumb.

A bad guy.

One who had connections with whoever was targeting Ellie.

Dean said, "Conroy and Mia seem to have managed to find a balance between work and their personal lives."

"Sure, because everything is going fine for their relationship."

"Ah. So you do want a relationship with Jess." Dean grinned like he wasn't taking any of this seriously.

"I'm not Conroy. And Jess is definitely not Mia." Ted shrugged.

"It'll work out." He didn't want to ask this question. "Anything on Dad?"

The skin around his brother's eyes flexed. An involuntary wince. "I found an arrest warrant in Nevada. If we see him, we need to tell Conroy."

He almost seemed relieved. And scared of their father—which Dean had known. He figured Ted had been strong armed into working one of the old man's schemes. Or many. Who knew how young he'd recruited Ted?

Yet, every email Dean had sent home to check in with him, Ted had replied that it was all fine. Everything was good. Nothing to worry about. As though that was all supposed to convince him not to worry.

Their father didn't have the first clue about email. So why had Ted lied to him? Unless he was ashamed. Or he thought Dean didn't know what their father was. *Was it worse than I even knew?*

Ted's attention snagged on something else. They watched Jess walk over, hanging up the phone. She said, "The arson inspector is on his way."

Dean nodded. "The blaze got seriously hot very quickly." Not to mention the broken window, and the smell. "I'm thinking it'd been deliberate. Where's Ellie?" He turned and scanned. There were so many people all over the front yard. Cops, spectators. First responders who'd wanted to see to him.

Dean was fine.

Or he would be if he knew where she was.

"Ellie didn't come back around the house?" Jess twisted to look around as he'd done. "I didn't see her. I assumed she ditched me while I was on the phone and came back over—"

Dean took a deep breath and yelled, "Sergeant Basuto!"

Ted and Jessica both flinched. The sergeant trotted over. "What is it?"

"I need everyone to look for Eleanor Ridgeman." Dean didn't waste any time heading for the side of the house.

Until someone grabbed his elbow. Dean swung around to find the doctor.

"What is it?"

"We just need to find Ellie. That's all."

The doctor gasped. "She's missing?" Not the first time Dean had seen him overact. What was his deal here?

"Let me go so I can find her, doc." This man was his mentor. Yet Dean had begun to sour toward the man recently. Or at least feel like things were…off. "Unless you'd care to share something pertinent?"

Jess skidded to a stop beside him. "What was that?"

"Nothing." Doctor Gilane shook his head. "You're right. You should find her, because the last thing she needs is a repeat of what happened to her before."

Ted said, "What do you mean doc?"

The older man blinked. "Nothing. It's just… being assaulted and all…"

Dean shot him one last look, then sprinted around the house to the back yard. He'd been out here before. The boundary line for the end of Chief Ridgeman's yard was beyond the trees surrounding his land. In the dark of night, there was nothing but black.

Dean cupped his hands around his mouth. "Ellie!"

Her sister called out to her.

Ted did the same.

Jess said, "Here."

He grasped what she held out. A flashlight. "Thanks. Spread out?"

"Copy that."

Being assaulted and all… Dean wanted to be sick. Ellie had been assaulted before? It had to have been years ago when she'd still lived here. Of course she would move away with her mother after a traumatic incident.

He'd seen in her eyes several times an edgy tension of someone unsure of the risk they were under. Wondering if she could trust him. Judging whether or not she was safe.

Beyond this open land there was a side road. Had she been taken? All these attempts to scare her off from finding what her grandfather had buried. And now the perpetrator had switched it up by destroying her grandfather's belongings.

This was an escalation.

Could be that after the success of the fire, the person who'd thrown that Molotov cocktail was high on adrenaline. He might've seen her, and she'd wandered closer to him but farther from her sister. Wrong place at the wrong time. He'd grabbed her from the yard and hauled her back into the trees.

Dean shuddered and realized he'd palmed his gun.

He swept the beam of his flashlight across the grass and pine needles, considering the temperature. Weather conditions. She would be okay for a while out here. Exposure came at much lower temperatures and, last time he checked, there was no storm forecasted.

If she got away from whoever had grabbed her, she could sit tight somewhere until he found her.

But she would have to wait there knowing he'd failed her. Dean hadn't protected her this time the way he'd protected her before—the time he'd been hurt himself. This time it was Jess who had been with her.

Dean ground his teeth together. He called out, "Anything?"

From his left, Jessica replied, "Nothing!"

"Me either." That was Ted, to his right. "Where is she?"

I don't know. Was Ellie even still alive? Nausea threatened to overwhelm him, just thinking about it. Kill Ellie, and no one was left with a vested interest and the skillset to find out what her grandfather wanted unearthed.

And yet, in hurting her, this guy would set an entire police department—and one angry former SEAL—on his path. There was no way they would allow whoever did this to get away with it. They would hunt him down like he'd hurt one of their own.

Because that was who Ellie was.

A strong, intelligent woman who had lived through an assault and still had the courage to trust him to take care of her. A Last Chance native. Someone he wanted to get to know better each time he was with her, and when he wasn't with her, missed her. Wondered what she was doing.

Face it, you've got it bad for her.

That was all well and good, as far as realizations went. But if he was going to do anything about it—starting with asking her to forgive him for falling down on his job—then he had to first find her.

Jessica let out a frustrated sound. "Ellie!"

Ted called out, "Ellie, where are you?"

Dean kept going. Scanning the ground, he prayed with everything in him that he would find her. *Assaulted.* He asked God to protect her from the same trauma she'd already been through—or worse. She'd protected herself all these years. And now, because of him and Jessica, she was vulnerable again.

Dean heard the smallest of sounds. He tucked the flashlight and lifted one arm, making a fist in the air.

Right. They didn't know what that meant.

"Ellie!"

He yelled, "Quiet for a minute." Not meaning to come across that harsh, but it was the night that made sound seem louder. And the trees. *Ellie.* "I thought I heard something."

Ted crashed through the pine needles on the ground to his side. "What is it?"

"I don't know. Be quiet for a second, yeah?"

His brother fell silent.

Dean listened. Nothing.

He moved forward again, sliding the beam of the light across the ground in front of him.

Until he saw it. A shoe. Dean raced for her. "Ellie!"

She was huddled against a tree, lying on her side. Dean gasped for air as he laid two fingers on her neck to feel for a pulse.

"Is she…" Jessica didn't finish.

Dean twisted to her. "She's alive. Ted, run and get the car. Bring it to the road up there." He pointed for a second, then gathered Ellie in his arms. Ted ran full speed. Dean ignored the screaming pain in his shoulder. She smelled like smoke, but worse than that—she was seriously cold.

"Let me see her." Jessica shone her flashlight on her sister's face and hissed. "She has marks on her neck."

"Come on." He struck out, using long strides to get to the street. "Let's get her out of here."

Twenty-Six

Ellie blinked, her eyes focusing on a ceiling light. Then the yellow glow stung, so she looked away from it.

"Hey."

She shifted on the bed and saw an armchair across the room. Dean sat up and set a thick book aside, like a textbook. She couldn't focus enough to read the title. "Hey." The word was thick and graveled, barely audible.

"Here." He moved to the side of the bed and handed her bottled water, twisting the cap off for her.

When she sat up on her elbow, he smoothed her hair off her shoulder.

Ellie drank, eyeing him as the room-temperature liquid soothed her scratchy throat. "I probably look like I was dragged backward through a rosebush."

"That sounds painful."

She made a face because he was right.

"How are you feeling?"

She sat up further and touched her neck. "Sore. But all right."

It couldn't be compared to what had happened before. She wasn't going to let her mind drift to that place. One happened a long time ago, and the other was yesterday—or however long she'd been asleep.

"I'll text Ted. He can tell Jessica you're all right."

Ellie groaned. "The house. Is it destroyed?"

"There's a lot of damage, but it's not structural. It can be repaired." He set the bottle of water on the end table where he had a lamp and an alarm clock. "When she hears you're awake, she'll want to come and get a statement about what happened."

"Maybe I'll text her myself. She can just copy and paste it into a report."

"I'm not sure it works like that."

Ellie said, "My sister is a police officer and my grandfather was the chief. There have to be *some* perks."

Dean smiled. "I guess that answers my question about how your throat is doing." Still, he lifted warm hands and probed at sore spots on her neck until she flinched. "Sorry. It looks bad."

"It hurts a bit when I swallow, but that's all."

"Looks worse than it is?"

Ellie shrugged. "Maybe."

Dean backed up and stood. "Hungry? I could make you tea and maybe some oatmeal? Something soft."

"I'll come with you." She shoved back the covers. "I'd like to stretch my legs."

He nodded, glancing around. Ellie scanned the room, a single man's bedroom. She imagined it was a lot like military barracks. Decorated in a style she figured should be called, "modern military warrior." Utilitarian furniture. Flags on the wall. A camo jacket had been hung on the back of the desk chair, and there was a collection of boots on the floor. In one corner, where the vaulted ceiling was highest, a paddleboard stood upright.

"It's not much, but it's home."

He thought she would look down on him for having a modest living space? Ellie said, "I bought my condo from an eighty-two-year-old lady moving into a retirement home. It came fully furnished." She paused. "And she hadn't changed the décor since the seventies. I just need a cat, and then I'll be the quintessential spinster history professor."

His lips twitched. "Yeah?"

She nodded. "I even have her dishes—those white ones with the blue design on that all old people seem to have."

He chuckled, then slipped his hand around hers and gently tugged her to the door. "You love it."

"It suits me." She chewed her lip for a second. "But that doesn't mean I don't wonder what I'm missing."

"You feel like something is?"

"Sometimes."

"Wondering is natural." He led her to a huge kitchen area with a massive fridge that should probably be in a restaurant. "But if you want a change, then just do it."

"Just like that?" She settled on a stool, shaking her head. "Staying where I am and doing the same things I've always done is way less scary."

"Life is supposed to be scary." He filled an electric kettle and switched it on. "That's how you know you're living it."

Ellie said, "I'm glad you and I have different definitions of scary. I don't think I can handle what you can, Mr. Navy SEAL."

"Seems to me like you handled yourself just fine. Things haven't been easy, but you came through it. Right?"

Ellie ran her thumbnail along the cement between two counter tiles. "I didn't fight him off. I just froze."

"Did you see his face?"

She closed her eyes for a second. "He was wearing a mask. He grabbed my neck and shoved me back against the tree. I don't know when I blacked out." She shook her head. "He probably didn't abduct me because he didn't want to carry me, unconscious."

Who knew all those squares of caramel chocolate would come in handy? For once she was glad she was too heavy to carry.

Dean said, "Good thing, since I got to do it instead."

He'd carried her? She looked at his huge bicep muscles—which she'd been trying to avoid staring at so far. "But your shoulder."

Dean set a steaming mug of tea in front of her. "Act now, worry later."

"It's the SEAL motto?"

He shook his head. "The SEAL motto is, 'The only easy day was yesterday.'"

"That sounds awful." Ellie sipped, looking around instead while he chuckled. Because she needed a second not thinking about that man if she was going to have to go over it multiple times. That was what happened before. Everyone wanted the story, and she wound up sick of talking about it.

Maybe that was why she'd quit therapy. There was nothing good about going over and over something, instead of just moving on from it.

"You counsel people." She realized she'd said it aloud when he nodded. "What if someone just wants to forget what happened to them?"

"Depends." He took a slow sip of his drink. "Are they self-destructing other parts of their life?"

"Like, is the trauma manifesting itself somewhere else? Drug addiction, or OCD."

"Among other things, yeah." He looked like she'd surprised him.

"Like the fear of change." She swallowed. "Or pushing aside emotion—*all* emotion—in favor of logical judgment."

Dean shrugged one shoulder, his expression soft. "The only person who can say what's right for you, is you."

Ellie continued her study of the room, processing what he'd said while she sipped her tea. It felt good on her throat. Which made her think of that man, squeezing her neck with his thick fingers. Some of the liquid got stuck. She coughed.

Dean started toward her.

She waved a hand. "I'm okay."

She twisted again on the stool. Against the wall were huge couches with oversized, dark blue cushions that seemed to invite her to sink into them. Two lamps. A giant entertainment center with huge speakers. A huge dining table with mismatched chairs. On the wall was another map of the town.

She was seeing those everywhere right now.

Dean must have seen her studying it. He said, "The map was on the wall when we moved in. Along with a few other things. We think this was the first house in Last Chance, an old military training facility that was abandoned somewhere in history. Probably the fifties or sixties. After mapping out the rest of the town, they all built their property and moved out."

"Wow." She looked around more and saw a photo on the mantel. Ellie wandered to it. "Who are they?" Four men stood together, arms around each other. Dirty fatigues, sweat and black paint on their faces. All of them had huge rifles.

"Echo Team. They live here, but they're off on a job right now." Dean said, "I met them in Afghanistan, and I told them about Last Chance. They moved here before I even got out of the Navy. Asked if I wanted to live with them, and with me came Ted. Stuart showed up a few months ago. Even though my brother lives here too, there's still there's room for another half dozen people at least, so we've let Pastor Daniels know that it's available and to send any guys who need a place to stay our way."

"Like Maggie does with Hope Mansion?"

Dean nodded. She set the photo down and picked up a gold Christmas ornament that sat beside it, completely out of place. He said, "A couple years back, a day before Christmas Eve, I get this call. An elderly lady had hurt herself, and she didn't want to bother the police or EMTs. When I got there, I discovered she'd tried to take a heavy box of decorations down from a closet shelf. She'd lost her husband a few months before and this was her first Christmas without him. He'd always gotten the decorations down for her."

"Was it bad?"

"A few bruises. I called the guys." He waved a hand toward the photo. He was treading carefully, trying not to upset her. She felt like she was on a knife edge. But despite years of trying to forget what had happened to her, it was back at the forefront.

She said, "Echo Team?"

Dean continued, "They came over, hauled out the Christmas tree and set it all up. All the decorations. They even hung lights on the front of her house."

She wanted to smile, but it wasn't there. When she tried to speak, the last words she thought she'd have said emerged. "He touched me."

Dean's gaze lowered to her neck.

"There was a group of them. It was a party, and I didn't even want to go in the first place, but it was Homecoming night and my friend dragged me." She thought of her former best friend, and how she hadn't spoken to her since. Nor had she had a best friend since. "They…herded me into a bedroom and—"

"Who?" He frowned. "When did this happen?"

"Junior year." She took a breath. "It was Ed Summers and a bunch of his friends."

Thunder rumbled across his expression. "They touched you?"

Ellie closed her eyes and nodded. "When that guy grabbed me from the yard, Jess didn't even notice." Her breath hitched. She didn't blame her sister—not the way she blamed her friend. "I saw his face." Her stomach clenched painfully. "Then I blinked, and it wasn't him. It was…"

"Ed Summers." Dean squeezed her hand. "Did he do more than touch you?"

Ellie shook her head. "The cops raided the party. I shoved at one of them, and he shoved back. I hit my head on a shelf." She lifted her fingers and massaged the spot on the back of her head. "The doctor had to staple it back together."

Dean hung his head.

"My grandfather found me bleeding and crying."

When he lifted his gaze, he held his arms open. Ellie walked into his hug. Why did she feel so safe with him? "Thank you."

His chest rumbled. "If he wasn't dead…"

"I know." She looked up at him. "Like I said. Thanks."

Ellie had never had a defender before. Her grandfather had been upset. He'd felt powerless to help since he hadn't gotten there fast enough to prevent it. Dean felt just as deeply and was just as protective as her grandfather. But his strength was obvious, even when he had been hurt himself. It didn't change who, and what, he was.

Dean lowered his head and touched his lips to hers. A soft kiss of comfort and compassion. He didn't pressure her, just kept it light. Sweet.

Until the doorbell rang.

Twenty-Seven

Dean looked back just before he opened the door. Ellie had turned away, though, denying him a glance at her face. After that kiss, as light and short as it was, he felt the flush on his own cheeks. It had been a while since he was attracted to anyone. He'd about given up on the idea of finding someone before he could prove he was the man everyone thought he was.

It turned out he just needed to wait for her to cross his path…in the process of her nearly being struck by a car.

Things weren't perfect, but he wasn't going to pass up the opportunity. Ellie was everything he wanted in a woman. And he wanted the chance to help her through her pain, to support her. Protect her. He'd thought that would turn him off. That he wouldn't want to feel like he was "working" with someone in a relationship. But with her, he was glad to do it.

The doorbell rang again, followed by a knock on the door. He didn't think he'd ever actually heard the bell ring before. It wasn't like people just stopped by here.

He hauled it open. On the porch, Doctor Gilane took half a step back.

Dean said, "Help you?"

Beyond the doctor was the yard, then the doctor's brand new BMW sport utility vehicle. Past that, Last Chance sprawled out in front of him, at the bottom of the hill. On either side, huge tall pines reached up for the sky.

"Uh, yes. I was just seeing if Ellie needed anything. If I could help her at all." He stammered a couple of the words but coughed to cover it.

Nervous. The doctor's normally perfectly-styled hair looked a little mussed. Like he'd been running his hands through it. He also hadn't put on his gold watch. Had he been wearing it when he'd come over to treat Dean's shoulder? He didn't remember.

The doctor took a step toward him.

Dean acted surprised, as though this man he was supposed to trust had shocked him with this uncharacteristic behavior.

Stuart was gone right now. Even Ted wasn't here. He was on his own. If the doctor tried anything, Dean would have to deal with it himself.

"Come in." His tone was pretty sarcastic, considering the doctor had basically invited himself in.

Dean moved ahead of him. When he got to the end of the hall where the open space began, he shifted and essentially barred the doctor's entry. Given what Ellie had just told him, Dean wasn't ready for anyone to be in her space right now.

Sure, he was going to be super overprotective of her now. Enough had happened, and she'd been abducted last night. He still didn't have the whole story about that. Until he'd settled, and she knew it would *never* happen again—as much as he could prevent it—they'd all just have to deal with him being antsy.

Ellie stared up at the map on the wall. He'd never really even looked at it, and the idea it had drawn her attention for some reason made him want to get her to talk through it with him. But first, he'd have to get the doctor to leave.

"As you can see, she's fine." Dean wasn't, but the doctor wasn't here to help him.

"Yes. I see." The doctor flashed him a bright smile…one that looked like it was about to crack.

Dean wanted to ask the doctor what was going on and why it seemed like he was off. Dean normally respected this man, and in all these years, Dean had received nothing but approval from him. Like his unequivocal support for the therapy center. Now it was like he was seeing through the dissonant fragments Gilane usually held together so well.

"Is everything okay?"

The doctor opened his mouth. Before he could say anything, Ellie said, "Yes. Listen to me, Jess. I need you to come and look at this."

Dean glanced at her. She was on the phone with her sister. After the day she'd had, even with the rest she'd gotten, there was still so much to do. Jessica would probably head over soon to take her statement now she knew Ellie was awake.

"I know. I'll come and look at it soon. But I'm not—" She paused. "—quite ready to leave here yet."

Dean's heart about melted. She felt safe here, and she wanted to stay longer. With him.

"Okay. That sounds good." Ellie hung up and turned. Her eyes widened and he shot her a look, as much of an apology over her finding them both staring at her as he could put into one expression.

"Doctor Gilane." She smiled but didn't cross the room to them.

"He was just checking on you." Dean turned to the doctor.

Ellie said, "Dean is taking good care of me."

The doctor shifted his stance. "That's good. There are a number of complications that can occur as a result of smoke inhalation, and it can prove to be even more of a potential threat when you add in having been choked. Even for a minute."

"It was more than a minute."

"I'm very sorry for what happened, Eleanor."

She said, "It wasn't your fault. Someone grabbed me. He shoved me against a tree and put his hands on my neck."

The doctor swallowed. "Like I said. I'm sorry about that."

Dean processed the fact that Ellie must have realized the same thing as he did about the doctor. That instinctual itch of an idea that something wasn't right. Now it was as though she intended to test the doctor. To push him to a point where he would reveal his true colors and what was actually going on.

"There's no need to be. Dean found me, along with his brother and my sister. They made sure I was all right." She lifted her chin.

"If Ellie has any problems, I'll drive her over to the emergency room." Dean wouldn't risk messing around. Not when a swollen windpipe could exacerbate itself later—even hours or days after it first occurred. That could turn deadly, fast. Just because something was off with the doctor didn't mean he would chance putting Ellie's life at risk.

He didn't have the means to intubate her here.

"Yes." The doctor nodded. "Of course."

"Howdy-ho!"

They all spun around. The doctor was clearly nervous.

Jessica strode down the hall, her wet hair pulled back and wearing her police uniform. Dean saw the doctor's glance at her weapon. It made him want to go fetch his own from on top of the refrigerator and slide the holster onto his belt.

Ellie stayed where she was. Jessica passed them, went all the way to her sister, and gave her a fierce hug. Dean's eyes burned. He blinked away the sting—and some eye sweat he wasn't going to admit to—and ushered the doctor to the hall.

"Let's leave them to it." Jess showing up was a great opportunity, one he wasn't going to waste. "They've been through a lot the past few days."

If the doctor had anything to do with that, Dean would be surprised. But he would want to know either way. Just as he wanted to make sure Ellie was safe for good. Not just for now.

Dean used his size and pure momentum to get the doctor out the front door. Gilane almost tripped over the front step, but Dean was done with him. If the doctor was just here to feel bad and make sure they all knew it— then he could just go.

"I'll let you know if we need anything."

Dean shut the door and strode back to the living area. The last *two* times Ellie had been out of his sight, something terrible had happened. First one, he'd been blown up along with the cabin. Second, she was abducted.

And then left alone.

Another scare tactic?

Jess planted her hands on her hips. "One of you talk to me."

Ellie spun around. Beside her, Jessica bristled.

Dean sighed. "Sit down, both of you."

"I need to tell Jess about the map."

He held up a hand. "Just give me a minute." Dean stared at her while his thoughts flipped through everything he knew at the moment. She was all right. His shoulder was on fire, and she looked paler than she should be.

Jessica still had a bandage on her forehead. Stuart was who-knew-where. Ted was afraid of their father.

He slumped back on the couch and shut his eyes, running his hands down his face while he took a rare moment to just breathe.

"Is he okay?"

Ellie replied to her sister's question. "Even Superman has vulnerabilities."

That was how she saw him? Dean stared at her. "I'm not an alien hero."

Jessica laughed. "No comment."

Ellie shoved her sister's shoulder. "You know I didn't mean that." But it had served to bring levity to the moment.

Jessica covered her sister's hand with her own. "Please tell us what happened. You were pretty out of it when we brought you here. I thought we were going to have to take you to the hospital."

Dean hadn't thought that, but he knew Jessica had been scared. "What did he do?"

The ghost in Ellie's eyes disappeared when she blinked. "I told you most of it."

Dean nodded.

"After he choked me for a second, my legs started to give out." Ellie pressed her lips together. He saw her squeeze her sister's hand. "I just don't think he wanted to carry me."

"It was another warning."

She locked gazes with Dean and nodded.

Jessica said, "Did he do anything, or say anything, after that?"

Ellie swallowed. Dean noted the discomfort, not worse, but he still didn't like it. She said, "I should have left it alone."

"So more of the same," Jessica said. "Warning you away from looking into Pop's past and whatever he wanted you to find."

Ellie made a face. "Everything I had that was going to give me an idea of what it was has now been destroyed. There's nothing left to find unless Mr. Holmford wakes up and tells us what it was."

"Conroy checked with the hospital," Jessica said. "It's looking like he won't wake up anytime soon. If at all."

Ellie let out a long sigh and slumped back in the seat where she was. Dean wished he was beside her, so he could pull her into his arms and just hold onto her. It would make both of them feel better. Kind of like that kiss had.

The two women on their side of the coffee table looked like they'd been through the wringer, and he imagined he did as well.

Jessica looked around. "I've never been in Ted's house before. It's huge in here."

"Ted's house?"

She shot him a look. Dean just shook his head.

Ellie got up and wandered back to the map. "Did you bring that picture with you?"

"Yes." Jess dug in her shirt pocket and pulled out her phone. "Though, why you're all hot on this map thing, I have no idea. If it had to do with what Pop wanted you to find, he'd have had one as well. Not just Mr. Holmford and the café."

"And here." Ellie held out her hand.

Jessica slapped her cell phone into it.

"It's a match."

Dean got up, stretching his shoulder while they were both turned away from him. *Ouch.* His wound still hurt, and he was past due for more antibiotics. "What's a match?"

Ellie said, "The coffee shop map and this map—" She pointed to his wall. "—they're the same. But the map at Holmford's was different."

"But Pop didn't have any maps. So what does it have to do with anything?"

"I want to look at the house."

Jess folded her arms. "Maybe when the fire investigator is done."

Ellie said, "I think it means something. Because one map is what they let the public see. One map is what the founder we know of—Holmford—had for himself."

"The truth, and the lie." Dean crossed the room. "What does Holmford have on his map that mine doesn't?"

Ellie looked up at him, excitement lighting her eyes. "A trail."

Twenty-Eight

It took a whole day for the fire inspector to be done with her grandfather's house—her sister's house now. Ellie went in first with Dean right behind her. He had his gun out. Ellie had been trying to convince him since her sister came over that they should walk up into the hills and check out this trail.

But first, she wanted to check over the damage. See if there was anything she could salvage.

"Thanks for coming with me." She glanced back over her shoulder.

"Where else would I be?"

Right. Because he was protecting her. Not for any other reason than he felt bad she'd been abducted, and he'd failed to prevent it. She understood how he thought now. With a protective streak that made him feel guilty for not having done enough.

Was that what her grandfather had felt...guilt? Unable to prevent something terrible, he'd kept that secret for years. Now it was up to her to discover it. To do what she thought was right with the information.

Ellie stopped at the doorway to the study and sighed. "Do you think he knew I'd be in danger doing what he asked?"

She didn't think her grandfather would have wanted that. Wouldn't he have at least considered the possibility she'd be at risk?

"If Holmford knew as well, as a founder, I don't see why your grandfather would have left you unprotected."

She glanced at Dean. Her grandfather's choice to receive the land around the cabin. *He didn't leave me unprotected.* She had the cabin—he had the land. Her grandfather had surrounded her with Dean. Intentionally? He can't have known they would be attracted to each other, yet her grandfather had placed them alongside each other.

She had to believe he'd known Dean would keep her from danger. He was a hero through and through.

Ellie said, "Then he had to have also left me a way to figure it out."

"The trail?"

She didn't want to discuss the trail right now that she was here at the house and had the chance to look through his things. But she had to climb over charred furniture. Someone hadn't wanted her to be able to look through any of this. Tried to destroy any chance she had of figuring it out.

The rational part of her wanted to rise to the challenge and hope for the best. To be brave. The rest of her felt a lot like a scared little girl. Or the teen who'd just had her naiveté torn to shreds. That part of her wanted to pray there was still hope.

"You believe, right?"

Dean just waited by the door. He shrugged one shoulder. "I always have. When I needed God *and* when He felt far away."

"Where does your ability end and God's help begin?"

"It's a good question. One a lot of people wrestle with."

She continued to move through the room while he spoke.

"He gave me the skills I have. And put me in a place to receive the training to be a SEAL, a medic, and a counselor. I can do a whole lot, but I can't prevent every bad thing. I can't save everyone

I want to. And like with Stuart, I can't help him unless he wants to get better."

"So where does faith come in?"

"I can pray. I do what I can, and I pray as much as I can."

"But you can just walk away." Like with her, he didn't need to be protecting her.

"Can I?"

So with him, it was imperative. Similar to how she *had* to chase this mystery. "That's why I have to do this. It's why I need to figure this out and go up that trail. Take a look around. Because my grandfather trusted me to do it."

"The way I trust the skills God gave me."

She nodded. "After…" She didn't say it. "I pushed everything out. And everyone. My mom decided to move, and she took me and Jess with her. I wanted to go. Jess wanted to stay, but she was too young to argue. I graduated from high school in New York. Went to college. It was easier to study than to feel."

She glanced around the burned remnants of everything she'd ever cared about. The life she'd had. Her family.

"It's always been easier to delve into history. Those events were real, but it doesn't tug at my emotions the way the present does. I can live my life and be knowledgeable, but I don't have to be emotionally invested. It already happened."

Until now. She was back. She'd faced her demons and passed out from a lack of oxygen. Ellie had to face the fact she would never be strong enough to defeat an attacker. But she could be strong through it. The way she was refusing to back down now.

Dean said, "I knew early there was something in me that was different. I could fight, and I usually won. My dad was always manipulating everyone. Everything. Still does, as far as I know. My battles were physical. Mind games…" He sighed. "I couldn't do it. Not when it messed with my head. I got so mixed up, I would get in fights at school just to try and distract myself."

She glanced at him. From the distant look in his eyes, she figured he was lost in memory.

"So I joined the Navy. Got all the way into the SEALs. Far enough I realized it wasn't my father who put in me what it was that I didn't like. It was just me." He paused to scrub his hands down his face. "I didn't want to fight all the time, even if I was good at it. So I walked away from that as well. I came home and decided to be someone I liked. A man I could respect."

"And you've done it." She respected him. He was a hero, the kind of guy who put others first constantly. Who waded into their messes. Injuries. Accidents. Traumas. He wasn't shy about the mess and focused on helping people.

They'd both run from who they were. She'd denied her emotion. He'd tried to become someone he wasn't. It was almost comforting knowing he wasn't as perfect as she'd thought. There were chinks in this hero's armor. And she respected him all the more for it.

They'd both had to fight for peace.

She was still fighting and maybe always would be. Dean had become who he wanted to be—and the therapy center was part of that.

"I'm still figuring it out." She crouched and rifled through scorched books. The journal. She lifted it, leafing through the pages. They were unreadable now.

"There's nothing left." She tossed it aside and picked up a music box by her feet.

"I'm sorry."

Tears rolled down her face, and she swiped them away. "I have to figure out how to deal with fear and this sadness. I feel like it's swallowing me."

"Ellie."

She squeezed the music box too hard. It splintered in her hands.

"Ellie, look at me."

He sounded so compassionate. She shook her head and dropped the box. "I have to do it myself."

The last thing she wanted was for him to feel like he had to counsel her. But he said, "I want to help."

She straightened and faced him. "You have plenty of things to do, and I don't want to be one of your patients."

"You're not." He closed the gap between them. "I've been protecting you for days through some pretty intense stuff. I'm invested in the outcome now."

"Then why do you look mad?"

Dean cracked a smile. "My shoulder hurts. And you have bruises on your neck. This guy got way too close." He swallowed, all the self-deprecating humor gone now. "He could have killed you."

"He didn't."

"He could have raped you."

Her breath hitched in her chest. "He didn't." The same way she'd been saved from worse, years before. "It was bad, but I think God kept me from worse. He allowed it to happen—that, but no more."

"For what reason?"

"You're the one who believes. Why would that be?"

"Psalms says, 'You have hedged me behind and before, and laid Your hand upon me.'"

"What does that mean?" she asked. "Hedges?"

"He puts boundaries around us. Evil happens, but He wants to use it for His glory. And for our good."

"Like your father?"

"I have to have faith." He took a breath. "I don't know the extent of what he did to Ted. But I can be here now, helping. Praying."

"Being a hero."

"Maybe it's too late."

She touched his arms. "It isn't. I'm proof of that."

"You can say that because you aren't the one who has to live with the fact you didn't catch him. And I didn't keep you from being taken in the first place."

"Yes." She squeezed his arms. "I can say that. Because you found me. You're right, no one can prevent what is supposed to happen. I just have to find the good. Like being here with my sister.

Putting a wrong, right. Sticking it to Professor Tumbleweed, because I'm going to write a better book than he ever could."

Dean grinned again.

"And I can do it because you're here."

"I'm not going anywhere."

"That's why I feel like I have the strength to go up that trail and find out the secret someone is willing to hurt me and destroy my grandfather's things over, in order to keep it hidden."

"I can't be your strength. But I will be here." His expression intensified. "Whoever it is, they're serious."

"I know." She touched her neck. "And they might destroy it before I can find out what it is."

"They probably already did, and this is a last ditch effort to keep anyone from finding out."

She said, "I need to try."

Dean pushed out a breath.

"I know this isn't what you want to be doing. You're supposed to be setting up your therapy center."

That was why her grandfather gave him that land. Not for some wishful idea of hers that she be hedged, behind and before. Protected by a hero.

He frowned.

"But I do need you." She wanted him to understand. "When it's done, you won't need to protect me anymore. I'll be gone." It hurt to say the words, considering what her heart seemed to want from Dean.

That wasn't the point though, was it?

She didn't live here. Now that fire had destroyed it all, Jess could rebuild. While Ellie figured out her own path.

And she wasn't going to run, the way she'd done before. Too quickly jumping at the chance to start over somewhere no one knew her. Hiding in books, in history. Pretending nothing bothered her. Ellie's mom had train wrecked her life, making poor choices. Driven by her emotions.

She refused to do the same.

As soon as she could get back to her life, she would figure out what was next for her. Ellie wanted to land somewhere she felt at home. Despite how her future seemed to fit in with Dean, too much had happened here.

She didn't feel safe.

She needed him. "Until this is over, I need your help. I don't think I can do this without you. I'm independent, and I want to think I'm strong…"

"But everyone needs someone to watch their back."

She nodded, pleased he understood. Dean didn't look happy, though. He looked kind of mad about it. "I can't help feeling like we're running out of time."

She shoved at a few more things on the floor, only succeeding in getting ash on her fingers. The music box. The books. She still had no idea what her grandfather's clues were.

She'd failed.

"Let's go check out that trail." He crouched beside her. "Okay?"

Ellie nodded, her gaze snagging on the box. "What is…"

Dean saw what she had zeroed in on. He scooped it up and pulled the bottom section of the box apart. "Looks like a secret compartment." He tugged out a folded paper. It disintegrated in his hands and fell to the floor.

A map.

Twenty-Nine

He had his gun holstered, but that didn't mean Dean couldn't have it up and firing in less than two seconds.

Which was the only reason he allowed Ellie to come up here.

There was no point considering whether he *should* have told her no. She thought he was her hero? Fine. Dean was going to walk up this mountain with her on a wild goose chase, uncovering a secret that could take her a lifetime to work out, and then this would be done.

He'd been thinking about it since she asked him about faith. About his skills versus God's strength.

Dean's skillset? Thanks to the SEALs and all his training, that was mission completion. And right now the mission was keeping Ellie safe. Which meant taking out the source of the attack. If God had brought her to him, and if Dean was supposed to do this, then he would do it.

Fastest way to mission completion? Draw out the attacker. Her abductor. The main suspect, whoever he was.

Force a confrontation.

Eliminate.

This wasn't the first time the mission might require him to take a life. He knew he could do it if the situation forced his hand. However, he'd thought he left that behind when he walked away from the Navy.

If the team were here, he'd have them all helping. Using their skills to set up a takedown. But they weren't. Which meant Dean was on his own. His job, his way.

Much better than a bunch of cops tromping up this trail with them.

"Everything okay?"

He whipped his head from the terrain behind him, around to her, and almost bumped into her. She'd stopped the steady pace she'd kept up for nearly an hour, ahead of him on the trail. Sunlight made her hair shine. "Sure," he said. "Everything's fine with me. How about you?"

She pushed her glasses up her nose. "You seem nervous, looking around constantly like a squirrel is going to jump out and bite you."

"I'm thinking it'll be a little bigger than a squirrel." When she didn't back down and didn't continue, he said, "Head on a swivel."

"What does that mean?"

"Keep going, and I'll tell you." He nodded her onward. When she turned and kept going, he scanned around them again. Just to be sure the trap wasn't about to snap shut—on him.

"Well?" She kept walking.

"Situational awareness. You never know which direction danger is going to come from. Given how fast bullets fly, you'll hit the floor dead before you even realize what's happening. So you keep your head on a swivel. Trying to circumvent some of the danger by being aware of everything. Then you'll spot inconsistencies. Danger lying in wait."

Her shoulder's stiffened, but to her credit she didn't seem to give in to the fear.

"Which is why I'm here, and you don't have to worry."

After years spent trying to run from that part of himself—the warrior—right now, Dean was actually glad it was in him.

Now all he needed was…*there.*

He kept the swivel. Made it look like he hadn't seen it. When he circled back around to that spot, he gave it a second.

Definitely a dark figure. Moving through the forest to their left, tracking their progress up the path. To do that, he had to be close enough to see them. Which meant Dean could also see him.

This person had no military training. Not even police training or anything else. Hunters wanted to be seen by people, not animals. That kept them safe. This guy had on a dark jacket and a ball cap. Dean could camouflage himself in such a way no one would see him until he was right on top of them.

He could let fly with the knife on his belt and nail this guy. If he came just a little bit closer.

After he'd strangled and terrorized Ellie, what did he expect? Clearly he knew nothing about Navy SEALs.

"You look a little…bloodthirsty."

"Good." Dean scanned the forest, tracking the guy's movements. "That's what is going to catch this guy and keep you alive."

Not just alive. Untouched, if he had anything to say about it.

"O-kay."

"Don't worry, Ellie."

"I'm not," she said, sounding a whole lot more confident. "Because I just found what we're looking for."

She came to a stop on the side of the mountain. More of a foothill really, considering he'd climbed much higher peaks than this. Hauling a whole lot more gear.

Should he have brought his rifle?

No. That sent a visual message. He needed this guy to keep believing he was unaware, untrained. A washed-up, former military therapist who dabbled in emergency medicine. Dean grinned. His God-given skills were going to come in handy, soon as he found a good spot to set up an ambush.

Maybe he should have Ellie pretend to sprain her ankle. Or him, even. There was an idea.

"Dean. It's a cave."

"Huh?" He looked around her and saw the entrance. "A mine. Let's get inside."

She would be protected, and he'd face down their pursuer. *Thank You, God.* His skills plus God's leading. There was no way this would fail.

"There are a lot of signs." She crossed the rocky terrain to the entrance. Little bigger than a barn door, signs had been nailed to posts on either side. "No trespassing. Danger, falling rocks." She read them all.

"Great." He ushered her toward the opening. "Let's get out of view."

She took two steps and spun around. "What's going on here?"

"Someone is following us. Move away from the entrance." He pulled a flashlight, flicked it on and handed it to her, then grabbed another and pulled his gun. He secured his flashlight to the top of his weapon. "Don't shine the beam outside. I want him to wonder where we went."

Until he saw the entrance. Then he would know where they'd gone.

"Someone is following us." Her words were quiet. Breathy.

He didn't like the fear he heard. "I'm protecting you, remember."

"But he's coming," she hissed.

Dean touched her shoulder. "Go deeper into the cave. Be careful, and don't go far. I don't want you out of earshot." He also didn't want her to get hurt.

"While you do…what?"

"Catch his guy." He grinned at her, not sure she could see his face since the light was to his back and probably left his face shadowed. "As soon as he steps into the trap I'm about to set."

"Oh. Is that a good idea?"

"Why wouldn't it be?"

"Because of your shoulder, and he's…" She didn't finish.

"There's no reason to be scared when I'm standing between you and this guy." He stepped closer to her, and their flashlight beams lit each other's faces. "Don't worry, Ellie. I've got this, and he isn't going to touch you again."

"I'm not up here to catch him. I'm up here to find whatever they hid."

She'd been right earlier about one thing. If it was him, whatever had been buried would have been destroyed way before now. There would be nothing left to find.

So why the worry, if there was nothing to find?

He figured the threats were to keep her from reading too much into her grandfather's writings—what he'd left for her. A concentrated effort most likely triggered by the lawyer reading the will. Holmford probably tipped off whoever was doing this. Snitched on Ellie and Jess, which only backfired on him. Then they'd beaten him and left him for dead in the cabin. Maybe to make it look like he was involved.

Instead, they'd revealed his affiliation as a founder to Jessica and Dean. But at the same time, he managed to keep him from talking since he was still unconscious.

"You think this is a wild goose chase."

Dean started to object. "No. That's not—"

"I'm going to look around. I don't need your help, and you're busy playing bodyguard anyway. You catch this guy, and I'll be fine."

Dean had to follow her. "Yeah, you will be. That's exactly the plan."

"But you only agreed to come up here so you could…what? Draw him out."

She was smart. He'd give her that.

It was likely he'd never be able to pull one over on her. She would ruin any chance of him throwing her a surprise birthday party.

"Ellie, slow down. I'm coming with you."

There was no way either of them should be walking around in here. Not when it was potentially unstable, and with no cell signal. He had a satellite phone and a police radio in his backpack, so there was the highest chance he'd be able to call for help if needed. So long as he could get outside.

Keep us safe.

"Can this wait?" He padded after her, but she was moving fast. "After I get this guy, we can look all around down here. But I'd like to make the situation safe first. Otherwise we can't look thoroughly enough while distracted."

"You're the one distracted," she fired back over her shoulder. Charging forward with confident strides in a place she'd never been before wasn't going to end well. Even with the flashlight illuminating her way.

The walls narrowed in a way he didn't like. Then they parted, and he had to wait while she decided which way to go.

"Please let's go back. You can hold up somewhere, and I'll get the drop on whoever was following us. Please." It was worth a try.

"No." She shook her head, charging forward into one of the tunnels with no apparent rhyme or reason to her decision. "I'm so close."

Maybe she did know where she was going. It was possible she'd seen or read something that informed her decision. He didn't know how her brain worked. Perhaps the knowledge was subconscious, and she just followed her instinct.

Dean glanced back. When he looked ahead again, she'd disappeared. "Ellie." He wanted to throw a tantrum in frustration, but he was a grown man. "Ellie!"

"In here."

He took a few more steps and saw the side room. It opened back on itself, so the person in the tunnel couldn't see in the room. Likewise, the person in the room couldn't see the tunnel. A blind corner.

"What is this place?" It wasn't a mine. That much was for sure.

"Could be an old cave. Maybe even from before the gold rush. Before the white man first walked on these mountains. I'd have to do some research into the history of this area and talk to the tribes." She sounded sad, all of a sudden. "But that's not what concerns me."

The room domed up on the ceiling until he could see a tiny funnel of light at the very top. A vent hole, possibly for a fire? If the weather was bad, someone could stay here for days or weeks. Until food supplies had to be restocked.

"What is it?"

She moved her flashlight to the center. "The dirt here has been disturbed."

"Probably a wild animal looking for buried food, or a place to sleep." He moved toward it, aware he'd have to go back in a minute if he was going to set up that ambush. Or he'd be doing it from here. And a blind corner wasn't ideal.

"You need to look at it, Dean."

He frowned at the impatience in her tone. The dirt had been disturbed. He shone his flashlight in circles from the mound, trying to find what she was…

"Oh."

Poking out of the dirt was a triangle of material, some kind of floral pattern. A sleeve. Emerging from the cuff was a hand. Gnarled. Shriveled.

"This isn't my area of expertise." Her words were measured, even, and way too emotionless. "But I'm thinking that hand belongs to a dead person."

Clothing swished, along with the echoed sound of boots clomping through the dirt.

Ellie gasped. Dean wanted to tell her to be quiet, but it was too late.

Someone was in the tunnel.

Thirty

Dean pulled off his backpack, took out several thumb-width glow sticks, and started cracking them. He tossed them on the floor around the room, illuminating the area with an eerie green glow. Ellie watched as he pocketed two things, slid a third into the back of his waistband, and looked at her.

"What?" She whispered the word, not wanting anyone to know she was in here.

Dean evidently didn't feel the same way. Apparently he was purposely trying to run into her abductor.

Ellie shivered. She could feel the tree against her back, and the closing of his fingers around her neck. The lump in her throat. The hitch of her breath. It made her want to cough, except that she would alert her whereabouts to whoever was in the tunnel.

No, she didn't want to see him.

"Stay here."

She had no problem with that. There was enough in here to deal with without adding her assailant to the situation.

Ellie slumped against the wall. Free of Dean's imposing size in such a confined area. She could take a full breath—even if she was sharing her space with a dead body now. No, she had no problem with Mr. Protector taking off after him and saving her. He was determined. He was skilled.

She would do the job she had come here to do.

She let her breath out slowly, wrinkling her nose. There was no way to tell how long this person had been deceased.

Except that clearly it had been a while.

All she could see was the sleeve of a man's shirt and a wrinkled, decomposing hand.

She shivered again. There was no avoiding this. Ellie's encounters with the deceased extended only to books. This was a little more in her face than she'd have liked, but if her grandfather had wanted her to find this, then he obviously thought she could handle it.

With Dean's help.

He'd disappeared into the hallway. Ellie heard nothing. She pulled her cell phone out—no signal. She walked around, holding it up, trying to find an area in this cave where there might be a glimmer of a signal to call for help.

The construction of the cave…she didn't know how to tell if it was man made or natural. Except maybe for tool marks on the walls. She ran her fingers down the wall. Dirt. Clay, maybe. It was dark mud, but hard packed.

A shuffle in the hall reached her ears.

Ellie moved quickly then, away from the door. Her foot caught something, and she toppled over onto her hands and knees. Dean's backpack. She untangled her foot and moved around to the uncovered hand.

Dean was taking care of the threat. That was his job, and he was good at it.

"Everything will be fine," she whispered to herself. That was better than talking to a dead body, right? *Keep telling yourself that.*

Her alternative was to, what? Pray? She supposed that might not be a bad idea. But when had talking to God ever helped her before? That was what desperate people did. Those who couldn't help themselves. She didn't need faith when she had her brain and the resources around her.

At least not right now, before things were beyond her ability to fix them. Or Dean's ability as a warrior to protect her.

Ellie let the shiver roll through her and shook it off. Then she heard another grunt. *Dean.* He was out there, she was in here. Would that be how their lives went? Clearly they were on different pages with different priorities.

After all, he didn't care one whit about helping her figure this out. He only wanted to protect her—which was great. She was all for not facing that guy again. But if she never found what her grandfather wanted her to find, then the threat would never be gone.

Ellie wasn't going to sit around, waiting to be safe. She was going to do what she could to make herself that way. Once all this was out in the light, exposed, there would be nothing anyone could do about it. No reason to hurt her.

Not like this person.

She crouched by the hand, not sure what she was expecting to discover. Whoever he was, he hadn't died under natural or peaceful circumstances. Unless being buried up here, in a cave in the mountains, had been the plan. She supposed it was possible.

The sleeve was ragged, but the pattern seemed pretty much like seventies-era fabric. A connection to the Vietnam era? That was what had brought the founders together—or so she had theorized.

Perhaps this person was one of them, a founder.

The dirty secret Last Chance was hiding.

Ellie sighed. This poor person, hidden up here for years. Unknown. Unnamed. While the world went on at the bottom of the mountain, this person was decomposing. A story never told. The guilty conscience they'd had to live with. One everyone was going to know about.

Then the police could figure out who this person was, and how they'd died.

"Were you murdered?"

A shuffle preceded a thump, out in the hallway. Muffled grunts reached her. Should she go and help Dean? He was injured. Mr. Protector might not think she could help him, but what if the person he fought hurt him? What if they fought dirty, and he was in too much pain?

Ellie swallowed back the lump in her throat. She looked at her phone. Still nothing. Then at Dean's backpack.

The body.

A corner of something caught her attention. Under the hand. Ellie covered her fingers with her sleeve and dug underneath. Then around. What emerged from the soil was a small green book. Like a little notepad, or logbook or…

"A passport."

She didn't want to mess with what might be a crime scene, but Ellie needed answers. She lifted the passport and saw English writing along with those now familiar curls and swirls.

Vietnam.

She stared at the hand. "Who were you?"

A Vietnamese man who'd come to America? Years ago. She shook her head and flipped through the pages to a photo. The gentle eyes of a young man stared back. Maybe eighteen, or in his early twenties, even. Dark brown hair fell over his ears. His eyes were wide set, his brows thick. Cheekbones. Chin. Lips.

She didn't know what to make of it.

This young man had come here. All the way to Last Chance. Only to be killed once he got here?

"This makes no sense."

She studied the photo some more but didn't recognize him. And why would she? He might have died before she was even born.

A young man, with all the promise that came his way. Here, in Last Chance.

Through her research, she knew there were a lot of Amerasians. Children of the war born to a Vietnamese mother and an American father—a US soldier. They grew up abandoned and marginalized, often bullied for what they were. Taunted with horrible names like, "half-breed." As though any one person was less valuable than someone else.

Was this boy one of them?

If he'd come here, perhaps he'd been looking for something.

Or some*one*.

"And all you found was death."

This was what her grandfather wanted her to find? A secret he'd trusted her with.

Dean cried out. She knew it was him. Ellie whipped around, looking at the blind corner that led back to the tunnel.

She clambered to her feet and stuffed the passport in the back of her waistband. Then she looked from the body to the backpack. Was there a weapon in there she should get, one she could use? Dean was a warrior. A former SEAL. With a massive shoulder injury.

She could feel that tree at her back. Just like the wall, pressed against it with Ed Summers in her face. Ellie's breath came quick and erratic until spots seemed to spark in her vision. *No.* She couldn't let the fear of facing him again paralyze her the way it had all these years. The way it had kept her from returning to Last Chance. So scared she'd run into Ed.

Now he was dead, so there was no threat.

Summers had been in jail when she'd come for the funeral. Sincc then, he'd been killed in prison.

Now a new threat rose like a specter. The last thing she wanted was to be haunted for years to come over a new person, her abductor. A guy who had stood by the side of the road and threatened her with gestures while someone else spoke to her on the phone.

Which meant there were two people she needed to fear.

And one of them was here.

She scrambled to the backpack, looking for a weapon of some kind. A gunshot rang out. Dust fell from the ceiling like a mist.

Ellie turned to the entrance too fast. Her back muscles cramped. Her fingers were on the backpack zipper when she saw someone enter.

"Dean." She lifted her flashlight and shone it at his face.

But it wasn't him.

It was Mark.

"You're the one who abducted me." She scrambled back, then realized she was standing right over the spot the body was buried. Ellie changed directions, moving toward the wall. Still clutching the backpack in one hand. She stuck her hand in and rooted around.

"Drop that now." He lifted a gun and pointed it at her face.

Ellie let go of the backpack, but her hand was inside still. She pulled out slowly. Palm out so he could see she held nothing. She didn't want to get shot. "Why are you doing this?"

He motioned to the body with his gun. "Get over there."

"What?"

Was he going to kill her and leave her here with the dead Vietnamese boy? "Where's Dean? Did you kill him?"

Surely that was what the gunshot had been. Dean was dead. Surprised and killed. Now he probably lay bleeding on the ground.

Leaving her alone. *Dean.* She couldn't grieve for him. Not yet. Not until she knew he was actually dead. "Is he bleeding out? Did you shoot him?"

Mark chuckled. He took a step toward her, every line of his body screaming *threat.* "All you need to know is that I'm going to kill you if you don't get over there."

She hesitated, then stood. Moving slowly, Ellie tried to figure out what to do while she took small steps around to the other side of the body. She wasn't far enough away and would for sure get hit by this guy—no matter how badly he aimed.

Her voice quavered. "Someone will find my body."

"Nobody found his." He motioned to the mound of dirt. "You think they'll find you? Or your hotshot bodyguard out there?"

She spotted a flash of teeth in the dim light. How could she talk him down? He already believed he could do whatever he wanted and get away with it. *Help.*

Ellie didn't know who she was talking to. But she needed aid. That was plain enough for anyone to see. Ellie had no fighting skills. Dean had plenty, and he was down. Incapacitated.

She tried to think past the fear. Tried to figure out what she was supposed to say. All that went through her mind was the strength of his body as he pushed her against that tree and put his hands around her neck.

She whimpered. It sounded too loud in this enclosed space.

Help.

"It's buried under the body."

She shook her head. "What?" She had no idea what he was even talking about. But she was alive.

"Dig. I want what's under there."

"What?"

He shifted the gun and fired a shot. The flash seemed to sear her eyes and the sound rattled the room. Ellie screamed, clapping her hands over her ears.

"Get me what's under there or you're dead."

Ellie whimpered. Her legs gave out, and she collapsed in the dirt.

"I said, 'dig.'"

Thirty-One

Dean cracked one eye open. He could hear muffled talking but couldn't make out the words. The tone was enough, though. A deep voice, the man who'd attacked him. The other, higher pitched.

Ellie.

He shifted, biting back the groan that wanted to emerge. The gunshot had sliced through his right side, just above his hip. Dean pressed a hand to his T-shirt, and it came away a bloody, damp strip. Just a graze.

Still, he'd pretended it felled him. The guy had bought it. Now Dean had the room he hadn't had before, fighting in close quarters with an armed man. He hadn't been able to draw his weapon because the guy had come at him so hard and fast.

Now he knew why. Like he now knew why the guy had gone for Ellie's throat.

Because either he didn't have the stomach for killing, or he had been ordered to not murder anyone that was a part of this. Someone was already dead, buried here long ago.

This was Mark. The gym receptionist, a kid who'd won wrestling trophies in high school and still trained at the gym in town. The man on the side of the road, the one who had nearly strangled Ellie? He needed her to confirm that.

Back when they'd been determined to warn her off. Scare her a little. Was the doctor his partner? Was the older man somehow the cause of this? Maybe they knew each other, and maybe they didn't. Dean figured Mark knew the doctor. But did either of them have connections to the founders?

Dean got to his feet. Dizziness struck, and he pressed a hand to the wall. There was no time for that, though. He had to get to Ellie. As soon as he knew what all this had to do with Mark, he would secure the guy.

A calculated gamble was still a gamble, but he counted on Mark not wanting to kill Ellie. Maybe he didn't have the stomach for it.

Dean trudged to the entrance that led into the room where Mark was with Ellie. And the dead body.

The second he'd reached for his knife, Mark had fired that gun. Dean had his gun out now that there was more space. Fighting hand-to-hand with a gun in such close quarters made it too easy to get shot yourself. Not to mention, damage your hearing like Mia, the police Lieutenant, had.

Please, let this work.

He wasn't content to just jump into the fight with no forethought. He needed a prayerful strategy. That was what would get him and Ellie out of this alive.

She was crouched on the far side, next to the body, pulling dirt from the hole with her cupped hands. Ellie didn't see him.

Nor did Mark, who had his back turned and was focused on Ellie, thinking he'd already taken care of Dean. Now he was about to get a surprise of his own.

"Dig faster!"

Dean frowned. Why hurry? And what was she looking for? Ellie whimpered, continuing to swipe dirt back out of the hole.

"There's nothing here."

His heart clenched in his chest hearing her cry. More painful than the nagging sting in his side. It felt like it was dripping blood. He inched forward. Mark still didn't notice his presence.

Dean wanted some more time to think about Ellie's attacker and the revelation of his identity, but there was no time. He could hurt her at any second. Even though he didn't believe that Mark had shot at him to kill. And though he'd had the opportunity to kill Ellie, he hadn't. He seemed content to simply wave the weapon around.

Still, Dean didn't want her to be in danger for even one second longer than necessary. He wanted this guy neutralized. But he also wanted answers.

Dean stepped into the room. "That's enough, Mark."

He'd gone carefully, spoken softly. Made noise at the last minute, by first clearing his throat.

Even still, Mark spun with the gun first. Dean spotted his finger, depressing the trigger. He was going to fire.

Dean squeezed back on his trigger. Two shots, center mass, before Mark could even fire. The man wasn't an experienced gunman. He dropped to the ground, dead before he hit it. Ellie screamed.

"I didn't want to do that." Dean wasn't sure why he'd said that aloud.

Ellie scrambled back, pale in a way that worried him. Dean moved, ignoring the sting in his side as he crouched in front of her and took her hands. "Hey. It's okay now."

She blinked at him, glassy eyes and nearly translucent skin. Or so it looked in the strange light. Her hands were caked with dirt, her nails crusted with it.

"It's okay." He kept talking, soft nonsense words that were supposed to reassure her. Instead, his mind wandered and he found himself saying, "He gave me no choice. I had to kill him before he killed one of us."

Dean tried to shift, planted one knee and hissed at the pain in his side.

"He hurt you."

"I'm fine. What happened? What did he say?"

"Nothing. There was something under the body he wanted me to dig out." She sucked in a choppy breath but didn't break down.

There was more, he thought. But she said nothing else. Dean pulled over his backpack. "Whatever is under there, we don't have to find it. I'll call Conroy."

He spoke slowly since she was in shock and probably having trouble processing. She needed gentleness. Especially considering they had two options right now. Stay here with the dead body, or hike back down the mountain to get to a spot where the police would meet them. He wasn't sure which would be better for Ellie.

"Here it is." He showed her. "I'll call with this satellite phone, but we need to do it outside."

She blinked at him.

"Ellie. We should go."

"I found what it was." She waved at it. A mound of material.

Dean tugged himself over, pulling at the wound on his side. He unwrapped the bundle, flipping open what appeared to be a bloody shirt, revealing what was inside. "It's old. A handgun. But I don't recognize the style." Buried for years next to the bloody material, the metal had tarnished.

Dean looked at the body. "Could be how this person died."

A murder weapon. Were there prints still on it? He didn't know the ins and outs of forensics but figured it was possible there would be physical evidence left here.

"We should go outside." He stood, holding out his hand for Ellie to go with him. "Before we disturb anything else."

She nodded and took his hand. Straightening her gaze, she glanced over his side. She gasped. "You're bleeding!"

"It's not bad." He said, even though his shoulder was on fire. "Can you get the backpack, though? There are medical supplies in there."

She snatched it up and then huddled close to him.

"Ready?"

"Let's get out of here."

He was right with her, stepping around Mark's body. Giving the dead man and the burial area a wide berth. They left the old weapon that had been wrapped up. No one needed to touch it until the police got here.

Had whoever killed and buried this victim used that gun? They could have buried the murder weapon with the body, assuming that no one would ever discover it, keeping their secret hidden. Like it was the perfect crime.

Everyone involved had moved on with their lives, and no one ever found out that the very people who set up this town as a safe haven were complicit in a murder.

And one was the killer.

Was it her grandfather? She was in shock, but it occurred to Dean that if she was being cagey, it might be because she had figured something out and didn't want to say.

Dean walked with her, backtracking through the tunnels until he could see the light of day. He blinked at the harshness.

Truth, brought out into the light.

"We need to look at your side. You're bleeding."

Dean said, "I know." Not sarcastic. He didn't want to get into an argument with her when he'd just saved her. She was helping him now. They were a team. "It's not too bad. There's nothing to worry about."

He had her sit with him on the grass, but that hurt.

"Lie down."

"Hand me the phone." Dean took it from her and laid back on the grass. "Keep an eye out for anyone who comes up here. I don't want to be caught unaware."

She didn't answer, though. Ellie tugged up the hem of his T-shirt, and he saw her eyes widen.

"Easy." He said, "Breathe, yeah?" He didn't need her passing out.

He could carry her down the mountain sure enough, even with the wound, but that didn't mean it would be a pleasant experience. For either of them.

"This isn't fine. It's *bad*."

"Define, 'bad.'" Mostly he figured that was a matter of opinion. Not to mention a lifestyle difference between a Tier 1 operator and a university professor.

"You're bleeding."

Dean didn't like the frantic tone of her voice. "Didn't any of those books you read tell you about battlefield medicine?"

"You want me to get a saw and cut your leg off?"

"Not especially." He grinned at her and saw the flash of a smile on her face. "But I'm game if you are."

"No." She shook her head, amusement clear on her face. "Stop distracting me and tell me what I'm doing. You're losing blood."

"Grab the gallon plastic bag. In there is a package. On the outside it says 'QC.' Get some gloves on, then tear it open. It's gauze with a clotting agent on it."

"Okay." She tore it open.

"How deep is it?" The gauze was meant to be poked into a wound, but he didn't think it was that bad.

She frowned. "Maybe half an inch in the deepest spot."

He gritted his teeth. "Doesn't sound too bad." She could make of that whatever she wanted. "Push the gauze in as far as it'll go. Pack the wound, and then cover it all with what's left of the gauze."

"Okay."

He nearly passed out as her gloved fingers pressed and shifted the wound.

"Sorry. I'm sorry."

"Just get it done without throwing up on me, and you'll be my hero for life." If he could sit up, he'd be doing this to himself, but it was occupying her right now. He said, "Now set one hand on the other and push hard. Keep the pressure and don't move or let up until I tell you to."

He set a timer on his watch for three minutes.

"Are you going to call Conroy?"

He took a couple of breaths so *he* didn't hurl, and nodded. It didn't take long for Conroy to understand and promise he would send multiple officers. Dean drew the line at the offer of a Life Flight helicopter to take him to the hospital.

Ellie whimpered.

"You're doing great."

She scrunched up her nose, her glasses slipping. "I don't like this."

"Because you can't investigate the history," he guessed. "You're too busy dealing with the here and now." Dean reached up and slid her glasses up her nose. "A strategic retreat doesn't make you weak. It makes you smart. You know what you can handle, and what you can't. And yet, I'm guessing right now you're blowing through everything you thought you could do. You faced down a gunman. You confronted gruesome. Now you're getting your First Aid merit badge. All in a day's work."

She laughed, but it also sounded like a groan. "There's nothing funny about this. I saw a dead body."

Two, actually.

"Help is on the way." He studied her face. "Everything will be fine. Things won't go back to normal, because now you know how strong you *can* be."

"I don't like it."

"Don't retreat on me." He touched her arm, feeling the flex of her triceps as she pressed the gauze into his wound. Soon enough the timer would go off, and they would both be able to relax. Until then, he was going to keep her talking. "Promise me."

"Promise you what?"

"That when we come out of this, you won't retreat into the past. I need you here with me, Ellie."

"I *am* here."

"Good. Stay." He realized what he'd said. The implication of it. "Stay with me."

Thirty-Two

Ellie pressed the tape down over the edges of the clean gauze. Essentially, it was gauze covered with a powdery clay to—according to the package—dry everything up, which served to cauterize the wound.

"Help is on the way, though. Right?"

Dean sat up and started to repack their bag, trash and everything. "They should be here in about fifteen minutes. But there's no point in me bleeding for that long." He touched her cheek with his thumb. "Thank you."

She nodded. For a second she wondered if he was going to kiss her, but he didn't. "Don't make me do that ever again."

He grinned. *Then* he pressed a quick kiss on her lips. "Deal."

Ellie sat back and tried to process everything that'd happened. A dead man—one her grandfather might have murdered. Now Mark, the receptionist guy from the gym, was dead as well.

She removed her gloves, mostly just so she could rub her hands down her face. But they shook.

"It's adrenaline bleeding away."

"Was that guy really the one doing this?"

"Mark?"

When he shrugged, she said, "I'm pretty sure he was my abductor, and he might've been the guy on the highway when I got that call on my cell phone. Plus he hurt you with the winch." She thought back to that night. The hood over his face and the shadows. The more she tried to remember, the surer she became. "It was dark as well then, but I think it was him. I remembered the sound of his voice."

"We can tell Jess when she gets here."

Ellie groaned. "She's going to ream me one good for putting my life on the line while she was at work."

"She knew you were up here."

"That doesn't mean she won't remind me that she told me so." Ellie blew out a long breath and looked around at the trees and mountains, since Dean didn't seem to be in a real hurry. He probably wanted to wait for Conroy.

She would rather have started walking. Aim for the car parked at the bottom of the trail. Anything that would get her life back on track and back to normal for the first time since her grandfather died. She was ready to feel like her old self again.

Except what had Dean said? She shouldn't expect normal. That was an illusion, maybe even a place of safety. Like the comfort zone everyone was supposed to be so eager to break free of. She liked her comfort zone. It was…you know, comfortable and stuff. Especially when she had a *lot* of reading to do. Sure, it was work reading. But her TBR pile was still out of control.

He'd been right about one thing, though. She was learning how strong she was. And her brain was having trouble keeping up with it all. Ellie needed about a week of nothing to get a handle on all she'd been through. *And* how she felt about it.

Dean shifted. She heard deep in his throat, the pain from the movement.

Ellie realized then what Dean was reacting to, so she snatched up the gun that'd been discarded on the grass, and pointed it at the man coming toward them. He was still nearly fifty feet away, but he saw what she held.

Doctor Gilane raised both hands. "Are you both okay?" He had a bag over one shoulder, a leather satchel, and a concerned look on his face. "I heard the call come over the police scanner in my car, and I was close."

Dean lifted the side of his shirt. He coughed, then moaned.

Ellie glanced at him. He hadn't coughed before. Was there something more serious wrong with him?

Dean reached over and squeezed her knee. He whispered, "Keep ahold on the gun."

Ellie said, "Okay." But she lowered it, easing off on the tension. At least, that was the plan. Just so the doctor would continue his slow walk toward them and check on Dean. Make sure he wasn't in worse medical danger.

She held the gun flush against her leg while Doctor Gilane crouched beside Dean. He reached into his duffel. Both of them flinched, but the doctor pulled out only a stethoscope. He checked Dean's vitals.

"Everything okay with you, Eleanor?"

"I'm not hurt." That was the only thing she could think to say. She had to swallow down the lump in her throat. The slow creep of fear that threatened to choke her. Cut off her airway, as Mark had done with his thick fingers. Squeezing her neck and—

"Ellie."

She flinched and her gaze settled on Dean's strong features.

"Easy." He said, "You okay?"

Tears gathered. Ugh, if this was supposed to be some kind of new "normal," she did not like it. *Please, let more adrenaline leave my body*. Ellie recalled then that she'd prayed to God. In the thick of it, with a gun pointed at her head, she had asked for help.

And Dean had come.

They were both safe.

"I'm okay." She grasped his hand with the one not holding the gun.

"That's good, Ellie." The doctor said, "I'm sure I have a granola bar or a protein bar in my medical bag."

"I'm so glad you were close. We have to wait for the police to get here."

"They should be on their way now." Doctor Gilane nodded. "I'm sure they'll bring help with them."

"And a forensics team."

The doctor's eyebrows rose. "Is there…something to investigate?"

Ellie nodded. "A young man who works at the gym. He came here. He's the one who tried to abduct me." She tilted her chin to indicate the bruises on her neck. "Dean had to kill him."

"How terrible."

She didn't mention the dead Amerasian boy, and Dean said nothing about the hand. Nor did the doctor ask. But she did see something flash across his eyes.

"Yes," Ellie said. "When anyone takes a life for any reason, it is terrible. But in defense of a life, it can be noble. If a person's life is in danger and another is forced to take the life that threatens that person, then it can even be a good thing."

She'd never have spoken those words out loud, even days ago. Still living her "normal" life. But now she'd seen it. She'd felt that visceral fear, and Dean had saved her from a gun. Not just assault like she'd experienced before—or even worse. No, he'd saved her from death.

Ellie wasn't ready to die.

No one was when they met their end. The split second when a person realized they would die. When they recognized what was happening to them.

She'd read many battlefield journals. But this was the first time she'd ever come close to experiencing it for herself.

Dean said, "Did you know Mark? You taught classes at the gym and the drop-in center, haven't you? I thought I saw that you were doing First Aid and CPR training."

Ellie shivered at just the thought of doing that again with the gauze. She'd had to press so hard, she must've hurt Dean a lot. More than his wound was bothering him.

"Mark, you said?"

Dean nodded in response to the doctor's question. "The receptionist."

"Ah. Nice young man, or so I thought." Tension flickered in the Gilane's temple and around his eyes. "Shame."

"Yes." Ellie said, "It is a shame since he's the one who attacked me. It still astounds me that people are so capable of hurting each other. And I've experienced it." The doctor didn't know she read thoroughly all kinds of accounts of history. Battles. Hostile assaults on invading armies. All the horrible things man perpetrated on other men—along with women and children, too.

"Did he…say why?"

There it was. Dean stiffened beside her. Ellie's fingers flexed on the gun she held.

She was about to speak when Jess broke through the tree line. "Ellie!"

Dean took the gun from her hand, and she jumped up to run to her sister. Sweetest hug ever. Ellie heard the whimper in her throat.

Jess made a similar sound then pulled back. "Are you okay?"

Ellie explained everything, including the dead male buried in the dirt. She left nothing out about coming up here, finding what was buried. About the guy from the gym holding her at gunpoint and making her dig.

She relayed it all in a rapid whisper, leaving out the passport and the buried man's possible identity. Later she could explain that. Her sister was a cop, and they both cared about their grandfather and his reputation in this town. If he really had done something awful, then Jess could help her mitigate the fallout.

"That doesn't make sense." Jess shook her head. "How would Mark have known? What got him involved in all this?"

Maybe he was the descendent of a founder, the way she and Jess were. Maybe he'd been following her this whole time. Keeping tabs on her, then accosting her in the forest outside her childhood home. Was she supposed to have already figured out everything?

The whole thing overwhelmed Ellie all over again, and her legs started to give out. She had more questions than answers right now. Still. Even after all this.

"Doctor Gilane!" Jess grabbed her waist and helped Ellie sit. It was more like an ungraceful tumbling to the ground.

"Ellie, are you okay?" Dean crouched by her, concern on his face that she liked a whole lot.

The doctor knelt on the other side. Her sister held her hand.

Ellie was about to say yes, but it didn't come out. She shook her head instead. How did she know what to say, and who to trust? Her grandfather trusted her to do the right thing. But what did that even mean?

Tears rolled down her face. She couldn't get control of herself. If she could calm her breathing, she'd be able to have a rational conversation. Think this through intelligently. Work out what to do about everything.

The police were going to dig up that boy. They would do all kinds of forensic tests and figure out how he died. What that old gun had to do with it.

A man called out, "Dean!"

Dean squeezed her shoulder. "Conroy is here. You okay?"

She sent him a watery, emotional smile.

Dean touched his lips to her forehead. "You'll be okay." Then he got up and moved away.

That left her with the doctor, and her sister who said, "You'll need to explain to me what all *that* was."

Ellie didn't want to. It was between her and Dean, and it was just a result of shared trauma. Not any real honest feelings that would've happened if her life hadn't been in danger. That only made her cry more.

"Doc, she's distraught."

"You're right." The doctor touched Ellie's forehead, wiping away the feel of Dean's kiss. He probably didn't mean to do that. It was just what it felt like. "I can give her something. Help her to calm."

Ellie's breath hitched. She wanted to tell them she was fine, but nothing was fine. It wouldn't be until she'd worked all this out. *What did you do, Grandpa?* He hadn't been guilty over nothing.

"I think that would be good." Her sister squeezed her arm. "Just until she can get to the hospital and get checked out."

"All right." The doctor rustled in his bag. He pulled out a small zippered pouch, and with a needle, pulled clear liquid from a tiny bottle and plunged the contents into her arm.

Ellie hissed at the sting, whimpering a little. Where had Dean gone?

"All right." The doctor used a soothing tone. He rubbed her arm where he'd injected her. "There we go. It'll be all right."

Thirty-Three

"It's this way." Dean didn't like leaving Ellie, but she was with Jessica, as well as the doctor. So he figured she was safe for now, at least. He would check on her, just as soon as he showed Conroy where the bodies were.

He led the police chief to the room by way of the tunnels and through the double-blind door. Some long-forgotten person's home. A place to shelter from the wind.

Now it was the final resting place of two people.

Dean stopped at the door and let Conroy go first, lighting the way with a flashlight. Inside the room, his glow sticks still illuminated the area enough to see. But not clearly.

Conroy turned back to the officer who'd come with him. One of the ones Dean didn't know that well. "Let's get some floodlights up here."

The officer said, "Yes, sir," and hustled out.

Dean hoped he didn't trip over his own feet in his haste to do his chief's bidding. He didn't want to look at the floor, and the man he'd killed. Or the man uncovered. Instead, Dean studied the room itself while Conroy moved around and muttered.

"Whoa."

He turned to see the police chief crouched over the hand, close enough to touch it if he reached out. But only barely.

"You weren't kidding about this being old. Whoever they are, they've been here years."

"Since the town was founded would be my guess."

Conroy stood. He nodded while he scratched at his jaw. "There's an archeologist at the university I know. He'll be an asset. I think I'll give him a call."

"An archeologist? Like, there's historical significance here?"

"Could be," Conroy said. "Better safe than sorry, and he'll have a better idea than any of us locals how to remove the body with the least amount of disturbance. To the victim *and* this room."

"Makes sense."

"As much as I love our small town, we're not experts on everything. To my knowledge, no one here has dealt with a victim this old." Conroy paused a second. "It might not even be a murder committed using the gun you found."

Dean had to concede that point to him.

He was ready to get out of here. Just as soon as he gave his statement to one of the cops, he could take Ellie down the mountain, and they could both get some rest. His side was throbbing. He was used to a get in/get out method the SEALs were best at. Cops seemed to meander anytime there wasn't an immediate threat.

But then, special operations military didn't have to worry so much about chain of evidence. Or preservation of the scene. Not when it was other people's job to worry about "why" or any of the other "w" words. They just followed orders. Point and shoot. The tip of the spear.

"Dean!"

Conroy tipped his head toward the door. "Go lead your brother in. The three of us need to get up to speed."

Dean found Ted in the hall. His brother had that frantic, flushed look on his face. "Hey."

Ted blew out a breath. He rolled his eyes as he approached.

"I'm fine."

"Yeah, that's why you have blood on your shirt." Ted gave him a loose hug.

Dean walked his brother back to Conroy.

The chief had Mark's wallet in his hands when he looked up. "Anything new on your end?"

"A few things." Ted nodded.

Dean waited for him to elaborate, but it was Conroy who said, "Add to the list. I need a full background on Mark Ayles."

"Copy that." Ted pulled out his phone and scrolled through to his notes app, which was chock full. "I've confirmed the lawyer, Peter Holmford, is one of the men pictured in that squad from Vietnam along with the former chief."

Dean said, "Is he awake yet?"

Ted shook his head. "As for the rest of them, I'm waiting to hear back from the Department of Defense as per our *official* request."

Dean wanted to chuckle. Ted was the kind of guy who bucked against normal constraints. Take his appearance, for example. He looked like he belonged at a Portland, Oregon used bookstore. Where he would be making coconut milk lattes with organic sugar. When he wore his glasses, it was even worse.

He seemed, by appearance, to better suit someone like Ellie. Her librarian thing wouldn't look out of place beside him.

Which made it curious to him why Dean was the one who'd gravitated toward her while Ted had a thing for Ellie's sister. After years thinking he and Ted were light years apart, and not just in age, he was beginning to think they might be closer knit than he'd thought. Which was probably what Ellie thought about her sister. The gap in age between them and their younger siblings didn't seem to stop the apparent connection.

Dean figured the four of them would get on well. But worrying about the dynamics at Thanksgiving dinner could wait for right now. First, he needed to convince her to stay.

He'd laid it all out.

Now it was her turn to respond. She had to want it, considering she'd be the one changing her whole life to be with him. He wouldn't want to do that for someone else unless he was sure.

Which made him wonder if he should be willing to leave Last Chance.

Could he do it?

"You still there?" Ted waved his hand in front of Dean's face. "You spaced out. Probably thinking about Ellie."

Dean wanted to slap his little brother upside the head but settled for just grasping the back of his neck until Ted winced.

"Okay. Maybe not."

Except he hadn't been wrong. "Do you need me for anything else, Conroy?"

The chief said, "Just a minute. I know you're eager to go check on her, but I'll need the weapon used."

They got it bagged as evidence.

Conroy said, "I just don't get what Mark has to do with this."

Dean figured it was a shame they couldn't ask him. But no one said that out loud. "Ellie said he was the one who attacked her." He shrugged. "He has to have some kind of connection to whoever killed this person and buried them here for all these years."

Conroy nodded. "Could have to do with West, considering the person who tried to break into the Ridgeman residence."

Dean nodded. "Another someone trying to scare Ellie. Put pressure on her and take the focus off one suspect."

"Except so far," Conroy said, "the suspect list we have is everyone in town over the age of fifty-seven. Which includes my future father-in-law." He shrugged. "Short of sitting them all down and asking who is behind the town's start, it's going to be hard to figure out."

Dean was about to ask how that could be when Conroy continued. The police chief said, "On paper, the town was founded by a corporation. Ted dug up all the paperwork, and there aren't any names listed. At least not for people still living, or who we've so far been able to track down."

"So we have no idea?" Dean glanced between them. "Is it just me, or is that crazy? I mean, we know Chief Ridgeman was one of the founders, and we know Holmford was too."

"Do we?" Ted shrugged. "Those are the conclusions we've come to. But are we even right?"

"All this…" Dean paced a couple of steps, then back. "I just can't put my finger on it."

"What?" Conroy shook his head.

"I've always respected Doctor Gilane. Except earlier, when he showed up at my house. He just seemed…off."

Ted said, "Does he have anything to do with Mark Ayles?" He motioned to the dead guy. "That might be a connection."

And yet…

Dean said, "We have no evidence."

"That's not exactly true." Conroy said, "We'll have to confirm. But I *think* Mark's mom was married to Gilane at one point." He thought for a moment. "Now that I think about it, I'm sure."

"That still doesn't implicate the doctor in threatening Ellie, right?" Dean said. "Not without evidence."

"True." Conroy nodded. "But we have to start with an informed theory. That's what cases start with."

"So you have an idea, and you set out to prove it."

"Not if you want the truth," Conroy said. "You'll miss something assuming you're right."

"I've been trying to keep an open mind about who is behind this." Dean shrugged. "Mark is the last person I thought was going to turn up here. I actually thought for a while that Doctor Gilane was the one behind it. He says he wasn't here when the town first started though. Maybe no one who lives here now was. Maybe there's no way to find out who was here when the town first began."

"Then there's the issue of this victim." Conroy waved toward the decomposing hand, barely more than a skeleton with a sleeve. "A lot of this rides on this person's identity, the manner in which they died, and how long they've been dead."

"So basically we have nothing."

Ted shifted. "Or, at least nothing that makes sense."

Dean groaned. "I want to be able to tell Ellie *something*."

"Sorry."

Dean shook his head at his brother's apologetic expression. "What about Dad?"

Ted just stared at him.

"What?"

"I have his number." Anxiousness flashed across Ted's face. "Maybe you could—"

Dean said, "Text me the number, I'll call him. If it turns out he was here when the town was founded, you can bet he knows what happened. Secrets are his specialty. The juicier, the better, as far as he's concerned."

The tension on Ted's face increased exponentially.

"I'll find out."

That comment didn't make things any better. Dean said, "Ted, is there something we need to talk about?"

His brother barked a nervous laugh. "No. Course not."

Dean shared a glance with Conroy. Neither of them was convinced. But Dean had to deal with his problems one at a time. "I'm thinking we can't be sure Ellie's life isn't still in danger."

"You could've told me that." Jess strode in. "Otherwise I'd have stayed outside with her."

Ellie was still surrounded by cops. But now Dean wanted, even more than before, to go out there and be with her.

Dean was about to comment as much when Jess saw the dead gym receptionist. "Mark Ayles?"

Conroy flashed a grin. "Welcome to the party."

"I'm not sticking around to hash it out all over again." Not when he wanted to get back to Ellie. To Conroy he said, "Can you let me know if you come up with anything?"

"In the interest of public safety, yes. All the pertinent details of the case? No."

"Good enough for me."

Jess spun around. "He really held a gun on my sister?"

Dean nodded.

Jess sighed. "Why is it always the cute ones that are psychos?"

Ted looked like he wanted to throw up. Dean said, "I'm thinking that's an overgeneralization."

She shrugged. "No great loss. He was always going on and on about his dad." She mimicked his low voice, "Bought me a boat, you know? But I needed something to pull it, so he got me a new fully-loaded truck. Wanna go for a ride?" She rolled her eyes. "As if I didn't know what that meant. He must've thought I was as dumb as he was."

Conroy said, "Remind me to never let you work homicide."

Before she could comment back to him, Dean said, "His father?"

Hadn't Conroy said Mark's mother had been married to the doctor?

"Yeah, he—"

Fear squeezed his chest like chains. "Where's Ellie?"

She shook her head. "The doctor gave her a sedative. He's going to take her to his car and get her to the hospital so she can get checked out."

Dean sprinted as fast as he could from the cave. He needed to catch up to them.

Before it was too late.

God, please tell me I'm wrong.

Thirty-Four

A low rumble was the first thing she recognized. The hum of an engine, tires on a road. Ellie blinked. Or tried to. *What's going on?* She had no idea if she was able to make a sound that would be coherent. Her thoughts felt like liquid swirling in a cup. Trying to find purchase, but unable to settle for long enough.

She shifted. A car. Right, she was in a car. She could see a blur of trees whizz past from where she lay in the backseat, looking out the window. Ellie tried to kick off the door with her feet and sit up. Her hands moved strangely. She managed to focus enough to realize they'd been tied together. She couldn't reach the knot of the silk tie, as it was on the back of one of her hands and too far for her fingers to reach.

Professor Tumbleweed had this tie. She'd imagined strangling him with it many times when he'd insisted on picking at her teaching style just for the sake of criticizing her.

Probably that wasn't what was happening here.

Think. She'd called for God's help before, but He hadn't done anything to save her. Dean was the one who'd come in. Her foggy brain wanted to have an idea about that, but she couldn't get a complete thought to manifest itself.

Her mind only wanted to scream that everything was *wrong.*

Ellie rolled. She got her hands under her and pushed up. Her elbows gave out, and her face smushed back against the seat. A breathy, "Oof," escaped her lips.

She heard a man curse loudly. Then he said, "You're awake."

Ellie knew that voice. Knew him. Her mind flashed back to the feel of a tree behind her. Hands on her throat. The face in front of hers was Ed Summers, though. No, that wasn't right. It was a different man. A dead man. She'd seen Dean kill him. Not Summers. The other one.

Ellie bit her lip. Hard enough the sting eclipsed her racing mind. *Think.* She had to think, or all this panic racing through her veins was going to lead to exactly what she feared. *What is happening?* Whatever it was, things were serious. They'd been up on the mountain, with her sister there. The doctor had given her a shot.

Was that why her head felt like this?

It should've calmed her. Surely she wasn't meant to feel this out of it. Like she couldn't string two thoughts together.

They were supposed to go…

"Hospital." That single word escaped her mouth. Ellie didn't even know if he heard her. They were supposed to be going there, so she could be checked out. Since she'd both found a body and seen a guy murdered. Never mind that Dean had been shot.

The blood. She remembered pushing that special gauze against his side. "Dean."

In the driver's seat, the doctor said, "You're out of luck. So is he."

"Where…going?"

"You should have just left it alone." The doctor pushed out a long sigh. "I told you to leave it alone."

It was Doctor Gilane? She wanted to think on that, but nothing would come. She only rolled and shifted on the seat as he took corners too fast. At one point, she nearly fell to the floor. Ellie rolled back, a flash of the interior roof, and then the sun in her eyes. Then she was facing the seat back.

The car screeched to a halt.

Ellie rolled toward the front. Her nose planted in the upholstery and one leg fell off the seat. Thankfully her shoe jabbed at the floor mat or she'd have tumbled off. Instead, she stopped, perched on the edge of the seat.

A door slammed.

Then another opened. "Come on." He grabbed her under her arms, hauling her out. It took him a couple of tries, and he nearly dropped her, but the doctor got her bound hands around his neck and brought her upright. Her head lolled to the side.

Get a grip. She had to fight him. To do that, she needed control of her limbs. But this stupid drug he'd given her was coursing through her veins. Everything was a blur, and she had hardly any motor control. She was probably going to pee herself. If she hadn't already done it. Why were heroines in movies always so glamorous? They either got rescued, looking fabulous. Or they kicked the bad guy's behind and saved themselves.

She was neither. And she was pretty sure that she had snot from her tears smeared on her face.

He set her feet down. Ellie locked her knees. She was pretty wobbly. When he took her arms from around his neck, she shoved him away so that he would back off—maybe even fall. Instead, she was the one who landed on the ground.

Her hip hit the dirt, and she cried out. With the pain came clarity.

Doctor Gilane moved toward her, intent clear on his face. He was resigned to do what he felt he had to do.

She held up both hands. "No!"

Her scream was followed by a flock of birds taking off from a nearby tree. Ellie looked around. They were on the side of a mountain. The road was nothing but a two-lane dirt track. On the far side was a hill. *Caution: falling rocks.*

On their side, beyond his parked BMW, was a drop-off.

She knew this place.

Ellie had grown up in Last Chance. This was Dead Man's Curve.

"Don't fight it. There's no point, Ellie." He sighed. "You didn't listen to me, and now I can't have you telling everyone once you find out."

Panic tightened her chest. *Once you find out.* She shook her head but managed to keep her mouth shut. He didn't know that she'd found the Amerasian boy.

Ellie didn't get up from the ground. That would take the energy she needed to think. She said, "So now what? I mean, it's not like I know what you did."

Except she just might. He didn't know that. Bluffing was the only chance she had to buy some time.

Doctor Gilane stared hard at her. It was the first time she'd seen his expression with dead eyes.

"Why bring me up here?" She motioned to the cliff. "If I don't know anything, just drop me off at the hospital and leave me alone. There's no reason to terrorize me."

He'd destroyed everything she had left that belonged to her grandfather. All, except, her memories—the things he'd taught her. Would that backbone of character keep her alive now? She'd doubted her grandfather's innocence. Why else feel so guilty, if he hadn't been a part of killing that boy and burying him there?

"You had to know someone would find him."

"So now you think you know everything?" He reached into his back pocket and pulled out that green passport she'd stuffed in the back of her jeans. Right before she'd lied by omission to Dean. Gilane said, "All because of this?"

"Tell me the truth." Why else bring her up here, unless his sole intention was to see her demise? "You can give me that, at least. Before you do whatever you're going to do."

"This means nothing." He tossed the passport by her feet. "It will prove nothing."

"Not that a young boy came here and ended up dead in that cave?" Her jaw clenched, but she managed to say, "Did you kill him?"

She'd believed, for a moment at least, that there was a chance her grandfather had done it. Now she knew what lengths the doctor was willing to go to keep it a secret.

"Did you hurt Peter Holmford?"

Doctor Gilane scoffed. "You experienced Mark's *hands-on* expertise." He lifted his left hand, the one holding the gun, and rotated it. Showing her. "Like I would damage these hands. I'm a doctor."

"One who took an oath to 'do no harm.' Isn't that how it goes?"

How could he justify terror and murder? Dean had saved her and defended his own life in taking Mark's. Jess had told her the police considered it self-defense even before they heard her version of the events. They knew Dean. His character. The man he was every day around town.

Would they say the same about the doctor?

That made her wonder what people would say about her. Ellie wanted to make a mark in academia. But if she did that while having no substance to the people around her? No legacy in relationships? Where was the value?

"How can I possibly help people, when everything I've built has been ruined?"

"You made a mistake, right?" She was guessing, but calling it that—or an accident—was the best way to explain that might defuse the situation. She just wanted to know what happened to the boy. But not if he killed her for knowing. "That boy came here. Who was he?"

"No one." The doctor spat the words out. "The result of a momentary pleasure on the other side of the world. And then he shows up here with a gun, ready to kill me and destroy everything." He laughed, but it held no humor. "He didn't like hearing it wasn't just me that kept her for the weekend. The spoils of war." His lips curled up. "We were kids, thrown into battle. Many things that happened there would be considered questionable here."

Her stomach roiled. Questionable? How about unconscionable. "So you killed him?"

"What choice did we have?"

"Who pulled the trigger?"

He laughed again. "Your grandfather was there. Is that what you want to know? I guess before you throw yourself off this cliff in despair over what he did, it's right for you to know the truth."

"No." She'd changed her mind.

"So holier-than-thou. Ridgeman and his *morals*."

"He knew what you did."

"Of course. Like I said, the spoils of war."

"And when the boy showed up here?" She wanted to be sick.

"It was his idea to leave the boy in that cave. No one needed to know. Holmford was *weak*." He tossed that word at her like a weapon. A threat.

"It was his word against yours."

"The kid wouldn't quit. He would've never stopped." His chest rose and fell rapidly. "We had to kill him."

"We?"

"Holmford. Me. The others."

"And my grandfather helped you bury him."

He sneered. "All because some chit told her spawn a story."

"Like the one you told Mark?" The idea fell from her lips barely formed. "Why else would he do this with you?"

"Another spawn. He was a mistake that never amounted to anything. In the end he was good for something, though. No one will ever connect us."

Ellie had more faith in the police and their powers of investigation than that. She'd grown up with the chief for a grandfather, and now her sister as a cop. They would eventually put all the pieces together, or they'd never rest.

Even if she was dead.

Maybe especially because she was dead.

"Holmford will wake up," she said. "He'll tell the police what you did."

Gilane scoffed. "Please. I'm a doctor, remember? He's in the hospital, and I'm due there later for work. Unfortunately for

Holmford, he won't be coming out of that coma I made sure he ended up in."

He was going to kill Peter Holmford.

"And you carry on with your life? No one knows who that boy was. No one ever asks questions."

"Hmm. Good point. Perhaps I could arrange for Holmford to wake up long enough to confess to me before he finally succumbs to his injuries." He considered it. "I'll have to work out a plan. I'm sure he can be useful, and I'm more than happy to make a statement to the police on what I heard."

"You disgust me." It had to be said. "You prey on people you consider less than you and discard them when they're no longer of any use to you."

"And in the meantime, everyone has a good time."

Bile rose in her throat. "I'm not."

"We could change that. I'm sure we have time."

"I'd rather you just shoot me right here."

"Why would I do that, when you could jump?" He said, "After, of course, you tell me all about your grandfather's sins. The ones you can no longer live with. Make them juicy. The story will sound better." He grabbed her arm.

Ellie cried out, but it was of no use. He dragged her to the edge. She didn't look down. "No. Don't do this. I won't tell anyone."

"Jump, or I push you. Your choice."

"No!" She shook her head while Gilane stared down at her.

"Hey!"

A gunshot rang out. Gilane's body jerked, and he let go of her. Another shot blasted right by her, washing the world in front of her in a flash of fire.

Ellie fell over the edge.

Thirty-Five

Dean got in Conroy's face. "Get out of my way."

"You don't know that he has her."

He gritted his teeth, hands fisted by his sides to keep from shoving the police chief away from him. Dean would end up arrested. And then where would Ellie be?

He spun to Jessica. "Talk some sense into him!"

Tears rolled down her face. For the first time, the young police officer looked scared. Ted moved to her, sliding his arm around her shoulders. Jessica grasped a handful of his brother's shirt and held on so tight her knuckles turned white.

Dean turned back to Conroy.

"I know what you're gonna say." Conroy held up one hand, palm out. "We'll find her. There's a BOLO out for the doctor and his car, as well as Ellie. She won't get far when everyone we have is out looking for her. It's all over town that we need to find them ASAP."

"So let's go."

He wanted to be comforted by Conroy's words, but the sick feeling in his stomach wouldn't ease. It had nothing to do with the sharp ache in his side from the gunshot graze and everything to do with the fact he'd trusted Gilane with Ellie. A man he'd respected had betrayed him. And for what?

Dean checked his backpack, ready to hoof it down the mountain.

"When you're ready, we'll head out. Mia will meet us at the parking lot."

Dean started walking, zipping up the pack as he moved. He swung it over his shoulders and got his rifle from where he'd left it.

Ted said, "Dean."

He shook his head and headed for the path.

"I'm coming with you."

Dean nodded but didn't spare even a second to glance at Jessica.

Every second he stayed there on the side of that mountain was a second Ellie might not have left to live. He knew how to press on and get the mission done. Dean had seen the aftermath of too many innocents caught in the crossfire.

The cops didn't need him to stay there. And they weren't going to stop him from finding her.

He stretched out his stride, tempted to run, but it was all downhill. He made quick but steady progress, praying he didn't twist an ankle. Praying Ellie was alive.

That she'd be alive when he got there.

Behind him, Conroy and Ted carried on a breathy conversation about GPS on the doctor's phone.

Dean couldn't get rid of the mental picture of him sitting across the table in the coffee shop, telling him he was all the way on board with the therapy center. Was it nothing but a ruse? A way to keep Dean close, so he'd know what Dean was doing. What he knew.

No, that was when he'd barely met Ellie. So it couldn't be about her grandfather's will.

But it could be about the time he'd spent with the former chief.

Maybe the doctor had been feeling him out, trying to discover whether the chief told him anything before he died.

Whatever the reason, the result was that he'd been played. The doctor didn't care about Dean's therapy center. He'd only had his own agenda.

And Dean never knew.

He never saw even a crack in the doctor's façade.

His chest hitched.

"She'll be okay."

Dean wasn't sure he agreed with Jessica. Maybe she was only trying to reassure herself. All he could think was that he just might've cost Ellie her life. When he'd been so determined to protect her. So interested in what he could get out of it. He hadn't even considered what else might be going on.

The trail spilled out into the parking lot. A police department truck was parked at a right angle to them. Dean pulled open the back door and climbed in just as his phone started ringing.

The number was Stuart's. "Hello?"

Jessica frowned at him. She let his brother climb in the center seat next to him and then got in, shutting the door behind her while Conroy got in the front passenger seat.

Mia hit the gas and pulled out. "Where am I going?"

Stuart's voice filtered through the haze of Dean's thoughts. "Don't… could…"

"Stu. Talk to me, what's going on?"

Something was wrong. But was Stuart on his own thing—in danger—or was he having one of his traumatic episodes, or did this have to do with Ellie?

Dean squeezed the bridge of his nose, holding his phone to his ear so hard he could probably crack the thing. "Talk to me, Stu."

He heard his friend breathe into the phone. It sounded like he was in pain.

Beside him, Ted whispered, "I'll trace the call."

Dean nodded. He waited while Stuart figured out what he was saying. After a minute that seemed like forever, his friend said, "I need help." He groaned. "She…"

Dean said, "Did you see Ellie? The doctor took her."

"Gone."

His heart sank. He couldn't mean that Ellie was gone, as in dead. Right? Just that she was gone. Which he already knew. "Where are you?"

The line was quiet.

"Stuart. Where are you?" He wanted to throttle the guy but had to rein in his desperation when he knew it wouldn't help and might make things worse. "I need to know where you are so I can help."

"Too late." Stuart gasped.

Dean moved the phone away from his mouth. "I think he's hurt." He also thought Stuart had seen Ellie. Or, he hoped she had.

"West side of town." Ted's screen continued to move as it tracked the signal for Stuart's phone. He'd wired in to the local cell towers, just in case. Now Dean was grateful his brother was entirely paranoid and had encouraged so many people in town to opt in, allowing a way for the police department to find them in an emergency. Including Dean. And Stuart.

"I need your help, Stuart. You need to tell me what's happening."

"I'm sorry." His friend whimpered. "I'm sorry, Brad. I couldn't stop it. I couldn't save her." Dean recognized the thought cycle Stuart was stuck in, going round and round in his past. His friend, Brad, was a regular topic in their therapy sessions. Stuart's one regret.

"Brad knew you loved him." That was the history Stuart had to live with. But right now Dean needed him to concentrate on the present. "Is she hurt?" He wasn't going to ask if "she" was dead.

"She fell."

There had been no woman in Stuart's last mission—the mission that had broken him so thoroughly. Could he have seen Ellie?

"Stuart," Dean began, speaking carefully, "have you seen Doctor Gilane?"

His friend hissed, a sound of disgust more than distress. "He was going to hurt her."

"Is he there?"

"Drove away."

"Stuart, where is Ellie?"

"She fell."

Dean fisted his free hand. He wanted out of the truck, or he was going to explode. There was no room to punch the window and neither was he going to jab his fist at the seat in front of him where the chief's fiancé was driving.

"I got it." Ted wasted no time saying, "Dead Man's Curve."

Dean let out a frustrated cry. He couldn't hold it back. "Stuart said she fell."

Mia must've pressed the gas pedal to the floor because the truck sped up.

Dean didn't want to wait however long it would take them. Minutes felt like hours. Ellie could be gone or seriously injured.

"Stuart, can you hear me?"

"Yeah." His friend sounded like he was fading.

"Are you hurt?"

"Blood." Stuart whimpered. "I'm sorry, Brad."

"I know you are." Dean gritted his teeth. "I forgive you."

He heard a sniff and realized Stuart was crying.

"Everything is going to be okay now." Dean said, "We'll be there in a couple of minutes."

"Brad."

"There was nothing you could do. Some things just happen, and they're out of our control." Dean didn't bring faith into his counseling if the person wasn't receptive, but Stuart knew where he stood. He'd seen Dean live out what he believed. "What we have to do is trust that God has it in His hands. That's what keeps us sane when things get dark. Knowing God is in control."

Dean needed the reminder as much as Stuart right now. *Ellie is in Your hands. Please keep her safe until I can get there.*

"I'm sorry I couldn't save her. I tried, but the doctor shot me."

Dean spoke to Conroy. "Stuart was shot."

"An ambulance is meeting us there." Conroy said, "Two minutes."

Dean nodded and focused back on the call. "We're almost there, Stuart. Where are you sitting?"

"Trees." The word was muffled. Dean heard a crackle, and then nothing.

"Stuart."

Silence.

"Stuart, can you hear me?"

Mia hit the brake and pulled to the side of the road. Dean got out on the hill, opposite the side that dropped off. "Look for Stuart!"

He rounded the back of the car and headed for the side of the road where the edge fell away. Dead Man's Curve.

A number of people had committed suicide here over the years. The metal barrier erected ten or so years ago kept cars from careening off the edge in an accident, but that only meant the last couple of deaths were those who'd intentionally jumped.

It wasn't a sheer cliff edge, but also not a gentle slope.

Dean scanned the hillside below. Loose gravel. Trees. Anyone who fell would hit obstacles on the way down. He looked for a trail. Any sign someone had disturbed the earth as they'd fallen.

"Are we sure she was here?"

Jessica studied the drop-off the same way he did, looking for her sister. Conroy had his attention on the ground. "Someone peeled out of here in a hurry, heading back toward town."

"The doctor?"

"Conroy!" That was Mia. "I found him!"

Dean wanted to go to Stuart, but he also didn't want to quit searching for Ellie. He moved along the edge, looking. Seeking. If he found her, he'd need a rope. Some way to rappel down the way he'd done so many times in the Navy.

But this time, he would be doing it to bring back the woman he loved.

"We need to find her." Jessica whimpered.

"Keep looking."

He wasn't going to stop. No matter what, he would find her.

Ted trotted over to him. "Stuart was shot in the shoulder. He's unconscious."

An ambulance pulled up behind Mia's vehicle. The EMTs got out, carrying a stretcher and duffel bag between them over to where Conroy waved. Stuart was up there, as he'd said over the phone. On the hill, where the trees were.

Did that mean he was also right about where Ellie was?

She fell.

Dean went back to his scanning search for her of the hill below. They wouldn't even know to look here if it wasn't for Stuart. It could only be God that his friend had been in the right place at the right time. Had he really seen the doctor and Ellie? Dean might be jumping to erroneous conclusions.

Please.

It was all the prayer he could pull together right now.

"There!"

At Jessica's cry, Dean and Ted raced to where she stood, farther down the road's edge. Dean reached her side and looked. "Where?"

Jessica pointed down the hill. "There. That's her jacket."

Dean saw the material. With the trees, he couldn't even tell if it was Ellie. He pulled off his backpack. "Get me a rope."

Ted started. "Dean—"

"Guys, I have to get down there. Get me a rope!"

There was nothing in the world that would keep him from getting to her.

Thirty-Six

The door opened. Ellie had expected Dean. When Jess was the one who walked in, dressed in her uniform with her police gun on display, she tried not to be disappointed and said, "Hi."

Jess came over to the side of her hospital bed, not quite able to hide the wince.

"I get it. I look awful."

Not only did Ellie have both hands bandaged, but she also had a bandage on her right leg from a nasty cut on the outside of her thigh. Her lip had a gash in it, and they'd taped down yet another bandage on her temple. She also had a broken big toe on her right foot.

Ellie was a mess.

But considering she'd thought for sure she was dead, she wasn't about to complain. Not when the medicine she'd been given made her feel all warm and floaty.

The only downside? She'd been awake hours now, and Dean still hadn't come in.

Jess said, "That's not it."

"Not going to tell me you told me so?" Ellie made a face. "You thought I shouldn't go up there. Just admit you were right."

Truth was, she wished she hadn't gone up there. After what she'd seen, and what she had learned, she would go back and tell herself not to walk up that mountain if she could.

Jess slumped into a chair beside the bed, on the side where she could see the door.

"You're here to protect me?"

"Until we find Gilane, yes."

Ellie smoothed down the blanket with her fingers.

"Stuart was shot. When he woke up, partway through the doctors stitching him up, he freaked out. Dean had to help them calm him down, otherwise they'd have had to give him a shot that would knock him out."

A shudder rolled through her, flooding her with memories of the doctor giving her one, causing her to pass out. When she'd come to, in the car, she hadn't even been able to think. She felt a million times better now, and it was nothing she'd wish on anyone.

"That's why he hasn't come to see you since you woke up."

Ellie shrugged one shoulder. Even she was nervous of the doctors right now, so she didn't exactly blame Stuart for freaking out. If that was what'd happened. His PTSD probably didn't help the situation.

"You're avoiding what's going on here."

Her sister was officially the queen of conversations coming out of left field. "Jess—"

"He would be here if he could." Her sister gave her a hard stare. "He rappelled down the side of a mountain, found you, and carried you back up to the road. On his back."

"So now you're on 'Team Dean?' Is that it?"

"You have been a fan of his this whole time. Now that he's proven he can take care of you, you want to jump ship? Just because he has more people than you to help." Jess shot her a look. "You're gonna be one of those needy women who insist their partner has one priority—them—and no one else should matter."

"That's not what this is."

"Then explain it. Because you found the answer, and he saved you. What's the problem?"

"This isn't over." She didn't get why Jess thought it was. "The doctor…" Tears gathered, along with a lump in her throat.

"Tell me what he said."

She studied her sister's face. It wasn't a compassionate invitation. More like an offer to listen so she could immediately refute anything Ellie said. Jess was frustrated, maybe even angry. Itching for an argument.

Ellie shook her head.

"What am I supposed to think? Gilane killed whoever that was in the cave. Pop knew about it, but for some reason never did anything. And the doctor tried to keep you from finding out. When you did, he tried to kill you." Jess lifted her hands. "I need you to explain this, Ellie. Because I'm pretty confused. And I don't want to wait for the tell-all exposé bestseller you're gonna write."

Ellie rolled her eyes.

"There you are." As though getting a reaction from her was the whole point of having said all that. "Whatever it is, you can trust me. But I need to understand."

"As the investigating police officer taking my statement, or as my sister?"

Jess said, "Do I have my notepad out?"

"You could be wearing a wire."

"You think I'd lie to you like that? Or you just can't risk anyone but me hearing this?"

Ellie studied the blanket again.

"Tell me what you know."

She relayed what the doctor told her about the weekend in Vietnam. It made her sick to think her grandfather had been there while a woman was being victimized, let alone that he might've participated.

Jess's lips thinned.

"He had to have been her son. The child of one of the men in that picture, though likely the doctor's. Or he's the one who killed the man."

"The body in the cave is a raped woman's child?"

Ellie said, "The doctor took his passport. I don't know his name, it was in Vietnamese, but his picture was young. Maybe eighteen, certainly no more than twenty-one. He traveled all this way, figuring out how to bring a gun along with him. They killed him."

"Detective Wilcox told me the deceased was a young man, and there's an indication he was shot multiple times."

Ellie squeezed her eyes shut. "Gilane killed his son."

"I didn't know you'd seen more than the hand."

"I found the passport right before Mark made me dig for the gun." She shook her head, still trying to figure it all out. "I'm sorry I hid it, but I was so worried about Grandpa's part in it. What I don't get is that Mark knew about there being a gun buried with the body. But he wasn't old enough to have been there when the crime took place."

"We'll figure it all out." Jess said, "We have a theory that Gilane is Mark's father, or his stepfather maybe. That gives us a connection between them. The doctor probably told him."

"Why would he do that?"

"People confess for all kinds of reasons." Jess shrugged. "Maybe he'd been drunk one night and said more than he'd wanted to."

"Then he'd have killed Mark, too."

"Maybe he brought him in on the secret. The way Pop did with his will."

Some gift that had been. He had to have known she would be in danger trying to uncover the secret. And she didn't believe he'd thought that covering her with Dean's protection by giving him the land surrounding the cabin would be a good enough plan.

Had he really not thought it would come to this?

She would never know what he'd left among his belongings, and at the cabin. It was all destroyed. But she'd managed to find the boy.

Maybe that was enough.

"It doesn't matter what the doctor says when you guys find him," Elle said. "Not when he could just lie through his teeth like he already has. Maybe Pop wasn't there for any of it, and he found out later. He might've been so distraught over it that he hadn't known before he was on his deathbed that he wanted me to put it right."

"After what happened to you?"

"I'm sorry I never told you."

Jess shook her head, so much gentleness on her face. "I'm not. I mean, I'm glad the question has been answered. But I didn't have any kind of right to know. It's your life." She frowned. "I'm just sorry that Pop thought it was a good idea to give you this."

Ellie shook her head. "I'm glad he did. I'm still grateful that he trusted me, even if I may wind up wishing I'd never found out. It's for the best."

Jess didn't look convinced.

"And I'm not writing a book about this."

Jess's lips twitched.

"There's none of it that I want to relive. Not my own experience, or the time I spent in that cave, thinking I was going to die. Then believing I was safe, only to have the doctor drug me and turn on me. No one, especially not someone with control over whether people live or die, should get to make decisions that go against what a person wishes."

"Don't do that. Don't make it abstract."

"What if—"

"Don't, El. It's not someone else's life. It's yours."

"He was going to kill me."

Her sister got up. She moved in close and held Ellie's hand. "Say it."

"I didn't want him to hurt me."

"Why?"

"Because I don't like it when it hurts."

"We're going to catch him."

"You don't know that." Ellie shook her head. "I can't protect myself."

"From everything? None of us can. That's why we stick together. That's why we have friends and family and emergency services." Her sister squeezed her hand. "But it won't work if you don't stick around."

"I'll be safer back at home, where Gilane can't find me."

"That's a gamble. Here, we'll *know* you're safe." Jess said, "You think Dean went to all that trouble to get you back only to watch you leave. Or let you swing again, unprotected?"

She wanted to say she didn't care what Dean thought. Or what he wanted.

But that wasn't true, was it?

She'd been awake for hours, and she hadn't even *seen* him yet. "I don't care."

Jess nearly laughed.

"I mean it. I don't care."

"When are you going to figure out that you care more than *everyone*? That's why you became a teacher. Because you get to care, but from a safe distance."

"It's not from a distance."

"Because you've chosen to get involved. To be a part of your students' lives." Jess paused. "The way you could also do here. Teaching at the high school."

"As if."

No one had invited her to think about doing that. Or simply told her to. She wasn't just going to…what? Put in an application? That was crazy.

Her sister pinned her with a knowing stare that Ellie didn't like that much, and said, "Stay here."

Ellie started to object.

"No. I want you to think about it. Not just because I could use the company from family right now. I also have to deal with repair on the house. And you could oversee fixing up the cabin."

If she even wanted to do that. Ellie wasn't sure if it was worth salvaging, especially considering Dean owned the land all around it. Who knew what would happen with that?

She knew what she wanted. But when had that ever happened?

If she had hope—the kind that ignored reality—then she would be back with that childish faith. The one that trusted God despite everything around her. She'd lost that after Ed Summers cornered her with his friends. Now she'd been through far worse.

She was here. They weren't.

Ellie realized she could be thankful for that much. There was a lot to think through right now, and a lot that might never be resolved unless they could get Doctor Gilane to tell the truth. But faith?

"On Sunday," she began, "do you think I could come to church with you?"

"I haven't been in a while. I work a lot on Sundays. But I can ask for it off, and we can go together. Safety in numbers."

Ellie felt the same way. Then she realized that her sister was right. It was what her life would be like if she remained in Last Chance.

Even if it was only for a few months while she took her sabbatical.

She reached for her sister's hand then. "I'll stay in Last Chance." She gave Jess's hand a gentle squeeze. "Until I'm due back to the university, and I'll reassess then." She even added, "Maybe the position at the high school will still be open."

Jess's expression lit up. "That would be…" She let out a noise that sounded like a squeal.

Ellie tried to ignore her. Apparently younger sisters were the same whether you were thirteen or almost thirty.

"Dean will come around. I just know he will."

"It doesn't matter. I'm doing this for me." *For us.*

Ellie needed to stay. This time, instead of leaving, she was going to let being here heal her. This town wasn't going to scare her anymore.

They would find the doctor. She would figure out what to do with her feelings for Dean. Help her sister rebuild her home. See if faith was something she wanted to resurrect. Finally put her grandfather's legacy to rest.

And start building the rest of her life.

Thirty-Seven

Dean closed the door to Stuart's room quietly, trying not to wake him. Conroy was headed down the hall toward him. When he spotted Dean, the police chief gave him a chin lift.

"Anything?"

Conroy shook his head. "No sign of Gilane. He's in the wind."

"He nearly killed her. And Stuart."

"I know." Conroy said, "How is he?"

"Calm now. He probably saved her life."

"Seems like a good guy—with a lot of stuff to work through."

Dean said, "So…pretty much like all of us then."

Conroy cracked a smile. "I guess that is true."

Dean's phone rang. He pulled it out but didn't recognize the number. "Probably about the car warranty I don't have." He swiped to answer the call. "Cartwright."

"So she's alive?" The voice was shaky. Nothing like the man he thought he knew.

"Gilane."

Conroy whipped out his phone and punched a button. If Dean had to guess, Conroy was calling Ted for another trace on Dean's phone.

Dean said, "Yeah. She's alive. So is the man you shot."

"Well. That's that I guess."

"Tell me where you are." Dean wasn't pulling any punches. "I'll come and get you, and we can go together to explain all this to Conroy."

Gilane huffed, audible over the phone line. "It's too late for that. I'll be gone by the time you get here."

Dean heard the unmistakable sound of the slide being pulled back on a Sig. "Don't do this."

"I'm not going to jail. For a boy who meant nothing? Coming here with the ridiculous notion that he'd get revenge?" He exhaled against the phone mic again.

Conroy made a circle motion with one hand and mouthed, "Keep him talking."

Dean nodded. He figured Ellie would want to know, so he said, "And Chief Ridgeman? What was his part in all this?"

Gilane was quiet.

"Might as well set the record straight." At least until the police found him, and he was arrested and given the right to a lawyer. "Tell your side of the story."

"My side? You sound like Ridgeman, trying to get me to confess. Like he was my priest? He should've just kept his mouth shut. Like Holmford should have. Old men and their weak stomachs. Now, suddenly, they can't handle what they've had to live with *all these years*." His tone shifted higher, and he mocked someone whining. "Oh, they had it harder than me? Please. I was the one who started this whole town. It was my idea. And when I started handing out the money to do it? No one had a problem then. Did they?"

Conroy's brows lifted. Dean saw the earbud in the police chief's right ear. He was following the conversation.

"Ridgeman suspected who the boy was, but he could never prove anything. Besides, what was the point? Back home no one cared. Until the boy showed up. Tried to kill me. I knew Ridgeman wasn't going to accept money to keep that quiet as well, so I had Holmford help me bury the kid." Gilane pushed out a breath. "Only, Ridgeman found us before we could get him in the ground. By that time, it was too late for him to save the boy. He tried to arrest me but halfway back to town, he gets a call. His wife is in labor and bleeding everywhere. So who is going to help her?"

Gilane started to chuckle.

"He let you go."

"I was the only doctor. I managed to save the baby, but his wife died. Never forgave me for that. Tried for years to prove I'd done something to her."

"Did you?"

"I didn't need to. By the time we got there, all I could do was save that baby."

Dean squeezed the bridge of his nose. He pleaded with Conroy, without words, to be able to hang up and be done with this conversation.

"Ridgeman had nothing, and we gave him everything. All he had to do in return was keep his mouth shut about it. Couldn't even do that when he was dying."

"Did you help him end it?"

Conroy's face lost all its color.

Dean said, "Well? Did you?"

"It's not illegal everywhere. Helping someone drift into the beyond, at peace." Gilane paused. "Mine won't be quite so peaceful."

"Surely there's a statute of limitations on murder? You can't still be held responsible."

Conroy shook his head, and mouthed, "Yes, he can."

Gilane just chuckled. "What's dead is my reputation. I'll never practice again, and no one will ever look at me to heal them."

That was all he was concerned about? "You have done good in this town."

"Your father was right about you."

"What—"

"I'd rather die than live losing everything I've worked for." The line crackled. A sudden blast of sound that was much too loud. *Gunshot.* Dean winced, moving the phone away from his ear.

Conroy pulled out the earbud. "He killed himself."

Dean tossed his cell phone onto the nearest chair. It bounced on the seat, tumbled over, and landed on the floor.

There was satisfaction in the crack as his screen shattered.

But it would've felt even better to have kicked the chair. Or punched the wall.

Instead he strode toward Ellie's room.

"Dean!"

He ignored Conroy and let himself into her room. Jess lifted her brows and stood. "I'll give you guys a minute."

Dean paced. He didn't even look at Ellie, he couldn't just yet. Too many thoughts swirled in his head. The doctor. What had happened. The chief. His father. Dean shook his head.

"I know. I look hideous, right?"

He whirled around to her. It wasn't a shock, seeing the bandages. He'd checked on her before he went to sit with Stuart. When she was still out.

"What happened?"

"I should be helping you feel better."

"Dean."

"What?"

She held out her hand. "Come here."

Dean took her hand and sat on the bed in the spot Jess had vacated. No doubt she was hearing the whole story from Conroy. Hopefully they'd recorded the conversation. Dean could explain it to Ellie, but if she could listen to the conversation herself, then she'd be able to think on each of the things Gilane had said. She would finally be able to put this to rest. To know she was finally safe.

"He's dead." Dean swallowed. "He killed himself."

Ellie closed her eyes for a second.

"You're safe now."

"I know." She tugged on his hand.

Dean leaned in, and Ellie wrapped him in her arms. He sighed and laid his forehead on her shoulder. "Ellie."

"It's over."

"I should be telling you that."

She chuckled. "When I forget, you can tell me."

"I'll always protect you." He lifted his head so he could look at her. He wanted to see her face. "I think I'm halfway in love with you at this point."

"We haven't known each other long."

"You think that you're not exactly the kind of person I would be interested in?"

She didn't answer. Not that it was really a question. He didn't mind if she wanted to guard her heart while he said what he needed her to hear.

"I've never met anyone like you. And I don't think I ever will, because I won't be looking anymore."

He wanted to ask her to stay. It was on the tip of his tongue, but he couldn't bring himself to put that much pressure on her.

Instead, he said, "I'm going to look at selling the land your grandfather gave me. I can start my therapy center anywhere. People can travel to me, and I'll get to be where I want to be."

"Which is here."

She didn't want him to move. He said, "Ellie—"

"Which is where *I'll* be." She held onto his hand in a strong grip. "I'd love to spend more time with you. Maybe when we're not in danger."

He returned her smile, wanting to kiss her but also content to let her finish.

"Get to know each other better when crazy isn't swirling around us."

"Are you sure?" Not only with what she'd just said, but about moving to Last Chance.

"I want to spend more time with Jess as well. And I trust my heart, so I want to find out if this thing between you and I could be something."

"It can. It is."

She smiled wider. "There has to be a reason why you suddenly feel like this is what 'home' should feel like." Ellie had found something with her sister. A lot had changed for their relationship over the past week.

He realized she was right to tread cautiously. Even as they were making a huge promise to each other just now with this simple conversation.

"Can I kiss you?"

She nodded.

Dean laid his lips on hers. He let it go on as long as he could before he had to pull back, before it would be too much for right now. It was new, and early. If they took care of this delicate love sprouting between them, then it would grow deep roots and stretch high with strength. Like a tree that could withstand all the storms that came its way, finding itself so much stronger than if it had never faced a single drop of rain.

Epilogue

Eight Months Later

"I don't see why we have to go so far. It's almost dark, and the food is going to get cold."

Dean smiled to himself. Ellie was right behind him, trudging up the path to the spot where her grandfather's cabin had exploded.

She'd had a long day at her computer. It was probably just as tiring after all that mental exertion than how he'd felt after a day of training in the Navy. "It's not too much farther."

"I know where we're going. You aren't fooling me, mister. Let's just eat right here." She motioned toward a downed tree.

He glanced over his shoulder. "Ants."

Her eyes widened.

She didn't know there were no ants out when it was this cold, and tonight was the last clear night before a big snow storm was going to roll in. Thanksgiving and Christmas had come and gone. She was still here and had begun talking to the principal about the history teacher position that was available for the next school year.

He knew she was waiting for him to commit. Truth was, with everything that'd happened before the holidays, he was more than ready to commit. Forever.

Ellie was all the family he needed.

And he wanted to make a life with her that was just theirs.

"It's just a little farther," he said again, grabbing her hand so he could tug her along.

She hadn't been up here since he came up with her several months prior so she could see with her own eyes just how thoroughly it had been damaged. There had been little to salvage, and she'd asked him to oversee it being cleared away.

At the clearing where her grandfather's cabin had stood, another structure had been built.

Ellie gasped. "Dean." Beside him, she lifted a hand and covered her mouth.

In the spot where the cabin had been now stood a gazebo. A sign above the steps on this side of it read, *For those we have loved and lost.*

Her voice was full of wonder. "What did you do?"

"I've been busy." He walked her over to it and set the cold bag containing their dinner down, along with his backpack which had the blanket in it.

"It's beautiful." She stared in wonder at the gazebo.

Dean flipped a switch and the inside illuminated with Christmas lights he'd strung up.

Ellie swiped a tear from her face. "I love you."

He was very glad she'd said that.

Dean waved her to one side. "Come here." They stood at the rail, and he pointed out the markers that had been staked into the ground. "That's where the therapy center will be." Beyond it was an ATV they would use to get back to town after dinner. "I had the road paved first and the parking area graveled over so the construction guys can get in and out easily."

"It's going to be amazing."

Dean took her hand. He turned her to face him. Then he pulled out what was burning a hole in his pocket and lowered to one knee.

Her eyes widened, and she shoved her glasses up her nose. "You made me walk all the way up here. I'm all sweaty, and now I'm crying!"

Dean chuckled. "Every time I look at you, I think to myself that you can't possibly be any more beautiful. And every time you prove me wrong."

He lifted her hand. "When I put this ring on your finger—?"

Dean slid it on. "And when we say, 'I do'—?"

He touched her shirt, right over her stomach. "And when our baby is growing in here—?"

Tears rolled down her cheek.

"There won't be one second of the rest of my life that I won't know in my heart that you proved me wrong." He stood, pulling her close. "Because you were right. This is home."

Keep turning pages for all the fun news

Last Chance book 4 is coming in July!

EXPIRED HERO

Sign up for my newsletter to get an email as soon as it's up on pre-order.

Did you enjoy this book?

Please consider leaving a review on your favorite book retailer! You could also share about the book on Facebook! Your review will help other book buyers decide what to read next.

Visit www.authorlisaphillips.com where you can sign up for my NEWSLETTER and get a free copy of Sanctuary Buried!

About the author

A British ex-pat who grew up an hour outside of London, Lisa attended Calvary Chapel Bible College where she met her husband. He's from California, but nobody's perfect. It wasn't until her Bible College graduation that she figured out she was a writer (someone told her). Since then she's discovered a penchant for high-stakes stories of mayhem and disaster where you can find made-for-each-other love that always ends in happily ever after.

Lisa can be found in Idaho wearing either flip-flops or cowgirl boots, depending on the season. She leads worship with her husband at their local church. Together they have two children and an all-black Airedale known as The Dark Lord Elevator.

Lisa is the author of the bestselling Sanctuary (WITSEC town series), the Double Down series, and more than a dozen Love Inspired Suspense novels. Her 2019 series of Northwest Counter-Terrorism agents was a big hit.

2020 is sure to be a lot of fun!

Find out more at www.authorlisaphillips.com where you can:

SIGN UP FOR MY NEWSLETTER

FIND A COMPLETE LIST OF BOOKS

SEE WHAT'S COMING NEXT

Lisa Phillips also writes Christian thriller supernatural novels under the name JL Terra

You can find these at www.jlterra.com

Made in the USA
Monee, IL
21 July 2020

36817630R00163